AN OATH OF BROTHERS

(BOOK #14 IN THE SORCERER'S RING)

MORGAN RICE

D1159221

Copyright © 2014 by Morgan Rice

All rights reserved. Except as permitted under the U.S. Copyright Act of 1976, no part of this publication may be reproduced, distributed or transmitted in any form or by any means, or stored in a database or retrieval system, without the prior permission of the author.

This ebook is licensed for your personal enjoyment only. This ebook may not be re-sold or given away to other people. If you would like to share this book with another person, please purchase an additional copy for each recipient. If you're reading this book and did not purchase it, or it was not purchased for your use only, then please return it and purchase your own copy. Thank you for respecting the hard work of this author.

This is a work of fiction. Names, characters, businesses, organizations, places, events, and incidents either are the product of the author's imagination or are used fictionally. Any resemblance to actual persons, living or dead, is entirely coincidental.

Jacket image Copyright RazzoomGame, used under license from Shutterstock.com.
ISBN: 978-1-63291-062-2

Books by Morgan Rice

THE SORCERER'S RING
A QUEST OF HEROES
A MARCH OF KINGS
A FATE OF DRAGONS
A CRY OF HONOR
A VOW OF GLORY
A CHARGE OF VALOR
A RITE OF SWORDS
A GRANT OF ARMS
A SKY OF SPELLS
A SEA OF SHIELDS
A REIGN OF STEEL
A LAND OF FIRE
A RULE OF QUEENS
AN OATH OF BROTHERS

THE SURVIVAL TRILOGY
ARENA ONE (Book #1)
ARENA TWO (Book #2)

the Vampire Journals
turned (book #1)
loved (book #2)
betrayed (book #3)
destined (book #4)
desired (book #5)
betrothed (book #6)
vowed (book #7)
found (book #8)
resurrected (book #9)
craved (book #10)
fated (book #11)

CHAPTER ONE

Darius looked down at the bloody dagger in his hand, at the Empire commander dead at his feet, and he wondered what he had just done. His world slowed as he looked up and saw the shocked faces of the Empire army spread out before him, hundreds of men on the horizon, *real* men, warriors with *real* armor and *real* weaponry, scores of them mounted on zertas. Men who had never known defeat.

Behind Darius, he knew, were his few hundred paltry villagers, men and women without steel, without armor, left alone to face this professional army. They had implored him to surrender, to accept the maiming; they didn't want a war they could not win. They didn't want death. And Darius had wanted to oblige them.

But deep down in his soul he could not. His hands had acted on their own, his spirit had risen up on its own, and he could not have controlled it if he tried. It was the deepest part of himself, the part that had been oppressed his entire life, the part that thirsted for freedom as a dying man thirsts for water.

Darius looked out at the sea of faces, never feeling so alone, yet never feeling so free, and his world spun. He felt outside of himself, looking down on himself. It all felt surreal. He knew this was one of those pivotal moments of his life. He knew it was a moment that would change everything.

Yet Darius had no regrets. He looked at the dead Empire commander, this man who would have taken Loti's life, who would have taken all of their lives, who would have maimed them, and he felt a sense of justice. He also felt emboldened. After all, an Empire officer had fallen. And that meant that any Empire soldier could fall. They might be bedecked in the greatest armor, the greatest weaponry, but they bled like any other man. They were not invincible.

Darius felt a rush of strength within him, and he burst into action before any of the others could react. A few feet away was the small entourage of Empire officers who had accompanied their commander, and they stood there in shock, clearly never expecting anything but surrender, never expecting their commander to be attacked.

Darius took advantage of their surprise. He lunged forward, drew a dagger from his waist, slashed one's throat, then spun around and in the same motion, slashed another.

The two of them stared back at him, eyes wide open, as if unbelieving this could happen to them, blood pouring from their throats, as they dropped to their knees, then collapsed, dead.

Darius braced himself; his bold move had left him vulnerable to attack, and one of the officers lunged forward and slashed his steel sword, aiming for his head. Darius wished at that moment that he had armor, a shield, a sword to block it—anything. But he did not. He'd left himself vulnerable to attack, and now, he knew he was going to pay the price. At least he would die a free man.

A sudden clang cut through the air, and Darius looked over to see Raj standing beside him, blocking the blow with a sword of his own. Darius glanced over and realized that Raj had taken the sword from the dead soldier and had rushed forward and blocked for him at the last moment.

Another clang tore through the air, and Darius looked to his other side to see Desmond blocking another blow meant for him. Raj and Desmond rushed forward, slashing back at their attackers, who had not expected the defense. They swung like men possessed, the clanging of their swords sparking as they met their attackers', driving them back, then each landing a deadly blow before the Empire soldiers could fully defend.

The two soldiers dropped down, dead.

Darius felt a rush of gratitude toward his brothers, elated to have them here, fighting at his side. He no longer faced the army alone.

Darius reached down, snatched the sword and the shield from the dead commander's body, then joined Desmond and Raj as they rushed forward and attacked the six remaining officers of his entourage. Darius swung the sword high, and relished the weight; it felt so good to wield a real sword, a real shield. He felt invincible.

Darius lunged forward and blocked a mighty sword slash with his shield and at the same time slipped a sword thrust between the kinks of an empire soldier's armor, stabbing him in the shoulder blade; the soldier grunted and dropped to his knees.

He turned and swung his shield, blocking a blow from the side, then spun around and used the shield as a weapon, smashing another attacker in the face and felling him. He then spun around with his sword and slashed his other attacker across the stomach, killing him just before the soldier, hands raised above his head, could land a blow on Darius's neck.

Raj and Desmond charged forward, too, at his side, going blow for blow with the other soldiers, the clanging sharp in his ears. Darius thought back to all their sparring with wooden swords, and he could see now, in battle, what great fighters they were. As he swung himself, he realized how much all of their sparring had sharpened him. He wondered if he could have won without it. And he was determined to win on his own, with his own two hands, and to never, ever, draw upon the magic power that lurked somewhere deep inside him and that he did not fully understand—or *want* to understand.

As Darius, Desmond, and Raj felled the remainder of the entourage, as they stood there alone in the midst of the battlefield, the hundreds of other Empire soldiers in the distance finally rallied. Collecting themselves, they let out a great battle cry and charged down on them.

Darius looked out, standing there, breathing hard, the bloody sword in his hand, and he realized there was nowhere to run. As the perfect squadrons of soldiers burst into action, he realized that that was death coming his way. He stood his ground, as did Desmond and Raj, wiped the sweat off the back of his brow and faced them. He would not back down, not for anyone.

There came another great battle cry, this time from behind, and Darius glanced back and was happily surprised to see all of his villagers, charging, rallying. He spotted several of his brothers in arms rushing forward, scavenging swords and shields from the fallen Empire soldiers, racing to join their ranks. The villagers, Darius was proud to see, covered the battlefield like a wave, scavenging, arming themselves with steel and weaponry and soon, several dozen of them were armed with real weapons. Those that did not have steel wielded makeshift weapons carved of wood, dozens of the younger ones, Darius's friends, wielding short, wooden spears that they had sharpened to a point, and small wooden bows and arrows at their sides, clearly hoping for a fight such as this.

They all charged together, as one, each and every one fighting for their lives as they joined Darius to face the Empire army.

In the distance a huge banner waved, a trumpet sounded, and the Empire army mobilized. The clanging of armor filled the air as hundreds of the Empire soldiers marched forward as one, well-disciplined, a wall of men, shoulder to shoulder, holding ranks perfectly as they marched toward the crowd of villagers.

Darius led his men in the charge, all of them fearlessly beside him, and as they neared the empire ranks, Darius shouted:

"SPEARS!"

His people let their short spears fly, soaring over Darius's head, flying through the air and finding targets across the clearing. Many of the wooden spears, not sharp enough, hit armor and bounced off harmlessly. But more than a few found kinks in the armor and hit their mark, and a handful of Empire soldiers cried out, dropping in the distance.

"ARROWS!" Darius cried out, still charging, sword held high, closing the gap.

Several villagers stopped, took aim, and unleashed a volley of sharpened wooden arrows, dozens of them arcing high in the air, across the clearing, to the surprise of the Empire, who clearly had not expected a fight—much less for the villagers to have any weapons. Many bounced harmlessly off the armor, but enough found their marks, striking soldiers in the throats and in their joints, felling several more.

"STONES!" Darius yelled.

Several dozen villagers stepped forward and, using their slings, hurled stones.

A barrage of small stones hailed through the skies, and the sound of rocks hitting armor filled the air. A few soldiers, hit in the face by stones, dropped, while many others stopped and raised their shields or hands to stop the assault.

It slowed the Empire and added an element of uncertainty to their ranks—but it did not stop them. On and on they marched, never breaking ranks, even with arrows and spears and stones assailing them. They simply raised their shields, too arrogant to duck, marching with their shining steel halberds straight up in the air, their long, steel swords swinging at their belts, clanging in the morning light. Darius watched them advance, and he knew that was a professional army coming toward him. He knew it was a wave of death.

There came a sudden rumbling, and Darius looked up and saw three huge zertas break from the front lines and come charging toward them, one officer riding each, wielding long halberds. The zertas charged, fury on their faces, kicking up waves of dust.

Darius braced himself as one bore down on him, the soldier sneering as he raised his halberd and suddenly hurled it right for him. Darius was caught off guard by the speed, and at the last moment he dodged it, barely getting out of the way.

But the villager behind them, a boy he knew from growing up, was not so lucky. He cried out in pain as the halberd pierced his chest, blood gushing from his mouth as he dropped to his back, staring up at the sky.

Darius, in a rage, turned and faced the zerta. He waited and waited, knowing that if he did not time it perfectly, he would be trampled to death.

At the last second Darius rolled out of the way and swung his sword, chopping the zerta's legs out from under him.

The zerta shrieked and dropped face-first to the ground, its rider flying off it, landing in the group of villagers.

A villager broke from the crowd and rushed forward, hoisting a large rock high overhead. Darius turned and was surprised to see it was Loti—she held it high, then smashed it down on the soldier's helmet, killing him.

Darius heard galloping and turned to find, bearing down on him, another zerta, the soldier astride it raising his spear and aiming it down at him. There was no time to react.

A snarl ripped through the air, and Darius was surprised to see Dray suddenly appear, leaping forward, high into the air, and biting the soldier's foot just as he hurled the spear. The soldier lurched forward and his spear throw went straight down, into the dirt. He wobbled and fell sideways off the zerta, and as he hit the ground he was pounced on by several villagers.

Darius looked to Dray, who came running to his side, forever grateful to him.

Darius heard another battle cry and turned to find yet another Empire officer charging him, raising his sword and bringing it down on him. Darius turned and parried, knocking the other sword away with a clang before it could reach his chest. Darius then spun around and kicked the soldier's feet out from under him. He fell to the ground, and Darius kicked him across the jaw before he could rise, knocking him out for good.

Darius watched Loti race past him, throwing herself headlong right into the thick of the fight as she reached down and snatched a sword from a dead soldier's waist. Dray lunged forward before her to protect her, and it concerned Darius to see her in the thick of the fight, and he wanted to get her to safety.

Loc, her brother, beat him to it. He rushed forward and grabbed Loti from behind, making her drop the spear.

"We must go from here!" he said. "This is no place for you!"

"This is the *only* place for me!" she insisted.

Loc, though, even with his one good hand, was surprisingly strong, and he managed to drag her, protesting and kicking, away from the thick of battle. Darius was more grateful to him than he could say.

Darius heard a clang of steel beside him and he turned to see one of his brothers in arms, Kaz, struggling with an Empire soldier. While Kaz had once been a bully and a thorn in Darius' side, now, Darius had to admit, he was happy to have Kaz by his side. He saw Kaz go back and forth with the soldier, a formidable warrior, clang for clang, until finally the soldier, in a surprise move, bested Kaz and knocked the sword from his hand.

Kaz stood there, defenseless, fear in his face for the first time Darius could remember. The Empire soldier, blood in his eyes, stepped forward to finish him off.

Suddenly, there came a clang, and the soldier suddenly froze and fell, face-first, down to the ground. Dead.

They both looked over, and Darius was shocked to see Luzi standing there, half Kaz's size, holding a sling in his hand, empty from having just fired. Luzi smirked at Kaz.

"Regret bullying me now?" he said to Kaz.

Kaz stared back, speechless.

Darius was impressed that Luzi, after the way he'd been tormented by Kaz in all their days of training, had stepped up and saved his life. It inspired Darius to fight even harder.

Darius, seeing the abandoned zerta stomping wildly through his ranks, rushed forward, ran up alongside it, and mounted it.

The zerta jerked wildly, but Darius held on, clutching it tight, determined. Finally, he got control of it, and he managed to turn it and direct it toward the Empire ranks.

His zerta galloped so fast he could barely control it, taking him out beyond all his men, leading the charge single-handedly into the thick of the Empire ranks. Darius's heart slammed in his chest as he neared the wall of soldiers. It seemed impenetrable from here. And yet, there was no turning back.

Darius forced his courage to carry him through. He charged right into them and as he did, he slashed down wildly with his sword.

From his higher vantage point, Darius slashed side to side, taking out scores of surprised Empire soldiers, who had not expected to be charged by a zerta. He cut through the ranks with blinding speed, parting the sea of soldiers, carried by his momentum—when suddenly, he felt a horrific pain on his side. It felt as if his ribs were being torn in two.

Darius, losing his balance, went flying through the air. He hit the ground hard, feeling a searing pain in his side, and realized he'd been smashed with the metal ball of a flail. He lay there on the ground, in the sea of Empire soldiers, far from his people.

As he lay there, his head ringing, his world blurry, he looked out in the distance and noticed his people getting surrounded. They fought valiantly, but they were just too outnumbered, too outmatched. His men were getting slaughtered, their screams filling the air.

Darius's head, too heavy, dropped back down to the ground and as he lay there, he looked up and saw all the Empire men closing in on him. He lay there, spent, and knew his life would soon be over.

At least, he thought, he would die with honor.

At least, finally, he was free.

CHAPTER TWO

Gwendolyn stood on the crest of the hill, looking out at the breaking dawn over the desert sky, and her heart pounded in anticipation as she prepared to strike. Watching the Empire confrontation with the villagers from afar, she had marched her men here, skirting the battlefield the long way, and positioned them behind Empire lines. The Empire, so focused on the villagers, on the battle below, had never seen them coming. And now, as villagers began to die below, it was time to make them pay.

Ever since Gwen had decided to turn her men around, to help the villagers, she had felt an overwhelming sense of destiny. Win or lose, she knew it was the right thing to do. She had watched the confrontation unfolding from high in the mountain ranges, had seen the Empire armies approaching with their zertas and professional soldiers, and it brought back fresh feelings, reminding her of the Ring's invasion by Andronicus, and then, Romulus. She had watched Darius step forward by himself, to face them, and her heart had soared as she had witnessed him kill that commander. It was something that Thor would have done. That she herself would have done.

Gwen stood there now, Krohn snarling quietly beside her, Kendrick, Steffen, Brandt, Atme, dozens of Silver and hundreds of her men all behind her, all wearing the steel armor they'd had since they'd left the Ring, all bearing their steel weaponry, all patiently awaiting her command. Hers was a professional army, and they had not had a fight since they'd been exiled from their homeland.

The time had come.

"NOW!" Gwen cried.

There arose a great battle cry as all of her men, led by Kendrick, raced down the hill, their voices carrying like a thousand lions in the early morning light.

Gwen watched as her men reached the Empire lines and as the Empire soldiers, preoccupied with fighting the villagers, slowly turned, baffled, clearly not understanding who could be attacking them or why. Clearly, these Empire soldiers had never been caught off guard before, and certainly not by a professional army.

Kendrick gave them no time to collect themselves, to process what was happening. He lunged forward, stabbing the first man he encountered, and Brandt and Atme and Steffen and the dozens of Silver at their side all joined in, shouting as they plunged their weapons into the soldiers. All of her men carried a great grudge, all had been itching for a fight, craving vengeance against the empire and cooped up from sitting idle too many days in that cave. They had been craving, Gwen knew, to let their wrath out on the Empire ever since they'd abandoned the Ring—and in this battle, they'd found the perfect outlet. In each of her people's eyes there burned a fire, a fire that held the souls of all the loved ones they'd lost in the Ring and the Upper Isles. It was a need for vengeance that they had carried across the sea. In many ways, Gwen realized, the villagers' cause, even halfway around the world, was their cause, too.

Men cried out as they fought hand-to-hand, Kendrick and the others using their momentum to slash their way thick into the fray, taking out rows of Empire soldiers before they could even rally. Gwen was so proud as she watched Kendrick block two blows with his shield, spin around and smash one soldier in the face with it, then slash another across the chest. She watched as Brandt kicked a soldier's legs out from under him, then stabbed him, on his back, through the heart, driving his sword down with both hands. She saw Steffen wield his short sword and chop off a soldier's leg, then step forward and kick another soldier in the groin and head-butt him, knocking him out. Atme swung his flail and took out two soldiers in one blow.

"Darius!" cried the voice.

Gwen looked over to see Sandara standing beside her, pointing to the battlefield.

"My brother!" she cried.

Gwen spotted Darius on the ground, on his back, and surrounded by Empire, closing in. Her heart leapt with concern, but she watched with great satisfaction as Kendrick rushed forward and held out his shield, saving Darius from an axe blow right before it hit his face.

Sandara cried out, and Gwen could see her relief, could see how much she loved her brother.

Gwendolyn reached over and took a bow from one of the soldiers standing guard beside her. She placed an arrow, pulling it back and taking aim.

"ARCHERS!" she yelled.

All around her a dozen of her archers took aim, pulling back their bows, awaiting her command.

"FIRE!"

Gwen shot her arrow high into the sky, over her men, and as she did, her dozen archers fired, too.

The volley landed on the thicket of remaining Empire soldiers, and cries rang out as a dozen soldiers dropped to their knees.

"FIRE!" she yelled again.

There came yet another volley; then another.

Kendrick and his men rushed in, killing all those men who had dropped to their knees from the arrows.

The Empire soldiers were forced to abandon attacking the villagers and instead turn their army around and confront Kendrick's men.

This gave the villagers an opportunity. They let out a loud cry as they charged forward, stabbing in the back the Empire soldiers, who were now getting slaughtered from both sides.

The Empire soldiers, squeezed between two hostile forces, their numbers dwindling quickly, finally began to realize they were outmaneuvered. Their ranks of hundreds soon dwindled to dozens, and those who remained turned and tried to flee on foot, their zertas either killed or taken hostage.

They did not make it very far before they were hunted down and killed.

There arose a great shout of triumph from both the villagers and Gwendolyn's men. They all gathered together, cheering, embracing each other as brothers, and Gwendolyn hurried down the slope and joined them, Krohn at her heels, bursting into the thick of it, men all around her, the smell of sweat and fear strong in the air, blood running fresh on the desert floor. Here, on this day, despite everything that had happened back in the Ring, Gwen felt a moment of triumph. It was a glorious victory here in the desert, the villagers and the exiles of the Ring joined together, united in defiance of the enemy.

The villagers had lost many good men, and Gwen had lost some of hers. But Darius, at least, Gwen was relieved to see, was alive, helped unsteadily to his feet.

Gwen knew the Empire had millions more men. She knew a day of reckoning would come.

But that day was not today. Today she had not made the wisest decision—but she had made the bravest one. The right one. She felt it was a decision her father would have made. She had chosen the hardest path. The path of what was right. The path of justice. The path of valor. And regardless of what might come, on this day she had lived.

She had really lived.

CHAPTER THREE

Volusia stood on the stone balcony looking down, the cobblestone courtyard of Maltolis spread out below her, and far below she saw the sprawled out body of the Prince, lying there, unmoving, his limbs spread out in grotesque position. He seemed so far away from up here, so minuscule, so powerless, and Volusia marveled how, just moments before, he had been one of the most powerful rulers in the Empire. It struck home how frail life was, what an illusion power was—and most of all, how she, of infinite power, a true goddess now, wielded the power of life and death over anyone. Now, no one, not even a great prince, could stop her.

As she stood there, looking out, there arose all throughout the city the cries of his thousands of people, the touched citizens of Maltolis, moaning, their sound filling the courtyard and rising up like a plague of locusts. They wailed and screamed and slammed their heads against the stone walls; they leapt to the floor, like irate children, and tore the hair from their scalps. From the sight of them, Volusia mused, one would think that Maltolis had been a benevolent leader.

"OUR PRINCE!" one of them screamed, a scream echoed by many others as they all rushed forward, leaping onto the mad Prince's body, sobbing and convulsing as they clutched it.

"OUR DEAR FATHER!"

Bells suddenly tolled all throughout the city, a long succession of ringing, echoing each other. Volusia heard a commotion and she raised her eyes and watched as hundreds of Maltolis's troops marched hurriedly through the city gates, into the city courtyard, in rows of two, the portcullis rising to let them all in. They all aimed for Maltolis's castle.

Volusia knew she had set in motion an event that would forever alter this city.

There came a sudden, insistent booming at the thick oak door to her chamber, making her jump. It was an incessant slamming, the sound of dozens of soldiers, armor clanging, slamming a battering ram into the thick oak door of the Prince's chamber. Volusia, of course, had barred it, and the door, a foot thick, meant to withstand a siege, nonetheless buckled on its hinges, as the shouts of men came from the other side. With each slam it bent more.

Slam slam slam.

The stone chamber shook, and the ancient metal chandelier, hanging high above from a wooden beam, swayed wildly before it came crashing down to the floor.

Volusia stood there and watched it all calmly, expecting it all. She knew, of course, that they would come for her. They wanted vengeance—and they would never let her escape.

"Open the door!" shouted one of his generals.

She recognized his voice—the leader of Maltolis's forces, a humorless man she had met briefly, with a low, raspy voice—an inept man but a professional soldier, and with two hundred thousand men at his disposal.

And yet Volusia stood there and faced the door calmly, unfazed, watching it patiently, waiting for them to crash it down. She could of course have opened it for them, but she would not give them the satisfaction.

Finally there came a tremendous crash, and the wooden door gave way, bursting off its hinges, and dozens of soldiers, armor clanging, rushed the room. Maltolis' commander, donning his ornamental armor, and carrying the golden scepter that entitled him to command Maltolis' army, led the way.

They slowed to a quick walk as they saw her standing there, alone, not trying to run. The commander, a deep scowl set on his face, marched right up to her and stopped abruptly a few feet away.

He glared down at her with hatred, and behind him, all his men stopped, well-disciplined, and awaited his command.

Volusia stood there calmly, staring back with a slight smile, and she realized her poise must have thrown them off, as he seemed flustered.

"What have you done, woman?" he demanded, clutching his sword. "You have come into our city as a guest and you have killed our ruler. The chosen one. The one who could not be killed."

Volusia smiled back, and replied calmly:

"You are quite wrong, General," she said. "*I* am the one who cannot be killed. As I have just proved here today."

He shook his head in fury.

"How could you be so stupid?" he said. "Surely you must have known we would kill you and your men, that there is nowhere to run, no way to escape this place. Here, your few are surrounded by hundreds of thousands of ours. Surely you must have known that your act here today would amount to your death sentence—worse, your imprisonment and torture. We do not treat our enemies kindly, in case you haven't noticed."

"I have noticed indeed, General, and I admire it," she replied. "And yet you will not lay a hand on me. None of your men will."

He shook his head, annoyed.

"You are more foolish than I thought," he said. "I bear the golden scepter. All of our armies will do as I say. *Exactly* as I say."

"Will they?" she asked slowly, a smile on her face.

Slowly, Volusia turned and looked through the open-air window, down at the Prince's body, now being hoisted upon the shoulders of lunatics and bore throughout the city like a martyr.

Her back to him, she cleared her throat and continued.

"I do not doubt, General," she said, "that your forces are well-trained. Or that they will follow he who wields the scepter. Their fame precedes them. I know, too, that they are vastly greater than mine. And that there is no way to escape from here. But you see, I do not wish to escape. I do not need to."

He looked back at her, baffled, and Volusia turned and looked out the window, combing the courtyard. In the distance she spotted Koolian, her sorcerer, standing there in the crowd, ignoring all the others and staring only up at her with his glowing green eyes and wart-lined face. He wore his black cloak, unmistakable in the crowd, his arms folded calmly, his pale face looking up at her, partially hidden behind the hood, awaiting her command. He stood there, the only one still and patient and disciplined in this chaotic city.

Volusia gave him a barely discernible nod, and she saw him immediately nod back.

Slowly, Volusia turned, a smile on her face, and faced the general.

"You can hand me the scepter now," she said, "or I can kill you all and take it for myself."

He looked back at her, astounded, then shook his head and, for the first time, smiled.

"I know delusional people," he said. "I served one for years. But you…you are in a class of your own. Very well. If you wish to die that way, then so be it."

He stepped up and drew his sword.

"I am going to enjoy killing you," he added. "I wanted to from the moment I saw your face. All that arrogance—it is enough to make a man sick."

He approached her, and as he did, Volusia turned and suddenly saw Koolian standing in the room beside her.

Koolian turned and stared at him, startled at his sudden appearance out of thin air. He stood there, stumped, clearly not expecting this, and clearly not knowing what to make of him.

Koolian pulled back his black hood and sneered back at him with his grotesque face, too pale, his white eyes, rolling back in his head, and he slowly raised his palms.

As he did, suddenly, the commander and all his men dropped to their knees. They shrieked and raised their hands to their ears.

"Make it stop!" he yelled.

Slowly, blood poured from their ears, and one by one, they dropped to the stone floor, unmoving.

Dead.

Volusia stepped up slowly, calmly, reached down, and grabbed the golden scepter from the commander's dead hand.

She lifted it high and examined it in the light, admiring the weight of it, the way it glistened. It was a sinister thing.

She smiled wide.

It was even heavier than she had imagined.

*

Volusia stood just beyond the moat, outside the city walls of Maltolis, her sorcerer, Koolian, her assassin, Aksan, and the commander of her Volusian forces, Soku, behind her, and she looked out at the vast Maltolisian army assembled before her. As far as she could see, the desert plains were filled with Maltolis's men, two hundred thousand of them, a greater army than she'd ever laid eyes upon. Even for her, it was awe-inspiring.

They stood there patiently, leader-less, all looking to her, Volusia, who stood on a raised dais, facing them. The tension was thick in the air, and Volusia could sense that they were all waiting, pondering, deciding whether to kill her or to serve her.

Volusia looked out at them proudly, feeling her destiny before her, and slowly raised the golden scepter up overhead. She turned slowly, in every direction, so they could all see her, all see the scepter, glistening in the sun.

"MY PEOPLE!" she boomed out. "I am the Goddess Volusia. Your prince is dead. I am the one who bears the scepter now; I am the one you shall follow. Follow me, and you shall gain glory and riches and all your hearts' desires. Stay here, and you will waste away and die in this place, under the shadow of these walls, under the shadow of a corpse of a leader who never loved you. You served him in madness; you shall serve me in glory, in conquest, and finally have the leader you deserve."

Volusia raised the scepter higher, looking out at them, meeting their disciplined glances, feeling her destiny. She felt that she was invincible, that nothing could lie in her way, not even these hundreds of thousands of men. She knew that they, like all the world, would bow down to her. She saw it happening in her mind's eye; after all, she was a goddess. She lived in a realm above men. What choice could they have?

As sure as she envisioned it, there came a slow clanking of armor, and one by one, all of the men before her took a knee, one after the other, a great clang of armor spreading across the desert, as they all knelt down to her.

"VOLUSIA!" they chanted softly, again and again.

"VOLUSIA!"

"VOLUSIA!"

CHAPTER FOUR

Godfrey felt the sweat pouring down the back of his neck as he huddled inside the group of slaves, trying not to stick to the middle and not be seen as they wound their way through the streets of Volusia. Another crack cut through the air, and Godfrey screamed out in pain as the tip of a whip lashed his behind. The slave beside him screamed much louder, as the whip was mostly meant for her. It lashed her solidly across the back, and she cried and stumbled forward.

Godfrey reached out and caught her before she collapsed, acting on impulse, knowing he was risking his life in doing so. She steadied herself and turned to him, panic and fear across her face, and as she saw him, her eyes opened wide in surprise. Clearly, she had not expected to see him, a human, light of skin, walking freely beside her, unshackled. Godfrey shook his head quickly and raised a finger to his mouth, praying she'd remain silent. Luckily, she did.

There came another crack of a whip and Godfrey looked over and saw taskmasters working their way up the convoy, mindlessly lashing slaves, clearly just wanting to keep their presence known. As he glanced back, he noticed, right behind him, the panicked faces of Akorth and Fulton, eyes darting about, and beside them, the calm, determined faces of Merek and Ario. Godfrey marveled that these two boys showed more composure and bravery than Akorth and Fulton, two grown, albeit drunk, men.

They marched and marched, and Godfrey sensed they were nearing their destination, wherever that might be. Of course, he could not let them arrive there: he had to make a move soon. He had accomplished his goal, had managed to get inside Volusia—but now he had to break free from this group, before they were all discovered.

Godfrey looked about, and noticed something he took to heart: the taskmasters were now congregating mostly at the front of this convoy of slaves. It made sense, of course. Given that all the slaves were shackled together, there was clearly nowhere they could run, and the taskmasters clearly felt no need to guard the rear. Aside from the lone taskmaster walking up and down the lines lashing them, there was no one to stop them from slipping out through the back of the convoy. They could escape, slip out silently into the streets of Volusia.

Godfrey knew they should act quickly; and yet his heart pounded every time he considered making the bold move. His mind told him to go, and yet his body kept hesitating, never quite working up the courage.

Godfrey still could not believe they were here, that they had really made it inside these walls. It was like a dream—yet a dream that kept getting worse. The buzz from the wine was wearing off, and the more it did, the more he realized what a profoundly bad idea all of this was.

"We have to get out of here," Merek leaned forward and whispered urgently. "We have to make a move."

Godfrey shook his head and gulped, sweat stinging his eyes. A part of him knew he was right; yet another part of him kept waiting for exactly the right moment.

"No," he replied. "Not yet."

Godfrey looked around and saw all manner of slaves shackled and dragged throughout the streets of Volusia, not only those of darker skin. It looked as if the Empire had managed to enslave all manner of race from all corners of the Empire—everyone and anyone who was not of the Empire race, everyone who did not share their glowing yellow skin, extra height, broad shoulders, and the small horns behind their ears.

"What are we waiting for?" Ario asked.

"If we run out into the open streets," Godfrey said, "we might be too conspicuous. We might get caught, too. We must wait."

"Wait for what?" Merek pressed, frustration in his voice.

Godfrey shook his head, stumped. He felt as if his plan were falling apart.

"I don't know," he said.

They turned yet another corner, and as they did, the entire city of Volusia opened up before them. Godfrey took in the sight, in awe.

It was the most incredible city he'd ever seen. Godfrey, as the son of a king, had been to big cities, and grand cities, and wealthy cities, and fortified cities. He had been to some of the most beautiful cities in the world. Few cities were able to rival the majesty of a Savaria, a Silesia, or most of all, King's Court. He was not easily impressed.

But he had never seen anything like this. It was a combination of beauty, order, power, and wealth. Mostly wealth. The first thing that struck Godfrey were all the idols. Everywhere, placed throughout the city, were statues, idols to gods that Godfrey did not recognize. One appeared to be a god of the sea, another of the sky, another of the hills…. Everywhere were clusters of people, bowing down to them. In the distance, towering over the city, was a massive golden statue, rising up a hundred feet, of Volusia. Hordes of people bowed low before it.

The next thing that surprised Godfrey were the streets, paved with gold, shining, immaculate, everything fastidiously neat and clean. All the buildings were made of perfectly hewn stone, not a stone out of place. The city streets stretched forever, the city seeming to sprawl to the horizon. What took him aback even more were the canals and waterways, interlacing through the streets, sometimes in arches, sometimes in circles, carrying the azure tides of the ocean and acting as conduits, the oil which made this city flow. These waterways were packed with ornate golden vessels, making their way gently up and down them, crisscrossing through the streets.

The city was filled with light, reflecting off the harbor, dominated by the ever-present sound of crashing waves, as the city, shaped in a horseshoe, hugged the harbor shoreline, and waves crashed right up against its golden seawall. Between the sparkling light of the ocean, the rays of the two suns overhead, and the ever-present gold, Volusia positively dazzled the eyes. Framing it all, at the entrance to the harbor, were two towering pillars, nearly reaching to the sky, bastions of strength.

This city was built to intimidate, Godfrey realized, to exude wealth, and it did its job well. It was a city which exuded advances and civilization, and if Godfrey had not known of the cruelty of its inhabitants, it would have been a city he would have loved to live in himself. It was so different from anything the Ring had to offer. The cities of the Ring were built to fortify, protect, and defend. They were humble and understated, like their people. These cities of the Empire, on the other hand, were open, fearless, and build to project wealth. It made sense, Godfrey realized: after all, the Empire cities had no one from whom to fear an attack.

Godfrey heard a clamor up ahead, and as they twisted down an alleyway and turned a corner, suddenly, a great courtyard opened up before them, the harbor behind it. It was a wide, stone plaza, a major crossroads in the city, a dozen streets emerging from it in a dozen directions. All of this was visible in glimpses through a stone archway about twenty yards up ahead. Godfrey knew that once their entourage passed through it, they would all be out in the open, exposed, with everyone else. They wouldn't be able to slip out.

Even more disconcerting, Godfrey saw slaves pouring in from all directions, all being ushered in by taskmasters, slaves from all corners of the Empire and all manner of races, all shackled, being dragged towards a high platform at the base of the ocean. Slaves stood up high on it, while rich Empire folk studied them and placed bids. It looked like an auction block.

A cheer rose up, and Godfrey watched as an Empire noble examined a slave's jaw, a slave with white skin and long, stringy brown hair. The noble nodded in satisfaction, and a taskmaster came up and shackled the slave, as if concluding a business transaction. The taskmaster grabbed the slave by the back of the shirt and threw him, face-first, off the platform and down onto the ground. The man went flying, hitting the ground hard, and the crowd cheered in satisfaction, as several soldiers came forth and dragged him away.

Another entourage of slaves emerged from another corner of the city, and Godfrey watched as a slave was shoved forward, the largest slave, a foot taller than the others, strong and healthy. An Empire soldier raised his ax and the slave braced himself.

But the taskmaster chopped the shackles, the sound of metal hitting stone ringing through the courtyard.

The slave stared at the taskmaster, confused.

"Am I free?" he asked.

But several soldiers rushed forward, grabbed the slave's arms, and dragged him to the base of a large golden statue at the base of the harbor, another statue of Volusia, her finger pointed to the sea, waves crashing at her feet.

The crowd gathered close as the soldiers held the man down, his head pushed down, face-first, on the statue's foot.

"NO!" the man screamed.

The Empire soldier stepped forward and wielded his ax again, and this time, decapitated the man.

The crowd shouted in delight, and they all dropped to their knees and bowed down to the ground, worshipping the statue as the blood ran over its feet.

"A sacrifice to our great goddess!" called out the soldier. "We dedicate to you the first and choicest of our fruits!"

The crowd cheered again.

"I don't know about you," came Merek's voice in Godfrey's ear, urgent, "but I'm not going to be sacrificed to some idol. Not today."

There came another crack of a whip, and Godfrey could see the entranceway getting closer. His heart pounded as he considered his words, and knew Merek was right. He knew he had to do something—and fast.

Godfrey turned at a sudden movement. From the corner of his eye, he saw five men, wearing bright-red cloaks and hoods, walking quickly down the street in the other direction. He noticed they had white skin, pale hands and faces, saw that they were smaller than the hulking brutes of the Empire race, and immediately, he knew who they were: Finians. One of Godfrey's great skills was being able to commit tales to memory even while drunk, and he had listened thoroughly over the past moon as Sandara's people had recounted stories of Volusia many times over the fire. He had listened to their descriptions of the city, of its history, of all the races that were enslaved, and of the only free race: the Finians. The only exception to the rule. They had been allowed to live free, generation after generation, because they were too rich to kill, too connected, too able to make themselves indispensable, and to broker in the trading of power. They were easily noticeable, he had been told, by their too-pale skin, by their bright red cloaks and fiery red hair.

Godfrey had an idea. It was now or never.

"MOVE!" he called out to his friends.

Godfrey turned and leapt into motion, running out from the back of the entourage, to the baffled looks of the shackled slaves. The others, he was relieved to see, followed on his heels.

Godfrey ran, huffing, weighed down by the heavy sacks of gold at his waist, as were the others, jingling as they went. Up ahead he spotted the five Finians turning down a narrow alleyway; he ran right for them, and only prayed they could turn the corner undetected from Empire eyes.

Godfrey, his heart slamming in his ears, turned the corner and as he saw the Finians before him, without thinking he leapt into the air and pounced on the group from behind.

He managed to tackle three of them down to the ground, his ribs hurting as he hit the stone and went rolling with them. He looked up and saw Merek, following his lead, tackle another, Akorth jump down and pin down one of them, and watched Fulton leap for the last one, the smallest of the bunch. Fulton, Godfrey was annoyed to see, missed, and instead he went groaning and tumbling down to the ground.

Godfrey knocked out one of them on the ground and held down another, yet he was panicked to see the smallest one still running, breaking free, about to turn the corner. He glanced up out of the corner of his eye and watched as Ario stepped forward calmly, reached down and picked up a stone, examined it, then reached back and threw it.

A perfect shot, it struck the Finian in the temple as he was turning a corner, knocking him down to the ground. Ario ran over to him and stripped him of his cloak and began to put it on, realizing Godfrey's intentions.

Godfrey, still struggling with the other Finian, finally reached up and elbowed him across the face, knocking him out. Akorth finally grabbed his Finian by the shirt and smashed his head into the stone floor twice, knocking him out too. Merek choked his long enough make him lose consciousness, and Godfrey looked over and watched Merek roll onto the final Finian and hold a dagger to his throat.

Godfrey was about to yell at Merek to stop, but a voice cut through the air, beating him to it:

"No!" commanded the harsh voice.

Godfrey looked up to see Ario standing over Merek, scowling down.

"Do not kill him!" Ario commanded.

Merek scowled back.

"Dead men don't talk," Merek said. "I let him go, all of us die."

"I don't care," Ario said, "he did nothing to you. He will not be killed."

Merek, defiant, slowly rose to his feet and faced Ario. He got in his face.

"You're half my size, boy," Merek seethed, "and I hold the dagger. Don't tempt me."

"I may be half your size," Ario replied calmly, "but I'm twice as quick. Come at me and I will snatch that dagger from you and slice your throat before you finish swinging."

Godfrey was amazed at the exchange, most of all because Ario was so calm. It was surreal. He didn't blink, or move a muscle, and he spoke as if he were having the calmest conversation in the world. It made his words all the more convincing.

Merek must have thought so, too, because he did not make a move. Godfrey knew he had to break it up, and quick.

"The enemy is not here," Godfrey said, rushing forward and lowering Merek's wrist. "He is out there. We fight each other, and we stand no chance."

Luckily, Merek allowed his wrist to be lowered, and he sheathed his dagger.

"Hurry now," Godfrey added. "All of you. Strip their clothes and don them. We are Finians now."

They all stripped the Finians and donned their bright-red cloaks and hoods.

"This is ridiculous," Akorth said.

Godfrey examined him and saw his belly was too big, and he was too tall; the cloak ran short, exposing his ankles.

Merek snickered.

"Should have had one less pint," he said.

"I'm not wearing this!" Akorth said.

"It's not a fashion show," Godfrey said. "Would you rather be discovered?"

Akorth grudgingly backed down.

Godfrey stood there and looked at the five of them standing there, wearing the red cloaks, in this hostile city, surrounded by the enemy. He knew their chances were slim, at best.

"Now what?" Akorth asked.

Godfrey turned and looked out at the end of the alleyway, leading out into the city. He knew the time had come.

"Let's go see what Volusia is all about."

CHAPTER FIVE

Thor stood at the bow of the small sailing vessel, Reece, Selese, Elden, Indra, Matus, and O'Connor seated behind him, none of them rowing, the mysterious wind and current making all effort futile. It would carry them, Thor realized, where it would, and no amount of rowing or sailing would make a difference. Thor glanced back over his shoulder, watched the massive black cliffs marking the entrance to the Land of the Dead fading farther and farther away, and he felt relieved. It was time to look forward, to find Guwayne, to start a new chapter in his life.

Thor glanced back and noted Selese sitting in the boat, beside Reece, holding his hand, and he had to admit, the sight was disconcerting. Thor was thrilled to see her back in the land of the living again, and thrilled to see his best friend so elated. Yet it also, he had to admit, gave him an eerie feeling. Here was Selese, once dead, now brought back to life. He felt as if they had somehow changed the natural order of things. As he examined her, he noticed she had a translucent, ethereal quality, and even though she was really there, in the flesh, he could not help but see her as dead. He could not help but wonder, despite himself, if she was really back for good, how long her time here would last before she returned.

Yet Reece, on the other hand, clearly did not see it that way. He was totally enamored of her, Thor's friend joyous for the first time in as long as he could remember. Thor could understand: after all, who wouldn't want the chance to make wrongs right, to make amends for past mistakes, to see someone one was sure he would never see again? Reece clutched her hand, staring into her eyes, and she caressed his face as he kissed her.

The others, Thor noticed, looked lost, as if they'd been to the depths of hell, to a place they could not easily shake from their minds. The cobwebs lingered heavily, and Thor felt them, too, shaking

32

flashbacks from his mind. There was an aura of gloom, as they all mourned the loss of Conven. Thor, especially, turned over and over in his mind if there was anything he could have done to stop him. Thor looked out to sea, studying the gray horizon, the limitless ocean, and he wondered how Conven could have made the decision he had. He understood his deep grief for his brother; yet Thor would never make the same decision. Thor realized he felt a sense of grief for the loss of Conven, whose presence had always been felt, who had always seemed to be by his side, ever since his first days in the Legion. Thor recalled his visiting him in prison, his talking him into a second chance at life, all of his attempts to cheer him up, to snap him out of it, to bring him back.

Yet, Thor realized, no matter what he'd done, he could never quite bring Conven back. The better part of Conven was always with his brother. Thor recalled the look in Conven's face as he'd remained behind and the others left. It was not a look of regret; it was a look of pure joy. Thor felt that he was happy. And he knew he shouldn't hold too much regret. Conven had made his own decision, and that was more than most people got in this world. And after all, Thor knew they would meet again. In fact, maybe Conven would be the one waiting to greet him when he died. Death, Thor knew, was coming for them all. Maybe not today, or tomorrow. But one day.

Thor tried to shake the somber thoughts; he looked out and forced himself to focus on the ocean, scouring the waters every which way, looking for any sign of Guwayne. He knew it was likely futile to look for him here, on the open sea, yet still, Thor felt mobilized, filled with a newfound optimism. He knew now, at least, that Guwayne was alive, and that was all he needed to hear. He would stop at nothing to find him again.

"Where do you suppose this current is taking us?" O'Connor asked, reaching over the edge of the boat and skimming the water with his fingertips.

Thor reached down and touched the warm water, too; it rushed by so fast, as if the ocean could not bring them wherever it was taking them fast enough.

"As long as it is far from there, I don't care," Elden said, glancing back over his shoulder in fear at the cliffs.

Thor heard a screeching noise, high up, and he looked up and was thrilled to see his old friend, Estopheles, circling high above. She dove down in broad circles around them, then lifted back up into the air. Thor felt as if she were guiding them, encouraging them to follow her.

"Estopheles, my friend," Thor whispered up to the sky. "Be our eyes. Lead us to Guwayne."

Estopheles screeched again, as if answering, and spread her wings wide. She turned and flew off into the horizon, in the same direction the current was taking them, and Thor felt certain they were getting closer.

As Thor turned he heard a gentle clanging at his side, and he looked down and saw the Sword of Death hanging at his waist, and it was shocking to see it there. It made his trip to the land of the dead feel more real than ever. Thor reached down, felt its ivory hilt, crossed with skulls and bones, and tightened his grip on it, feeling its energy. Its blade was inlaid with small black diamonds, and as he held it up to examine it, he saw them sparkling in the light.

As he held it, it felt so right in his hand. He hadn't felt this way about a weapon since he'd wielded the Destiny Sword. This weapon meant more to him than he could say; after all, he had managed to escape that world, and so had this weapon, and he felt they were both survivors of an awful war. They had been through it together. Entering the land of the dead and returning had been like walking through a giant spider web and pulling it off. It was off, Thor knew, and yet somehow he still felt it sticking to him. At least he had this weapon to show for it.

Thor reflected on his exit, on the price he'd paid, on the demons he'd unleashed unwittingly on the world. He felt a pit in his stomach, sensing he'd unleashed a dark force on the world, one not so easily contained. He felt he'd sent something out, like a boomerang, that would one day, somehow, return to him. Perhaps even sooner than he thought.

Thor gripped the hilt, prepared. Whatever it was, he would meet it in battle fearlessly, would kill whatever came his way.

But what he truly feared were the things he could not see, the invisible havoc the demons might wreak. What he feared most were the spirits unknown, the spirits who fought by stealth.

Thor heard footsteps, felt their small boat rock, and he turned and saw Matus walk up beside him. Matus stood there sadly, looking out at the horizon with him. It was a dark, grim day, and as they looked out, it was hard to tell if it was morning or afternoon, the whole sky uniform, as if this entire part of the world were in mourning.

Thor thought of how Matus had quickly become a close friend to him. Especially now, with Reece fixated on Selese, Thor felt the partial loss of one friend, and the gaining of another. Thor recalled how Matus had saved him more than once down there, and he already felt a loyalty to him, as if he had always been one of his own brothers.

"This vessel," Matus said softly, "was not made for the open seas. One good storm, and we shall all be killed. It is just an outboat from Gwendolyn's ship, not meant to traverse the seas. We must find a bigger boat."

"And land," O'Connor chimed in, coming up on Thor's other side, "and provisions."

"And a map," Elden chimed in.

"Where is our destination, anyway?" Indra asked. "Where is it we are going? Have you any idea where your son might be?"

Thor examined the horizon, as he had a thousand times, and reflected on all their questions. He knew they were all right, and had been thinking the same things. A vast sea lay before them, and they were a small vessel, with no provisions. They were alive, and he was grateful for that, but their situation was precarious.

Thor shook his head slowly. As he stood there, immersed in thought, he began to spot something on the horizon. As they sailed closer, it began to more distinctly come into view, and he felt certain it was something and not just his eyes playing tricks on him. His heart raced with excitement.

The sun broke through the clouds, and a shaft of sunlight poured down on the horizon and lit up a small island. It was a small land mass, in the middle of a vast ocean, with nothing else anywhere near it.

Thor blinked, wondering if it were real.

"What is it?" Matus asked the question on all of their minds, as they all saw it, all of them standing and staring.

As they came close, Thor saw a mist surrounding the island, sparkling in the light, and he sensed a magical energy to this place. He looked up and saw it was a stark place, cliffs rising straight up into the air, hundreds of feet, a narrow, steep, unforgiving island, waves crashing into the boulders that surrounded it, emerging from the ocean like ancient beasts. Thor sensed, with every ounce of his being, that this was where they were meant to go.

"That's a steep climb," O'Connor said. "If we even made it."

"And we don't know what's at the top," Elden added. "Could be hostile. Our weapons are all gone, except for your sword. We can't afford a battle here."

But Thor considered the place, and he wondered, sensing something strong here. He looked up high and watched Estopheles circling it, and he felt even more certain that this was the place.

"No stone must be left unturned in our search for Guwayne," Thor said. "No place is too remote. This island will be our first stop," he said. He tightened his grip on his sword:

"Hostile or not."

CHAPTER SIX

Alistair found herself standing in a strange landscape she did not recognize. It was a desert of sorts, and as she looked down the desert floor turned from black to red, drying up, cracking beneath her feet. She looked up, and in the distance she spotted Gwendolyn standing before a ragtag army, but a few dozen men, members of the Silver that Alistair once knew, all their faces bloody, their armor cracked. In Gwendolyn's arms was a small baby, and Alistair sensed that it was her nephew, Guwayne.

"Gwendolyn!" Alistair called out, relieved to see her. "My sister!"

But as Alistair watched there suddenly came an awful sound, the sound of a million flapping wings, growing louder, followed by a great squawking. The horizon turned black and there emerged a sky filled with ravens, flying her way.

Alistair watched in horror as the ravens arrived in one huge flock, a wall of black, swooped down and snatched Guwayne from Gwendolyn's arms. Screeching, they lifted him up into the sky.

"NO!" Gwendolyn shrieked, reaching for the sky as they tore at her hair.

Alistair watched, helpless, nothing she could do but watch them carry off the screaming baby. The desert floor cracked and dried further, and it began to split apart, until one by one, all of Gwen's men collapsed down into it.

Only Gwendolyn remained, standing there, staring back at her, her eyes haunted with a look that Alistair wished she had never seen.

Alistair blinked and found herself standing on a great ship in the midst of an ocean, waves crashing all around her. She looked about and saw she was the only one on the ship, and faced forward and saw another ship before her. Erec stood at its bow, facing her, and was joined by hundreds of soldiers from the Southern Isles. She was distressed to see him on another ship, and sailing away from her.

"Erec!" she called out.

He stared back, reaching out for her.

"Alistair!" he called back. "Come back to me!"

Alistair watched in horror as the ships drifted further apart, Erec's ship sucked away from her on the tides. His ship began to slowly spin in the water, and it spun faster and faster, Erec reaching out for her, Alistair helpless to do nothing but watch as his ship was sucked down by a whirlpool, deeper and deeper, until it disappeared from view.

"EREC!" Alistair cried.

There came another wail, to match hers, and Alistair looked down to see that she was holding a baby—Erec's child. It was a boy, and his wails rose to the heavens, drowning out the noise of the wind and the rain and the shrieking of men.

Alistair woke screaming. She sat up and looked around, wondering where she was, what had happened. Breathing hard, slowly collecting herself, it took her several moments to realize it was all just a dream.

She stood and looked down at the creaking floorboards of the deck, and realized she was still on the ship. It all came flooding back to her: their departure from the Southern Isles, their quest to free Gwendolyn.

"My lady?" came a gentle voice.

Alistair looked over and saw Erec standing beside her, looking back at her, concerned. She was relieved to see him.

"Another nightmare?" he asked.

She nodded, looking away, self-conscious.

"Dreams are more vivid at sea," said another voice.

Alistair turned to see Erec's brother, Strom, standing nearby. She turned further and saw hundreds of Southern Islanders all aboard the ship, and it all came back to her. She remembered their departure, their leaving a grieving Dauphine behind, whom they had left to be in charge of the Southern Isles with her mother. Ever since receiving that message, all of them felt they had no choice but to set sail for the Empire, to search for Gwendolyn and all the others of the Ring, duty-bound to save them. They knew it would be an impossible mission, yet none of them cared. It was their duty.

Alistair rubbed her eyes and tried to shake the nightmares from her mind. She did not know how many days had passed already on this endless sea, and as she looked out now, studying the horizon, she could not see much. It was all obscured by fog.

"The fog has been following us since the Southern Isles," Erec said, watching her gaze.

"Let's hope it's not an omen," Strom added.

Alistair gently rubbed her belly, reassured that she was OK, that her baby was OK. Her dream had felt too real. She did it quickly and discreetly, not wanting Erec to know. She hadn't told him yet. A part of her wanted to—but another part of her wanted to wait for the perfect moment, when it felt right.

She took Erec's hand, relieved to see him alive.

"I'm glad you're okay," she said.

He smiled back, as he pulled her close and kissed her.

"And why wouldn't I be?" he asked. "Your dreams are just fancies of the night. For every nightmare, there is also a man who is safe. I'm as safe here, with you and my loyal brother and my men, as I can ever hope to be."

"Until we reach the Empire at least," Strom added with a smile. "Then we shall be as safe as we can ever be with a small fleet against ten thousand ships."

Strom smiled as he spoke, seeming to relish the fight to come.

Erec shrugged, serious.

"With the Gods behind our cause," he said, "we cannot lose. Whatever the odds."

Alistair pulled back and frowned, trying to make sense of it all.

"I saw you and your ship being sucked down to the bottom of the sea. I saw you on it," she said. She wanted to add the bit about their child, but she restrained herself.

"Dreams are not always what they appear to be," he said. Yet deep in his eyes, she saw a flash of concern. He knew that she saw things, and he respected her visions.

39

Alistair took a deep breath, looked down to the water, and knew he was right. They were all here, alive after all. Yet it had seemed so true.

As she stood there, Alistair felt the temptation to again raise her hand to her belly, to feel her stomach, to reassure herself and the child she knew was growing within her. Yet, with Erec and Strom standing there, she did not want to give it away.

A low, soft horn cut through the air, sounding intermittently every few minutes, warning the other ships in his fleet of their presence in the fog.

"That horn might give us away," Strom said to Erec.

"To whom?" Erec asked.

"We know not what lurks behind the fog," Strom said.

Erec shook his head.

"Perhaps," he replied. "But the greater danger for now is not the enemy, but ourselves. We collide into our own, and we can bring our entire fleet down. We must sound the horns until the fog lifts. Our entire fleet can talk this way—and just as importantly, not drift too far from each other."

In the fog, a horn from another of the ships in Erec's fleet echoed, confirming its location.

Alistair looked out into the fog, and wondered. She knew they had so far to go, that they were on the other side of the world from the Empire, and she wondered how they would ever reach Gwendolyn and her brother in time. She wondered how long the falcons had took with that message, and wondered if they were even still alive. She wondered what had become of her beloved Ring. What an awful way for them all to die, she thought, on a foreign shore, far from their homeland.

"The Empire is across the world, my lord," Alistair said to Erec. "It shall be a long journey. Why do you stay up here on the deck? Why not go down below, to the hold, and sleep? You haven't slept in days," she said, observing the dark rings beneath his eyes.

He shook his head.

"A commander never sleeps," he said. "And besides, we are almost at our destination."

"Our destination?" she asked, puzzled.

Erec nodded and looked out into the fog.

She followed his gaze but saw nothing.

"Boulder Isle," he said. "Our first stop."

"But why?" she asked. "Why stop before we reach the Empire?"

"We need a bigger fleet," Strom chimed in, answering for him. "We can't face the Empire with a few dozen ships."

"And you will find this fleet in Boulder Isle?" Alistair asked.

Erec nodded.

"We might," Erec said. "Bouldermen have ships, and men. More than we have. They despise the Empire. And they have served my father in the past."

"But why would they help you now?" she asked, puzzled. "Who are these men?"

"Mercenaries," Strom chimed in. "Rough men forged by a rough island on rough seas. They fight for the highest bidder."

"Pirates," Alistair said disapprovingly, realizing.

"Not quite," Strom replied. "Pirates strive for loot. Bouldermen live for killing."

Alistair examined Erec, and could see in his face that it was true.

"It is noble to fight for a true and just cause with pirates?" she asked. "Mercenaries?"

"It is noble to win a war," Erec replied, "and to fight for a just cause such as ours. The means of waging such a war is not always as noble as we might like."

"It is not noble to die," Strom added. "And the judgment on nobility is decided by the victors, not the losers."

Alistair frowned and Erec turned to her.

"Not everyone is as noble as you, my lady," he said. "Or as I. That is not the way the world works. That is not the way that wars are won."

"And can you trust such men?" she finally asked him.

Erec sighed and turned back to the horizon, hands on his hips, staring out as if wondering the same thing.

"Our father trusted them," he finally said. "And his father before him. They never failed them."

"And does that mean they shall not fail you now?" she asked.

Erec studied the horizon, and as he did, suddenly the fog lifted and the sun broke through. The vista changed dramatically, their suddenly gaining visibility, and in the distance, Alistair's heart leapt as she saw land. There, on the horizon, sat a soaring island made of solid cliffs, rising straight up into the sky. There seemed to be no place to land, no beach, no entrance. Until Alistair looked higher and saw an arch, a door cut into the mountain itself, the ocean splashing right up against it. It was a large and imposing entrance, guarded by an iron portcullis, a wall of solid rock with a door cut into the middle of it. It was unlike anything she'd ever seen.

Erec stared at the horizon, studying it, the sunlight striking the door as if illuminating the entrance to another world.

"Trust, my lady," he answered finally, "is born of need, not of want. And it is a very precarious thing."

CHAPTER SEVEN

Darius stood in the battlefield, holding a sword made of steel, and looked all around him, taking in the landscape. It had a surreal quality. Even seeing it with his own eyes, he could not believe what had just happened. They had defeated the Empire. He, alone, with a few hundred villagers, without any real weapons—and with the help of Gwendolyn's few hundred men—had defeated this professional army of hundreds of Empire soldiers. They had donned the finest armor, had wielded the finest weapons, had had zertas at their disposal. And he, Darius, barely armed, had led the battle that had defeated them all, the first victory against the Empire in history.

Here, in this place, where he had expected to die defending Loti's honor, he now stood victorious.

A conqueror.

As Darius surveyed the field, he saw intermingled with the Empire corpses the bodies of scores of his own villagers, dozens dead, and his joy was tampered with sorrow. He flexed his muscles and felt fresh wounds himself, sword slashes in his biceps and thighs, and felt the sting of the lashes still on his back. He thought of the retaliation to come and knew their victory had come at a price.

But then again, he mused, all freedom did.

Darius sensed motion and he turned to see approaching him his friends, Raj and Desmond, wounded but, he was relieved to see, alive. He could see in their eyes that they looked at him differently—that all of his people now looked at him differently. They looked at him with respect—more than respect, with awe. Like a living legend. They had all seen what he had done, standing up to the Empire alone. And defeating them all.

They no longer looked to him as a boy. They now looked to him as a leader. A warrior. It was a look he had never expected to see in these older boys' eyes, in the villagers' eyes. He had always been the one overlooked, the one that no one had expected anything from.

Coming up alongside him, joining Raj and Desmond, were dozens of his brothers in arms, boys whom he had trained and sparred with day after day, perhaps fifty of them, brushing off their wounds, rising to their feet, and congregating around him. They all looked to him, standing there, holding his steel sword, covered in wounds, with awe. And with hope.

Raj stepped forward and embraced him, and one at a time, his other brothers in arms embraced him as well.

"That was reckless," Raj said with a smile. "I didn't think you had it in you."

"I thought for sure you would surrender," Desmond said.

"I can hardly believe we are all standing here," said Luzi.

They looked about in wonder, surveying the landscape, as if they all had been dropped down on a foreign planet. Darius looked at all the dead bodies, at all the fine armor and weaponry glistening in the sun; he heard birds cawing, and looked up to see the vultures already circling.

"Gather their weapons," Darius heard himself command, taking charge. It was a deep voice, a deeper one than he had ever used, and it carried an air of authority he had never recognized in himself. "And bury our dead."

His men listened, all of them fanning out, going soldier to soldier, scavenging them, each of them choosing the finest weapons: some took swords, others maces, flails, daggers, axes, and war hammers. Darius held up the sword in his hand, the one he had taken from the commander, and admired it in the sun. He admired its weight, its elaborate shaft and blade. Real steel. Something he thought he would never have a chance to hold in his lifetime. Darius intended to put it to good use, to use it to kill as many Empire men as he could.

"Darius!" came a voice he knew well.

He turned to see Loti burst through the crowd, tears in her eyes, rushing toward him past all the men. She rushed forward and embraced him, holding him tight, her hot tears pouring down his neck.

He embraced her back, as she clung to him.

"I shall never forget," she said, between tears, leaning in close and whispering in his ear. "I shall never forget what you have done this day."

She kissed him, and he kissed her back, as she cried and laughed at the same time. He was so relieved to see her alive, too, to hold her, to know this nightmare, at least for now, was behind them. To know that the Empire could not touch her. As he held her, he knew he would do it all again a million times over for her.

"Brother," came a voice.

Darius turned and was thrilled to see his sister, Sandara, step forward, joined by Gwendolyn and the man Sandara loved, Kendrick. Darius noticed the blood running down Kendrick's arm, the fresh nicks in his armor and on his sword, and he felt a rush of gratitude. He knew that if it hadn't been for Gwendolyn, Kendrick, and their people, he and his people surely would have died on the battlefield today.

Loti stood back as Sandara stepped forward and embraced him, and he hugged her back.

"I owe you all a great debt," Darius said, looking at them all. "I and all of my people. You came back for us when you did not need to. You are true warriors."

Kendrick stepped forward and placed a hand on Darius's shoulder.

"It is you who are a true warrior, my friend. You displayed great valor on the battlefield today. God has rewarded your valor with this victory."

Gwendolyn stepped forward, and Darius bowed his head as she did.

"Justice has triumphed today over evil and brutality," she said. "I take personal pleasure, for many reasons, in watching your victory and in your allowing us to take part in it. I know that my husband, Thorgrin, would, too."

"Thank you, my lady," he said, touched. "I have heard many great things about Thorgrin, and I hope to meet him some day."

Gwendolyn nodded.

"And what are your plans for your people now?" she asked.

Darius thought, realizing he had no idea; he hadn't been thinking that far ahead. He hadn't even thought he would survive.

Before Darius could respond there was a sudden commotion, and there burst forth from the crowd a face he knew well: there approached Zirk, one of Darius's trainers, bloodied by battle, wearing no shirt with his bulging muscles. He was followed by a half dozen village elders and a large number of villagers, and he did not look pleased.

He glared down on Darius condescendingly.

"And are you proud of yourself?" he asked disparagingly. "Look at what you've done. Look at how many of our people died here today. They all died senseless deaths, all good men, all dead because of you. All because of your pride, your hubris, your love for this girl."

Darius reddened, his anger flaring up. Zirk had always had it in for him, from the first day he'd met him. For some reason, he had always seemed to feel threatened by Darius.

"They are not dead because of me," Darius replied. "They had a chance to live because of me. To truly live. They died at the Empire's hands, not my own."

Zirk shook his head.

"Wrong," he retorted. "If you had surrendered, as we had told you to do, we all would be missing a thumb today. Instead, some of us are missing our lives. Their blood is on your head."

"You know nothing!" Loti cried out, defending him. "You were all just too scared to do what Darius did for you!"

"Do you think it's going to end here?" Zirk continued. "The Empire has millions of men behind this. You killed a few. So what? When they find out, they will return with fivefold these men. And next time, each and every one of us will be slaughtered—and tortured first. You have signed all of our death sentences."

"You are wrong!" Raj called out. "He has given you a chance at life. A chance at honor. A victory that you did not deserve."

Zirk turned to Raj, scowling.

"These were the actions of a foolish and reckless young boy," he replied. "A group of boys who should have listened to their elders. I never should have trained any of you!"

"Wrong," Loc yelled out, stepping forward beside Loti. "These were the bold actions of a *man*. A man that led boys to be men. A man that you pretend to be, but are not. Age does not make the man. Valor does."

Zirk reddened, scowling at him, and tightened his grip on the hilt of his sword.

"So says the cripple," Zirk replied, stepping threateningly toward him.

Bokbu emerged from the crowd and held out a palm, stopping Zirk.

"Don't you see what the Empire is doing to us?" Bokbu said. "They create division amongst us. But we are one people. United under one cause. They are the enemy, not us. Now more than ever we see that we must unite."

Zirk rested his hands on his hips and glared at Darius.

"You are just a foolish boy with fancy words," he said. "You can never defeat the Empire. Never. And we are not united. I disapprove of your actions today—we all do," he said, gesturing to half the elders and a large group of villagers. "Uniting with you is uniting with death. And we intend to survive."

"And how do you intend to do that?" Desmond asked back angrily, standing by Darius's side.

Zirk reddened and remained silent, and it was clear to Darius that he had no plan, just like all the others, that he was speaking out of fear, frustration, and helplessness.

Bokbu finally stepped forward, between them, breaking the tension. All eyes turned to him.

"You are both right and you are both wrong," he said. "What matters now is the future. Darius, what is your plan?"

Darius felt all eyes turn to him in the thick silence. He thought, and slowly a plan formed in his mind. He knew there was but one route to take. Too much had happened for anything else.

"We will take this war to the Empire's doorstep," he called out, invigorated. "Before they can regroup, we will make them pay. We will rally the other slave villages, we will form an army, and we will make them learn what it means to suffer. We might die, but we will all die as free men, fighting for our cause."

There came a great cheer out from behind Darius, from the majority of the villagers, and he could see most of them rallying behind him. A small group of them, rallying behind Zirk, looked back, unsure.

Zirk, clearly infuriated and outnumbered, reddened, released his grip on his sword hilt, and turned and stormed off, disappearing into the crowd. A small group of villagers stormed off with him.

Bokbu stepped forward and solemnly faced Darius, his face lined with worry, with age, with lines that had seen too much. He stared back at Darius, his eyes filled with wisdom. And with fear.

"Our people turn to you to lead them now," he said softly. "That is a very sacred thing. Do not lose their trust. You are young to lead an army. But the task has fallen upon you. You have started this war. Now, you must finish it."

*

Gwendolyn stepped forward as the villagers began to dissipate, Kendrick and Sandara by her side, Steffen, Brandt, Atme, Aberthol, Stara, and dozens of her men behind her. She looked upon Darius with respect, and she could see the gratitude in his eyes for her decision to come to his aid on the battlefield today. After their victory, she felt vindicated; she knew she had made the right decision, however hard it had been. She had lost dozens of her men here today, and she mourned their loss. Yet she also knew that, had she not turned around, Darius and all the others standing here would certainly be dead.

Seeing Darius standing there, so bravely facing off against the Empire, made her think of Thorgrin, and her heart broke as she thought of him. She felt determined to reward Darius's bravery, whatever the cost.

"We stand here ready to support your cause," Gwendolyn said. She commanded the attention of Darius, Bokbu, and all the others, as all the remaining villagers turned to her. "You took us in when we needed it—and we stand here ready to support you when you need it. We lend our arms to yours, our cause to yours. After all, it is one cause. We wish to return to our homeland in freedom—you wish to liberate your homeland in freedom. We each share the same oppressor."

Darius looked back at her, clearly touched, and Bokbu stepped forward in the midst of the group and stood there, facing her in the thick silence, all of their people watching.

"We see here today what a great decision we made to take you in," he said proudly. "You have rewarded us far beyond our dreams, and we have been greatly rewarded. Your reputation, you of the Ring, as honorable and true warriors, has held true. And we are forever in your debt."

He took a deep breath.

"We do need your help," he continued. "But more men on the battlefield is not what we need. More of your men will not be enough—not with the war that is coming. If you truly wish to help our cause, what we really need is for you to find us reinforcements. If we are to stand a chance, we will need tens of thousands of men to come to our aid."

Gwen stared back, wide-eyed.

"And where are we to find these tens of thousands of knights?"

Bokbu looked back grimly.

"If there exists anywhere a city of free men within the Empire, a city willing to come to our aid—and that is a big *if*—then it would lie within the second Ring."

Gwen stared back, puzzled.

"What are you asking of us?" she asked.

Bokbu stared back, solemn.

"If you truly wish to help us," he said, "I ask you to embark on an impossible mission. I ask you to do something even harder and more dangerous than joining us on the battlefield. I ask you to embark on your original plan, on the quest on which you were to embark today. I ask you to cross the Great Waste; to seek out the Second Ring; and if you make it there alive, if it even exists, to convince their armies to rally to our cause. That is the only chance we'd stand of winning this war."

He stared back, somber, the silence so thick that all Gwen could hear was the wind rustling through the desert.

"No one has ever crossed the Great Waste," he continued. "No one has ever confirmed the Second Ring even exists. It is an impossible task. A march to suicide. I hate to ask you. Yet it is what we need most."

Gwendolyn examined Bokbu, noted the seriousness on his face, and she pondered his words long and hard.

"We will do whatever is needed," she said, "whatever best serves your cause. If allies lie on the other side of the Great Waste, then so be it. We shall march at once. And we shall return with armies at our disposal."

Bokbu, tears in his eyes, stepped forward and embraced Gwendolyn.

"You are a true queen," he said. "Your people are fortunate to have you."

Gwen turned to her people, and she saw them all staring back solemnly, fearlessly. She knew they would follow her anywhere.

"Prepare to march," she said. "We shall cross the Great Waste. We shall find the Second Ring. Or we shall die trying."

*

Sandara stood there, feeling torn apart as she watched Kendrick and his people preparing to embark on their journey to the Great Waste. On her other side were Darius and her people, the people she

50

had been raised with, the only people she'd ever known, preparing to turn away, to rally their villages to fight the Empire. She felt split down the middle, and did not know which way to turn. She couldn't bear to see Kendrick disappear forever; and yet she couldn't bear to abandon her people, either.

Kendrick, finishing preparing his armor and sheathing his sword, looked up and met her eyes. He seemed to know what she was thinking—he always did. She could also see hurt in his eyes, a wariness of her; she did not blame him—all this time in the Empire she had kept her distance from him, had lived in the village while he lived in the caves. She had been intent on honoring her elders, on not intermarrying with another race.

And yet, she realized, she had not honored love. What was more important? To honor one's family's laws or to honor one's heart? She had anguished over it every day.

Kendrick made his way over to her.

"I expect you will remain behind with your people?" he asked, a wariness in his voice.

She looked at him, torn, anguished, and did not know what to say. She did not know the answer herself. She felt frozen in space, in time, felt her feet rooted to the desert floor.

Suddenly, Darius came up beside her.

"My sister," he said.

She turned and nodded to him, grateful for the distraction, as he draped an arm around her shoulder and looked at Kendrick.

"Kendrick," he said.

Kendrick nodded back with respect.

"You know the love that I hold for you," Darius continued. "Selfishly, I want you to stay."

He took a deep breath.

"And yet, I implore you to go with Kendrick."

Sandara looked at him, shocked.

"But why?" she asked.

"I see the love you hold for him, and he for you. A love like this does not come twice. You must follow your heart, regardless of what our people think, regardless of our laws. That is what matters most."

Sandara looked at her younger brother, touched; she was impressed at his wisdom.

"You really have grown since I've left you," she said.

"Don't you dare abandon your people, and don't you dare go with him," came a stern voice.

Sandara turned to see Zirk, overhearing and stepping forward, joined by several of the elders.

"Your place is here with us. If you go with this man, you shall not be welcome back here."

"And what business is it of yours?" Darius asked angrily, defending her.

"Careful, Darius," Zirk said. "You may lead this army for now, but you don't lead us. Don't pretend to speak for our people."

"I speak for my sister," Darius said, "and I will speak for anyone I wish."

Sandara noticed Darius clench his fist on the hilt of his sword as he stared down Zirk, and she quickly reached out and placed a reassuring hand on his wrist.

"The decision is mine to make," she said to Zirk. "And I have already made it," she said, feeling a rush of indignation and suddenly deciding. She would not let these people make a decision for her. She had been allowing the elders to dictate her life as long as she knew, and now, the time had come.

"Kendrick is my beloved," she said, turning to Kendrick, who looked back at her with surprise. As she said the words, she knew them to be true, and felt such a rush of love for him, felt a wave of guilt for not embracing him sooner before the others. "His people are my people. He is mine and I am his. And nothing, no one, not you, not anyone, can tear us apart."

She turned to Darius.

"Goodbye, my brother," she said. "I will join Kendrick."

Darius grinned wide, while Zirk scowled back.

"Never look upon our faces again," he spat, then turned and walked away, the elders joining him.

Sandara returned to Kendrick and did what she had wanted to do ever since the two of them had arrived here. She kissed him openly, without fear, in front of everyone, finally able to express her love for him. To her great joy, he kissed her back, taking her in his arms.

"Be safe, my brother," Sandara said.

"And you, my sister. We shall meet again."

"In this world or the next," she said.

With that, Sandara turned, took Kendrick's arm, and together, they joined his people, heading out toward the Great Waste, to a sure death, but she was ready to go anywhere in the world, as long she was by Kendrick's side.

CHAPTER EIGHT

Godfrey, Akorth, Fulton, Merek, and Ario, dressed in the Finians' cloaks, walked down the shining streets of Volusia, all on guard, bunched together, and very tense. Godfrey's buzz had long ago worn off, and he navigated the unknown streets, the gold sacks at his waist, cursing himself for volunteering for this mission and racking his brain for what to do next. He would give anything for a drink right now.

What a terrible, awful idea he had had to come here. Why on earth had he had such a stupid moment of chivalry? What was chivalry anyway? he wondered. A moment of passion, of selflessness, of craziness. It just made his throat run dry, his heart pound, his hands shake. He hated the feeling, hated every second of it. He wished he'd kept his big mouth shut. Chivalry wasn't for him.

Or was it?

He was no longer sure of anything. All he knew right now was that he wanted to survive, to live, to drink, to be anywhere but here. What he wouldn't give for a beer right now. He would trade the most heroic act in the world for a pint of ale.

"And who is it exactly we are going to pay off?" Merek asked, coming up beside him as they walked together through the streets.

Godfrey racked his brain.

"We need someone in their army," he finally said. "A commander. Not too high up. Someone just high enough. Someone who cares more for gold than killing."

"And where will we find such a person?" Ario asked. "We can't exactly march into their barracks."

"In my experience, there's only one reliable place to find someone of imperfect morals," Akorth said. "The taverns."

"Now you're talking," Fulton said. "Now, finally, someone is talking sense."

"That sounds like an awful idea," Ario retorted. "It sounds like you just want a drink."

"Well, I do," Akorth said. "And what's the shame in that?"

"What do you think?" Ario countered. "That you're just going to march into a tavern, find a commander, and buy him off? That it's that easy?"

"Well, the kid is finally right about something," Merek chimed in. "It's a bad idea. They'd take one look at our gold, kill us, and take it for themselves."

"That's why we're not bringing our gold," Godfrey said, deciding.

"Huh?" Merek asked, turning to him. "What are we going to do with it then?"

"Hide it," Godfrey said.

"Hide all this gold?" Ario asked. "Are you mad? We brought too much as it is. It's enough to buy half the city."

"That's precisely why we are going to hide it," Godfrey said, warming to the idea. "We find the right person, for the right price, that we can trust, and we'll lead him to it."

Merek shrugged.

"This is a fool's errand. It's going from bad to worse. We followed you in, God knows why. You're walking us to our graves."

"You followed me in because you believe in honor, in courage," Godfrey said. "You followed me in because, from the moment you did, we became brothers. Brothers in valor. And brothers do not abandon one another."

The others fell silent as they walked, and Godfrey was surprised at himself. He did not fully understand this streak of himself that surfaced every now and again. Was it his father talking? Or he?

They turned a corner, and the city opened up, and Godfrey was overwhelmed once again by the beauty of it. Everything shining, streets lined with gold, interlaced with canals of sea water, light everywhere, reflecting off the gold, blinding him. The streets were bustling here, too, and Godfrey took in the thick throngs, amazed. His shoulder got bumped more than once, and he took care to keep his head lowered so that the Empire soldiers would not detect him.

Soldiers, in all manner of armor, marched to and fro in every direction, interspersed with Empire nobles and citizens, huge men with the identifiable yellow skin and small horns, many with stands, selling wares up and down the streets of Volusia. Godfrey spotted Empire women, too, for the first time, as tall as the men and as broad-shouldered, looking nearly as big as some of the men back in the Ring. Their horns were longer, pointier, and they glistened an aqua blue. They looked more savage than the men. Godfrey wouldn't want to find himself in a fight with any of them.

"Maybe we can bed some of the women while we're here," Akorth said with a belch.

"I think they would just as happily cut your throat," Fulton said.

Akorth shrugged.

"Maybe they'd do both," he said. "At least I'd die a happy man."

As the throngs grew thicker, pushing their way through more city streets, Godfrey, sweating, trembling with anxiety, forced himself to be strong, to be brave, to think of all those back in the village, of his sister, who needed their help. He considered the numbers they were up against. If he could pull off this mission, perhaps he could make a difference, perhaps he could truly help them. It wasn't the bold, glorious way of his warrior brothers; but it was his way, and the only way he knew.

As they turned a corner, Godfrey looked up ahead and saw exactly what he was looking for: there, in the distance, a group of men came spilling out of a stone building, wrestling with each other, a crowd forming around them, cheering. They threw punches and stumbled in a way which Godfrey immediately recognized: drunk. Drunks, he mused, looked the same anywhere in the world. It was a fraternity of fools. He spotted a small black banner flying over the establishment, and he knew at once what it was.

"There," Godfrey said, as if looking at a holy mecca. "That's what we want."

"The cleanest-looking tavern I've ever seen," Akorth said.

Godfrey noticed the elegant façade, and he was inclined to agree with him.

Merek shrugged.

"All taverns are the same, once you're inside. They'll be as drunk and stupid here as they would be in any place."

"My kind of people," Fulton said, licking his lips as if already tasting the ale.

"And just how are we supposed to get there?" Ario asked.

Godfrey looked down and saw what he was referring to: the street ended in a canal. There was no way to walk there.

Godfrey watched as a small golden vessel pull up at their feet, two Empire men inside, and watched them jump out, tie the boat to a post with a rope, and leave it there as they walked into the city, never looking back. Godfrey spotted the armor on one of them and figured they were officers, and had no need to worry about their boat. They knew, clearly, that no one would ever be so foolish as to dare steal their boat from them.

Godfrey and Merek exchanged a knowing look at the same moment. Great minds, Godfrey realized, thought alike; or at least great minds who had both seen their share of dungeons and back alleys.

Merek stepped forward, removed his dagger, and sliced the thick rope, and one at a time, they all piled into the small golden vessel, which rocked wildly as they did. Godfrey leaned back and with his boot shoved them off from the dock.

They glided down the waterways, rocking, and Merek grabbed the long oar and steered, rowing.

"This is madness," Ario said, glancing back for the officers. "They might come back."

Godfrey looked straight ahead and nodded.

"Then we better row faster," he said.

CHAPTER NINE

Volusia stood in the midst of the endless desert, its green floor cracked and parched, hard as stone beneath her feet, and she stared straight ahead, facing off with the entourage from Dansk. She stood there proudly, a dozen of her closest advisors behind her, and faced off against two dozen of their men, typical Empire, tall, broad-shouldered, with the glowing yellow skin, the glistening red eyes and two small horns. The only noticeable difference of this people of Dansk was that, over time, they grew their horns out to the side instead of straight up.

Volusia looked out over their shoulders, and saw sitting on the horizon the desert city of Dansk, tall, supremely imposing, rising a hundred feet into the sky, its green walls the color of the desert, made of stone or brick—she could not tell which. The city was shaped in a perfect circle, parapets at the top of the wall, and between them, soldiers stationed every ten feet, facing every station, keeping watch, eyeing every corner of desert. It looked impenetrable.

Dansk lay directly south of Maltolis, halfway between the mad Prince's city and the southern capital, and it was a stronghold, a pivotal crossroads. Volusia had heard about it many times from her mother, but had never visited herself. She had always said that no one could take the Empire without taking Dansk.

Volusia looked back at their leader, standing before her with his envoy, smug, smirking down at her arrogantly. He looked different than the others, clearly their leader, with an air of confidence, more scars on his face, and with two long braids that descended from his head to his waist.

They had been standing this way in the silence, each waiting for the other to speak, no sound but that of the howling wind in the desert.

Finally, he must have tired of waiting, and he spoke:

"So you wish to enter our city?" he asked her. "You and your men?"

Volusia stared back, proud, confident, and expressionless.

"I do not wish to enter it," she said. "I wish to take it. I've come to offer you terms of surrender."

He stared back at her blankly for several seconds, as if trying to comprehend her words, then finally his eyes opened wide in surprise. He leaned back and laughed uproariously, and Volusia reddened.

"We?!" he said. "*Surrender!?*"

He screamed with laughter, as if he had heard the funniest joke in the world. Volusia stared back calmly, and she noted that all the soldiers joining him did not laugh—they did not even smile. They stared back at her seriously.

"You are but a girl," he finally said, looking amused. "You know nothing of the history of Dansk, of our desert, of our people. If you had, you would know that we have *never* surrendered. Not *once*. Not in ten thousand years. Not to *anyone*. Not even to the armies of Atlow the Great. Not once has Dansk been conquered."

His smile morphed to a scowl.

"And now you arrive," he said, "a stupid young girl, appearing from nowhere, with a dozen soldiers, and asking us to surrender? Why shouldn't I kill you right now, or take you to our dungeons? I think it is you who should be negotiating terms of surrender. If I turn you away, this desert will kill you. Then again, if I take you in, I might kill you."

Volusia stared back calmly, never flinching.

"I won't offer you my terms twice," she said calmly. "Surrender now and I will spare all of your lives."

He stared back at her, dumbfounded, as if finally realizing she was serious.

"You are deluded, young girl. You have suffered beneath the desert suns for too long."

She stared back, her eyes darkening.

"I am no young girl," she replied. "I am the great Volusia of the great city of Volusia. I am the Goddess Volusia. And you, and all beings on earth, are subservient to me."

He stared at her, his expression shifting, staring back at her as if she were mad.

"You are not Volusia," he said. "Volusia is older. I have met her myself. It was a very unpleasant experience. And yet I see the resemblance. You are…her daughter. Yes, I can see it now. Why is your mother not coming here to talk to us? Why is she sending you, her daughter?"

"*I* am Volusia," she replied. "My mother is dead. I made sure of that."

He stared back at her, his expression growing serious. For the first time, he seemed unsure.

"You may have been able to murder your mother," he said. "But you are foolish to threaten us. We are not a defenseless woman and your men of Volusia are far from here. You were foolish to venture so far from your stronghold. Do you think you can take our city with a dozen soldiers?" he asked, releasing and gripping the hilt of the sword as if thinking about killing her.

She smiled slowly.

"I can't take it with a dozen," she said. "But I can take it with two hundred thousand."

Volusia raised one fist high into the air, clutching the Golden Scepter, raising it ever higher, never taking her eyes off of him, and as she did, she watched the face of the Dansk envoy leader look out behind her, and morph to panic and shock. She did not need to turn around to know what he was looking at: her two hundred thousand Maltolisian soldiers, had rounded the hill upon her signal and stretched across the entire horizon. Now the Dansk leader knew the threat facing his city.

His entire envoy bristled, looking terrified and anxious to run back to the safety of their city.

"The Maltolisian army," their leader said, his voice fearful for the first time. "What are they doing here, with you?"

Volusia smiled back.

"I am a goddess," she said. "Why wouldn't they be serving me?"

He looked back at her now with a look of awe and surprise.

"Yet still, you wouldn't dare attack Dansk," he said, his voice quivering. "We are under the direct protection of the capital. The Empire army numbers in the millions. If you took our city, they would be obliged to retaliate. You would all be slaughtered in due course. You could not win. Are you that reckless? Or that stupid?"

She held her smile, enjoying his discomfort.

"Maybe a little bit of both," she said. "Or maybe I'm just itching to test my newfound army and sharpen their skills on you. It is your great misfortune that you lie in the way, between my men and the capital. And nothing, nothing, will lie in my way."

He glared her, his face turning into a sneer. Yet now, for the first time, she could see real panic in his eyes.

"We came to discuss terms, and we do not accept them. We will prepare for war, if that is what you wish. Just remember: you brought this upon yourself."

He suddenly kicked his zerta with a shout, and he turned, with the others, and galloped away, their convoy stirring up a cloud of dust.

Volusia casually dismounted from her zerta, reached over and grabbed a short, golden spear as her commander, Soku, reached over and handed it to her.

She held up one hand to the wind, felt the breeze, narrowed one eye, and took aim.

Then she leaned forward and threw it.

Volusia watched as the spear went flying in a high arc through the air, a good fifty yards, then finally she heard a great cry, and the satisfying thump of spear hitting flesh. She watched in delight as it lodged in the leader's back. He cried out, falling from his zerta, and landed on the desert floor, tumbling.

His entourage stopped and looked down, horrified. They sat there on their zertas, as if debating whether to stop and get him. They looked back and saw all of Volusia's men on the horizon, marching now, and clearly they thought better of it. They turned and galloped away, heading to the city gates, abandoning their leader on the desert floor.

Volusia rode with her entourage until she reached the dying leader, and dismounted by his side. In the distance she heard iron slam, and she noticed his entourage entering Dansk, a huge iron portcullis slamming down behind them, and the enormous iron double doors of the city sealed shut after them, creating an iron fortress.

Volusia looked down at the dying leader, who turned on her back and looked up at her in anguish and shock.

"You cannot wound a man who comes to talk terms," he said, outraged. "It goes against every law of the Empire! Never has such a thing been done before!"

"I did not intend to wound you," she said, kneeling down beside him, reaching out and touching the shaft of the spear. She shoved the spear deep into his heart, not letting go until finally he stopped squirming and breathed his last breath.

She smiled wide.

"I intended to kill you."

CHAPTER TEN

Thor stood at the bow of the small sailing vessel, his brothers standing behind him, his heart pounding with anticipation as the current carried them straight toward the small island before them. Thor looked up, studied its cliffs in wonder; he'd never seen anything like it. The walls were perfectly smooth, a white, solid granite, sparkling beneath the two suns, and they rose straight up, hundreds of feet high. The island itself was shaped in a circle, its base surrounded by boulders, and it was hard to think amidst the incessant crashing of the waves. It looked impregnable, impossible for any army to scale.

Thor held a hand up to his eyes and squinted into the sun. The cliffs seemed to stop at some point, to cap off in a plateau hundreds of feet high. Whoever lived up there, at the top, would live safely forever, Thor realized. Assuming anyone lived up there at all.

At the very top, hovering over the island like a halo, was a ring of clouds, soft pink and purple, blanketing it from the harsh rays of the sun, as if this place were crowned by God himself. A gentle breeze stirred here, the air pleasant and mild. Thor could sense even from here that there was something special about this place. It felt magical. He had not felt this way since he had reached the land of his mother's castle.

All the others looked up, too, expressions of wonder across their faces.

"Who do you suppose lives here?" O'Connor asked aloud the question on all of their minds.

"Who—or what?" Reece asked.

"Maybe no one," Indra said.

"Maybe we should sail on," O'Connor said.

"And skip the invitation?" Matus asked. "I see seven ropes, and there are seven of us."

Thor examined the cliffs and as he looked closely, he saw seven golden ropes dangling from the top down to the shores, glistening in the sun. He wondered.

"Maybe someone's expecting us," Elden said.

"Or tempting us," Indra said.

"But who?" Reece asked.

Thor looked up at the very top, all of these same thoughts racing through his mind. He wondered who could know they were coming. Were they being watched somehow?

They all stood in the boat silently, bobbing in the water, as the current brought them ever closer.

"The real question," Thor asked aloud, finally breaking the silence, "is if they are friendly—or if this is a trap?"

"Does it make any difference?" Matus asked, coming up beside him.

Thor shook his head.

"No," he said, tightening his grip on the hilt of his sword. "We will visit it either way. If friend, we will embrace them; if foe, we will kill them."

The currents picked up, and long, rolling waves carried their boat all the way to the narrow shore of black sand that surrounded the place. Their boat washed gently up, lodging on it, and as it did, everyone all jumped out at once.

Thor gripped the hilt of his sword, on edge, and looked about in every direction. There was no movement on the beach, nothing but the crashing of the waves.

Thor walked up to the base of the cliffs, laid his palm on them, felt how smooth they were, felt the heat and energy radiating off of them. He examined the ropes which rose straight up the cliff, sheathing his sword and grabbing hold of one.

He tugged on it. It didn't give.

One by one the others joined him, each grabbing a rope and tugging on it.

"Will it hold?" O'Connor wondered aloud, looking straight up.

They all looked up, clearly wondering the same thing.

"There is only one way to find out," Thor said.

Thor grabbed the rope with both hands, jumped up, and began his ascent. All around him the others did the same, all of them scaling the cliffs like mountain goats.

Thor climbed and climbed, his muscles aching, burning under the sun. Sweat poured down his neck, stung his eyes, and all of his limbs shook.

And yet at the same time, there was something magical about these ropes, some energy that supported him—and the others—and made him climb faster than he'd ever had, as if the ropes were pulling him up.

Much sooner than he'd imagined possible, Thor found himself reaching the top; he reached up and was surprised to find himself grabbing onto grass and soil. He pulled himself up, rolling onto his side, onto soft grass, exhausted, breathing hard, limbs aching. All around him, he saw the others arriving, too. They had made it. Something had wanted them up there. Thor did not know if that was cause for reassurance or for worry.

Thor took a knee and drew his sword, immediately on edge, not knowing what to expect up here. All around him his brothers did the same, all of them rising to their feet and instinctually getting into a semicircular formation, guarding each other's backs.

Yet as Thor stood there, looking out, he was shocked by what he saw. He had expected to see an enemy facing him, had expected to see a rocky and barren and desolate place.

Instead, he saw no one there to welcome them. And instead of rock, he saw the most beautiful place he had ever laid eyes upon: there, spread out before him, were rolling green hills, lush with flowers, foliage, and fruits, sparkling in the morning sun. The temperature up here was perfect, caressed by gentle ocean breezes. There were fruit orchards, lush vineyards, places of such bounty and beauty that it immediately caused all of his tension to fall away. He sheathed his sword, as the others relaxed, too, all of them gazing out as this place of perfection. For the first time since he'd set sail from the land of the dead, Thor felt as if he could truly relax and let down his guard. This was a place he was in no rush to leave.

Thor was baffled. How could such a gorgeous and temperate place exist in the midst of an endless and unforgiving ocean? Thor looked about and saw a gentle mist hanging over everything, looked up and saw, high above, the ring of gentle purple clouds covering the place, sheltering it, yet also allowing the sun to streak through here and there—and he knew in every ounce of his body that this place was magical. It was a place of such physical beauty that it put even the bounty of the Ring to shame.

Thor was surprised as he heard what sounded like a distant screech; at first he thought it was just his mind playing tricks on him. But then he felt a chill as he heard it again.

He raised his hand to his eyes and looked up, studying the skies. He could have sworn it sounded like the cry of a dragon—and yet he knew that was not possible. The last of the dragons, he knew, had died with Ralibar and Mycoples. He had witnessed it himself, that fateful moment of their deaths still hanging over him like a dagger in his heart. There wasn't a day that went by when he did not think of his good friend Mycoples, when he did not wish she was back at his side.

Was it just wishful thinking, his hearing that cry? The echo of some forgotten dream?

The cry suddenly came again, ripping through the skies, piercing the very fabric of the air, and Thor's heart lifted, as he felt numb with excitement and wonder. Could it be?

As Thor raised his hand to his eyes and looked up into the two suns, high up above the cliffs, he thought he detected the faint outline of a small dragon, circling in the air. He froze, wondering if his eyes were playing tricks on him.

"Is that not a dragon?" Reece suddenly asked aloud.

"It is not possible," O'Connor said. "There are no dragons left alive."

But Thor was not so sure as he watched the outline of the shape disappearing into the clouds. Thor looked back down and studied his surroundings. He wondered.

"What is this place?" Thor asked aloud.

"A place of dreams, a place of light," came a voice.

Thor, startled at the unfamiliar voice, wheeled around, as did all the others, and was shocked to see, standing before them, an elderly man, dressed in a yellow robe and hood, carrying a long translucent staff, inlaid with diamonds, a black amulet at its end. It sparkled so bright, Thor could barely see.

The man wore a relaxed smile, and he walked toward them in a good-natured way and pulled back his hood, revealing long, golden, wavy hair, and a face which was ageless. Thor could not tell if he was eighteen or a hundred years old. A light emanated from his face, and Thor was taken aback by its intensity. He had not seen anything like it since he had last laid eyes upon Argon.

"You are correct," he said, as he locked eyes with Thorgrin and walked right up to him. He stood but a few feet away, and his translucent green eyes felt as if they burned right through him. "To think of my brother."

"Your brother?" Thor asked, confused.

The man nodded back.

"Argon."

Thor gaped at the man, shocked.

"Argon!?" Thor said. "Your brother?" he added, barely able to get the words out.

The man nodded back, examining him, and Thor felt as if he were seeing into his very soul.

"Ragon is my name," he said. "I am Argon's twin. Although of course, we don't look much alike. I believe I am the more handsome one," he added with a smile.

Thor stared, speechless. He did not know where to begin; he'd had no idea that Argon had a brother.

Slowly, it all began to make sense.

"You brought us here," Thor said, processing it all. "Those currents, this island, those ropes… You planned for us to come here." Thor pieced it all together. "You've been watching us."

Ragon nodded back.

"Indeed I have," he said. "And I am very proud of you. I did control the tides here—it was my way of extending hospitality. Those who arrive here, on this isle, can only arrive because they deserve it. Being here is a reward: a reward to those who have displayed great valor. And you—*all* of you—have passed the test."

Thor suddenly heard the loud, definitive screech of a dragon—he was certain this time—and he looked up and was in awe to see a baby dragon, its wingspan hardly ten feet, diving down low, circling. It screeched, a young dragon's screech, and extended its wings as it flew in broad circles; then finally it landed, setting down just a few feet beside Ragon.

It sat there, facing Thor and the others, and lowered its wings, still and calm, staring back proudly.

Thor stared back in wonder.

"It can't be," he whispered, breathless, examining it. It was the most beautiful creature he'd ever seen. It looked positively ancient. "I saw the last of the dragons die. It saw it myself."

"But you did not see the egg," Ragon said.

Thor looked at him, puzzled.

"The egg?"

Ragon nodded.

"Of Mycoples and Ralibar. Their child. A girl."

Thor's mouth fell open in shock, and he felt tears well up as he examined the dragon in a whole new light, as he realized, for the first time, how much she resembled Mycoples. He knew there was something familiar about her.

"She's beautiful," Thorgrin said.

"You can pet her," Ragon said. "In fact, she has been looking forward to meeting you, very much. She knows all about what you did for her mother. She's been waiting for this day."

Thorgrin stepped forward, one step at a time, wary of her, yet anxious to meet her. She stared back at him proudly, unblinking, with light-red scales and glowing green eyes, and stood perhaps ten feet tall. He could not tell if she liked him or not, and he felt an intense energy radiating off of her.

As he approached, Thor raised a hand and gently stroked the side of her face, his palm touching her long scales. She purred contentedly as he did, lifted her chin as if to acknowledge him, and then suddenly lowered her head and, to Thor's delight, brushed it against his chest. With her long, scratchy tongue, she licked Thor's face.

It scratched the side of Thor's cheek, but he didn't mind. He knew it was a sign of affection, and he leaned down and kissed her on the head. Her scales were strong and smooth, young, still needing to be formed, softer than her parents' were. Seeing her brought back all his memories, made him realize how much he'd missed Mycoples—and made him feel as if he had her back again.

"I loved your mother," Thor said softly to her. "And I shall love you just as much."

The dragon purred again.

"You've made her quite happy, Thorgrin," Ragon said. "The only thing she needs now is a name."

Thor looked at him questioningly.

"Are you asking me to name her?"

Ragon nodded.

"She is young, after all," he replied. "And no one has come along to name her. I could have. But the task, I knew, awaited you."

Thor closed his eyes, trying to allow a name to come to him. As he did, he thought of Mycoples and Ralibar, and wondered what name they would have wanted, what name would best honor her parents.

"Lycoples," Thor heard himself blurt out. "We shall name her Lycoples."

Lycoples raised her neck and screeched, breathing fire straight up into the sky, a small flame, still young, and Thor jumped back, startled. She spread her wings wide, lowered her head, and she suddenly leapt up into the air, circling, flying high above, higher and higher, until Thor watched her disappear from sight, in wonder.

"Have I offended her?" Thor asked.

Ragon smiled and shook his head.

"On the contrary," he said. "She quite approves."

Ragon reached out and clasped a hand on Thor's shoulder and began to lead him on a walk.

"Come, young Thorgrin," he said. "We have much to discuss, and this isle is far bigger than it seems."

*

Thor and the others followed Ragon, winding their way through the island, taking everything in as they went. Thor could not believe how comforted he felt being here, in Ragon's presence, especially after their long sojourn across an endless, unforgiving ocean, after so many days with no hope or land in sight, and with their provisions running so low. And especially after emerging from the land of the dead. He felt as if he had been reborn, as if he had emerged from the deepest rungs of hell to the highest levels of paradise.

But there was more to it than that. Thor also felt deeply at home with Ragon, felt comforted in his presence, the same way he had always felt around Argon. In some ways he felt that having Ragon here was like having Argon back.

Thor also felt incredibly comforted by the sight of Lycoples, circling high above, screeching every so often to make her presence known. He looked up and spotted her and was thrilled to see her. It made him feel as if Mycoples were back with him again, as if a piece of himself had been restored.

And yet, even with all of this, there was still something more to this place, something else that Thor could not quite detect, lingering just beneath the surface. He sensed something here, a presence, something he could not quite put his finger on. He felt as if there were something here waiting for him, something that would make him whole again. He did not understand what it could be, here in this empty place the middle of nowhere, but it kept gnawing at him, his senses screaming at him that there was something crucial here, somewhere on this island.

They marched for hours, and yet strangely enough, Thor found that his legs were not tired in this place. It was the most idyllic place he'd ever seen, and they strolled through rolling hills, through lush fields of green, and Thor felt as if he were being cradled in the very arms of paradise.

They crested a hill, and as they did, Ragon came to a stop, and Thor stopped beside him. He looked out, and was shocked by the vista: there, in the distance, sat a castle made of light. It shone in the sun, sparkling, looking like a golden cloud, yet in the shape of a castle. It had a translucent feel to it, and Thor realized the castle was entirely composed of light.

He turned to Ragon in wonder.

"The Castle of Light," Ragon explained.

They all stared, silent, Thor not knowing what to say.

"Is it real?" Thor asked, finally breaking the silence.

"As real as you and I," Ragon replied.

"But it looks to be made of light," Reece said, stepping forward. "Can one enter?"

"As surely as you might enter any castle," Ragon replied. "It is the strongest castle known to man. Yet its walls are made of light."

"I don't understand how that can be," Thor said. "How can a castle at once be so light, yet so strong?"

Ragon smiled.

"You will find that many things here, on the Isle of Light, are not what they seem to be. As I said, this a place where only those who deserve it are allowed to enter."

"And what is that?" Matus asked.

Matus gestured to another building, and Thor turned with the others and saw another building of light, opposite the castle, built in a low arch.

"Ah," Ragon said. "I'm glad you pointed it out. It's where I plan to take you next: the armory."

"Armory?" Elden asked, hopeful.

Ragon nodded.

"It holds all manner of weaponry, weaponry which cannot be found anywhere else on earth," Ragon said. "Weaponry meant only for the deserved."

Ragon turned and looked at them all meaningfully.

"God smiles down on your valor," he said, "and it is time for your reward. Some rewards are reserved for the next life—and some for this one. It's not only the dead who get to enjoy themselves," he said with a wink.

The others looked at him in surprise.

"Do you mean there are weapons in there meant for us—" O'Connor began.

But Ragon was already off, hiking down the hill with his staff, mysteriously fast, a good fifty yards away already, although he seemed to walk at a leisurely pace.

Thor and the others looked at each other in wonder, then they all turned and hiked down the hill, hurrying to catch up.

They followed him right up to the soaring, golden double doors to the armory, and they watched as Ragon reached out with his staff and tapped on the doors.

As he did, there came a tremendous bang, echoing as if he were tapping on iron with a battering ram. Thor couldn't understand how it could be so; his staff had barely touched the doors of light.

Slowly, the doors opened wide, a light shining forth from the inside, temporarily blinding Thor, making him raise his hands. The light calmed and Ragon walked in, and one by one, they all followed.

Thor looked at the high-arched ceiling as he went, at the soaring room, a hundred feet deep, taking it all in in awe. An endless array of weaponry was lined up along the walls, rows and rows of it, weapons forged in gold and silver and steel and bronze and copper and metals Thor did not recognize. Beside this were all manner of armor, all brand-new, shining, shaped in the most unusual and intricate designs that Thor had ever seen.

"You have all been to the land of the dead and back," Ragon said. "You have all proved yourselves. You left your friends behind; you left your families behind; you left your comforts behind. You ventured forth only for each other, your brothers. You upheld your solemn oath. An oath of brothers is stronger than any weapon in the world. And that is something you have come to learn."

Ragon turned and gestured to the walls, to the rows and rows of weapons.

"You are men now. As much—even more so—than any other men, regardless of your age. It is time for you to have the weapons of men, the armor of men. This armory is yours, a gift from God. A gift from the One who watches over you.

"Choose," he said, turning and smiling, waving his staff. "Choose your weapons and your armor. It will be the weapon you are meant to wield for a lifetime. Each weapon here has a special destiny, and the weapon you choose is meant only for you. It can be wielded by no other. You can choose no other. Close your eyes and let your weapon summon you."

Thorgrin looked about the armory, and as he did, he felt his sword, the Sword of the Dead, vibrating in his hand. He drew it from its sheath and held it up, examining it in wonder, and as he did, he was shocked to see the skulls and crossbones around the hilt beginning to move, the mouth of ivory opening up as if it were crying. As he watched, he heard a noise emanate from it, and the mouth began to emit a moaning sound.

Thor looked down at his hand as if he held a creature squirming in it, and he did not know whether to throw it away or clutch it more firmly. He had never encountered a weapon like it; it was truly alive. It both intimidated and empowered him.

Ragon came up beside him.

"You hold one of the greatest weapons known to man," Ragon said. "A sword even demons are afraid to wield. You are not mistaken: it is very much alive."

"It looks as if it is weeping," Thor said, staring at it.

"It is as alive as you are," Ragon said. "That moaning you hear is the moaning of the souls it has taken; those tears are the tears of the dead. It is a hard weapon to wield, a weapon with a mind of its own, a history of its own. A weapon that must be tamed. Yet it is also a weapon that chooses, and it chose you. You would not be wielding it if it didn't want you to.

"There is no weapon out there to rival it. Learn to wield it, and to wield it well. The weapons here are for the others, not for you."

Thor nodded in understanding.

"I would wish for no other weapon," he replied, sheathing his sword, determined to learn how to master it.

Ragon nodded.

"Good," he said. "There is, though, armor here for you. Let it summon you, and you shall find it."

Thor closed his eyes and as he did, he felt an invisible force take hold of him. He opened his eyes and allowed the force to lead him to the far wall, each of his friends spreading out throughout the vast room, as each was led in a different direction.

Thor stopped before a set of golden armor. He looked up and saw two long, thin plates of circular armor, and he wondered what they were for.

Ragon came up beside him.

"Go ahead," he prodded. "They won't bite. Take them down."

Thor took them down off the wall gingerly and examined them.

"What are they?" he asked.

"Wrist guards," Ragon replied. "Made of a metal you shall never know."

"They are so light," Thor observed, skeptical.

"Do not be deceived, young Thorgrin," Ragon said. "These will stop a greater blow than the thickest of armor."

Thor examined them in awe.

Ragon stepped forward and took them from Thor, and as Thor held out his arms, he clasped one over each wrist. They were so long, they went up Thor's wrists and covered his forearms. Thor raised his arms, testing them, and he could not believe how light they were. They fitted perfectly, as if they had been made just for him.

"Use them to block an enemy's blow," Ragon said. "Just as you would a shield or a sword. Yet these are even stronger than the finest steel—and when you are in the thick of battle, they will anticipate your enemy, and will surprise you with unique qualities of their own."

"I don't know how to thank you," Thor replied, feeling ready to battle an army by himself.

O'Connor stepped forward, his eyes alight with excitement as he pulled a golden bow and quiver down from the wall. The quiver held the longest, sleekest arrows Thor had ever seen, and on it there draped a golden archer's glove. O'Connor held it up in awe and put it on. It was made of a super-light golden chain mail, its mesh designed to wrap around his middle finger and then to wrap around up his wrist and forearm. He closed and opened his fist, examining it in wonder.

He then raised the bow and held it to his chin.

"That bow is unlike any other," Ragon explained. "Arrows shot from it will fly twice as far, and pierce any armor known to man. You can fire them more quickly, and the weight of the bow is the lightest known to man."

O'Connor tested it, pulling the string, raising it up, and examining it in awe.

"It is magnificent," he said.

Ragon smiled.

"It is your reward, not mine," he said. "The best gratitude is to use it well in battle. Protect those who are too weak to protect themselves. And protect your brothers."

O'Connor slid it over his back and it fit perfectly, as if it were meant to be.

Matus, beside him, stepped forward and reached up and placed both hands on a long golden studded shaft, at the end of which dangled a long golden chain and three spiked golden balls. It was the most beautiful flail Thor had ever seen, and Matus held it up, chains rattling, and slowly swung it over his head. He marveled at the weight of it, and looked in wonder to Ragon.

"A hero's weapon," Ragon said. "That is no ordinary flail. Its chains expand and contract as needed, sensing your enemy's distance, keeping you out of their reach, and its balls detect their master, and will not strike you, or any of your group."

Matus swung them and they were dazzling in the light, making a soft whooshing noise as he spun them, so silent it was as if they were not even there.

Elden reached up and gingerly removed from the wall a long shaft—as long as he—with a small, gleaming golden axe-head at the end of it, its blade shaped in a razor-sharp crescent. He held it up and turned it, reflected in the light, not quite sure what to make of it.

"It's so light," Elden said. "And so sharp."

Ragon nodded.

"Long enough to kill a man from ten feet away," he said. "Your enemies shall not be able to approach you, and you can strike a man down from his horse before his lance can touch you. As a battle axe, it is unparalleled, longer, sleeker, and stronger than all others. You can cut through men or you can cut through a tree—always, in one chop. This axe never fails—and its blade never dulls."

Elden swung it overhead, and Thor felt its wind even from here as Elden seemed to swing it effortlessly, the longest axe he'd ever seen.

Indra reached out and grabbed hold of a long spear, resting horizontally on the wall, and carefully took it down. She held it up in the light, its shaft comprised of a translucent gold material, studded with diamonds, and ending in a long, sharp diamond tip. She turned it over in her hands, examining it in awe.

"There exists no sharper spear," Ragon said. "It is a spear that can fly farther than any other, that can pierce any man, any armor. It is befitting of you, a woman with skills to rival any man of the Legion."

"It is magical," she said in hushed tones.

"And loyal," he replied. "You can never lose it. With each throw, it shall return to you."

Indra examined it, even more impressed, clearly speechless.

Reece stepped forward and grabbed the most beautiful halberd Thor had ever seen, its three golden prongs glistening in the light, lodged into the end of a shaft of gold.

"A halberd to rival no other," Ragon explained. "Some call it the devil's pitchfork—yet in a true knight's hands it is a weapon of honor.

It is also incomparable in hand-to-hand combat. It is also deadly in the air: throw it, and its diamond shaft will dazzle and blind your enemy, stunning them. Take aim, and it will pierce anything in your way. And it will always return to you."

With only Selese left amongst the group, Ragon turned to her.

"For you, my dear," he said to her, holding out a small sack.

Selese held out her palm and he placed it inside it, and she looked down, and held it up. She opened it and poured it on her other palm, and Thor could see that it was fine golden sand. It fell through her fingers, back into the sack.

"You are not a fighter," Ragon explained, "but a healer. This sand will heal any man from any wound. Use it wisely: there is less in this sack than you think."

Selese bowed her head, eyes tearing up.

"A great gift, my lord," she said. "The only gift greater than the gift of death is the gift of life."

Thor looked over all his brothers and Indra and Selese, all of them decked with new weaponry, and he almost did not recognize them. They each looked, with their glistening, magical weapons, looked like formidable warriors. They looked like seven titans, like a group of warriors that any foe would be wise to stay far away from. Especially after emerging from the darkest hells, Thor felt as if they had all been reborn, ready to face the world.

And they had not yet even approached the wall of new armor.

Ragon looked them over approvingly.

"These are weapons to help find your way in a fierce world," he said. "Weapons to wield with honor, weapons of light in a sea of blackness, weapons strong enough to face the demons. Honor God and fight in His name, in the cause of the just, the cause of the oppressed, and you will prevail. Fight for power, or for riches, or for greed, or for lust, or for conquest, and you will lose. Stray from the light, and no weapon can save you. You shall wield these weapons only as long as you shall merit them."

Ragon turned to the wall of armor.

"Now go choose your armor, splendid armor, armor to match these glorious weapons."

One by one they all fanned out across the room, each looking up at the rows and rows of golden armor. Thor was about to join them, when suddenly he was struck by something. A sixth sense.

He turned to Ragon.

"I sense there is something more," he said, "something else you are withholding. Some great secret."

Ragon smiled wide.

"My brother was right," he said. "The power is indeed strong within you."

He sighed.

"Yes, young Thorgrin. I have one more surprise for you. The greatest surprise, and the greatest gift, of all. In the morning. You will stay the night here, all of you, in my castle. And in the morning, you will not believe the joy that is coming your way."

CHAPTER ELEVEN

Godfrey, on guard, kept his eyes peeled as they rowed in their small golden vessel down the canals of Volusia, the current taking them slowly, weaving in and out of the back streets of Volusia. Everywhere, he looked for a place to stash the gold. He needed some place reliable, some place discreet, some place where they would not be watched, some place he would remember. They could not stash it in the boat, and as the tavern loomed up ahead, he knew their time was running short.

Finally, something flashed and caught his eye.

"Stop rowing!" he called out to Merek.

Merek, standing at the rear, used his long oar to slow then stop the boat, and as he did, Godfrey pointed.

"There!" Godfrey said, pointing.

Godfrey looked down and saw, up ahead, something beneath the water. Sunlight cut through the water, and perhaps six feet down, Godfrey could see the hull of a vessel, capsized long ago, sitting on the bottom of the canal. It was just shallow enough to spot, and yet just deep enough to be discreet. Even better, beside it, on the shoreline, was a small golden statue of an ox—marking a spot he could not forget.

"Down there," Godfrey said, "beneath the water."

They all looked over the side of the boat.

"I see a capsized boat," said Akorth. "Stuck at the bottom."

"Exactly," Godfrey said. "That is where we shall leave our gold."

"*Underwater!?*" Akorth asked, flabbergasted.

"Have you gone mad?" Fulton asked.

"What if the current carries it away?" Merek said.

"What if someone else finds it?" Ario chimed in.

Godfrey shook his head as he hoisted a sack of gold, so heavy his arm shook as he lifted it, ensured it was tied tight, and dropped it in the water. They all watched as it sank quickly, resting cozily inside the bottom of the hull.

"It's not going anywhere," Godfrey said, "and no one's going to find it. Can you see it from here?"

They all peered into the water, and clearly they could not. Godfrey himself could barely make out the outline of it.

"Besides, who is going to go combing the waters for gold?" he asked. "Especially when the streets are paved with it?"

"No one touches the gold of the streets," Merek said, "because the soldiers would kill them. But free loot is another matter."

Godfrey reached out and dropped a second sack.

"The currents won't take it anywhere," he said, "and no one will ever know where it is—but us. Would you rather carry it into the tavern?"

They all looked out to the looming tavern up ahead, then back beneath the water, and finally, they all seemed to agree.

One by one, they each leaned forward, held out a sack, and dropped it.

Godfrey watched as they all sank. Then, suddenly, the brilliant sunlight shifted, hidden behind a cloud, and the waters became murky again. There was no visibility whatsoever.

"What if *we* can't find it?" Akorth asked, suddenly panicked.

Godfrey turned and looked over, and they all followed his glance to the towering statue of the ox on the street beside them.

"Look for the ox," he replied.

Godfrey nodded to Merek, and they continued rowing, and soon they turned a bend, and the waters brought them right to the tavern, straight ahead, the noise from the patrons audible even from here.

"Keep your heads down and your hoods lowered," Godfrey directed. "Stay close together. Do as I say."

"And what of drink?" Akorth said, panicked. "We've just hidden away all our gold. How are we supposed to buy a drink?"

Godfrey smiled and held out a coin.

"I'm not stupid," he said. "I saved one."

The boat docked, and they all jumped out, quickly abandoning it, and merged into the bustling crowd. The noise grew as they approached the bar, the men rougher here, the Empire soldiers and patrons clearly all drunk, scores of them bustling outside, laughing and shoving each other. A few of them smoked a strange pipe Godfrey had not seen before, and the heavy odor hung in the air.

Godfrey felt at home, finally, felt as he would outside any bar in the world. These people might all be miscreants, they might all have different colored skin than he, but they were drunk, carefree, and they were *his* people.

Godfrey led the way, his men following as he pushed his way through the crowd, lowering his head, and entered the tavern.

He was met by a rush of sounds and smells, similar to what he might find in any tavern anywhere: stale beer, old wine, men sweating the day away indoors. It was a familiar and strangely comforting smell. It was louder in here, the voices blending, people speaking multiple languages he did not recognize. The patrons seemed like a rough crowd, a mix of delinquent soldiers and the lower strata of the population. None of them, Godfrey was relieved to see, turned his way as he entered; they were all preoccupied with drink.

Godfrey kept his head down and cut his way through the crowd, the others on his heels, until he made his way to the bar. It was an old weathered bar, the kind he might have found back in the Ring.

He leaned an elbow against it, squeezing in between several patrons, reached out, and put the gold coin on the bar, hoping the bartender would accept it. It might be struck differently, but after all, gold was gold. As he saw mugs of ale being served, he began to salivate; he hadn't realized how badly he craved a drink.

"I'll take five," Godfrey said, as the bartender, a towering, humorless Empire man, approached.

"I don't drink," Merek said.

Godfrey looked at Merek in surprise.

"Then four," Godfrey corrected.

"Make it five," Fulton chimed in. "I'll drink yours."

"None for me, either," Ario said. "I never drank before."

Godfrey, Akorth and Fulton looked at him in astonishment.

"Never drank!?" Fulton said.

"Then today's your lucky day," Akorth said. "You will drink with us. Keep it at five," he said to the bartender. "In fact, make it six. I want double, too."

The bartender stood there, annoyed, then picked up the piece of gold and examined it, suspicious. Godfrey's heart pounded as he looked down at him, scrutinizing him.

"What gold is this?" he asked.

Godfrey felt himself sweating under his hood. He thought quick, and decided to act indignant.

"Should I take back my gold then!?" Godfrey demanded, gambling.

The bartender stared him down, then finally, to Godfrey's great relief, he must have decided that gold was gold. He placed it in his pocket, and shortly thereafter delivered six pints of ale. Godfrey took his, Akorth and Fulton each snatched two.

Godfrey chugged his, drinking greedily, realizing how badly he'd craved it. He savored every sip, realizing as he drank how different this ale tasted from the ale he knew back in the Ring; it was brownish in color, had a nutty, spicy aftertaste to it, tasting something of earth and ashes and fire. It also had a kick, an aftertaste which burned the back of his throat.

At first Godfrey did not know if he liked it or not; but as he finished it off and set it down, as he gave it a few moments to kick in, he decided it was the best ale he'd ever had. He didn't know if it just because he was parched, or nervous, or homesick—but he was sure he'd never had anything like it. He also, very quickly, realized it was the strongest ale he'd ever had, feeling light-headed after just one.

He turned and noticed the delighted eyes of Akorth and Fulton, and realized they loved it, too.

"Now I can die," Fulton said.

"I can live in this city," Akorth said.

"You won't ever get me to leave," Fulton added. "The Ring? Where's that?"

"Who cares?" Akorth said. "Give me a supply of this and I'll convert. I'll grow horns."

They turned and eyed the sixth and final mug of ale, sitting there on the bar untouched, waiting for Ario. Akorth reached out and slid it over to him.

"Drink while you can," Akorth said. "You may not get a second chance. A terrible thing, to die never having had a drink."

"And be quick about it," Fulton added. "You don't leave a full glass before me and think I won't drink it."

Ario, unsure, tentatively reached out and took the mug. He drank slowly, tasting it, and made a face.

"Uggh," he said. "This is awful."

Akorth laughed, reached out and snatched it from his hands, the foam spilling over the edge and onto his wrist.

"I won't ask you twice," he said, "and I won't let it go to waste. Try it again when you have hairs on your chest."

Akorth raised the pint to his mouth, but suddenly, unexpectedly, Ario reached out and snatched it from Akorth's hand. Akorth looked back at him, shocked, as Ario calmly lifted the pint and slowly and steadily drank the entire thing, his throat gulping as he did.

He didn't even wince as he gently put it back down, staring Akorth right in the eye.

Akorth and Fulton looked back at him, clearly shocked. Godfrey was, too.

"Where did you learn to drink like that, boy?" Godfrey asked, impressed.

"I thought you'd never had a drink?" Fulton pressed.

"I didn't," Ario answered calmly.

Godfrey examined him and wondered even more about this boy, so calm, so expressionless, yet always surprising him. He was a boy of few words, yet much action; he was so understated that one underestimated him—and that was his great advantage.

Godfrey ordered another round, and as it came, he took another long sip and, keeping his head low, he discreetly turned and surveyed his surroundings. Scores of Empire soldiers occupied the room, and he scanned the crowd, looking for any signs of an officer, of someone important. Someone who could be bought. He searched for a face that exuded corruption, greed—an expression that Godfrey, in all his years in the taverns, had come to recognize well.

Suddenly, Godfrey was jostled, a shoulder bumping him hard on his back. He stumbled forward, spilling the rest of his beer.

Annoyed, Godfrey turned to see who the offender was, and he saw a large Empire soldier, a foot taller than he, shoulders as wide as he, glaring down at him. His yellow skin turned orange, and Godfrey wondered if this was what happened when they were drunk—or mad.

"Don't get in my way again," he seethed to Godfrey, "or it will be the last time you do."

"I'm sorry—" Godfrey began, wanting to draw attention away, about to turn around—but suddenly Merek stepped forward.

"He wasn't in your way," Merek snapped, scowling at the man fearlessly. "You bumped him."

Godfrey's heart dropped as he watched Merek confronting the man. Merek, Godfrey was beginning to realize, was way too hotheaded. Maybe it had been a mistake to bring him. He was too unpredictable, too volatile—and he carried way too big of a chip on his shoulder.

"In fact," Merek added, "I think you owe my friend an apology."

The Empire soldier, after getting over his initial shock, grinned down at Merek, as he loosened his neck and cracked his knuckles. It was an ominous sound.

He stared down at Merek as if he were food or prey that had walked right into a trap.

"How about I tear out your heart and feed it to your friend. Would that work as an apology?"

Merek, fearless, sneered back, determined, even though the man was twice his size. Godfrey did not know what he was possibly thinking.

"You can try," Merek replied, stealthily reaching down and resting a hand on his dagger. "But your hands better be a lot quicker than your mind."

The Empire soldier now looked unamused; his face darkened.

"Merek, it's OK," Godfrey said, reaching out and placing a palm on his chest. Godfrey heard his own words slurring, and wondered just how strong that ale was. Now he regretted it; how he wished his mind was sharper.

"Should have had that drink," Akorth said, shaking his head. "That's what happens when you don't have any drink. You look for a fight."

"Well, you look for a fight when you drink, too," Fulton added.

The Empire soldier, annoyed, looked from Merek to Akorth to Fulton, and as he did, narrowed his eyes, as if realizing something. He reached up and abruptly lowered Godfrey's hood, revealing his face.

"First Finian I've seen without red hair," the soldier observed. He looked Godfrey up and down, suspiciously—then he looked them all over. "In fact, those cloaks don't fit at all, do they? And your skin: it's not half as pale as it should be."

The Empire soldier, realizing, grinned wide, and Godfrey gulped, the situation going from bad to worse.

"You're not Finians at all, are you?" he continued. Then he turned and yelled out over his shoulder. "Hey, fellas!"

The tavern quieted as a dozen Empire soldiers ambled their way over. Godfrey noticed with horror that, if possible, they were all even bigger than he.

They came up beside him.

"Now look what you've done with your big mouth," Godfrey hissed to Merek.

"Rather have a big mouth than cower in fear," Merek snapped back.

"Look what we have here!" the Empire soldier said loudly, as they all looked. "A bunch of humans in disguise!"

Godfrey swallowed hard, sweat pouring down the back of his neck, as another dozen soldiers crowded around. Godfrey looked for the exit, but the soldiers all crammed in so tight that they were completely surrounded.

Merek suddenly reached for his dagger, but two soldiers stepped up, grabbed his wrist, and yanked it away before he could do anything. Then they grabbed his arms, and he struggled uselessly to break free.

Godfrey was too scared to move. The Empire soldier leaned in close, just a few inches away, grinning down at Godfrey.

"Now what is a fat little white boy like you doing in our tavern? Disguised as a Finian?"

"I have gold!" Godfrey blurted out, knowing it was the wrong thing to say at the wrong time, but feeling desperate and not knowing what else to say.

The Empire soldier's eyes opened wide in amusement.

"He has *gold*, has he!?" he called out, laughing, and all the other soldiers broke into laughter. "I'm sure you do, fat boy. I'm sure you do."

"Wait, I can explain—" Godfrey began.

But before he could finish his words, Godfrey caught a glimpse of a fist, coming straight up, so fast, out of nowhere. The next thing he knew he felt it smashing into his chin, felt his teeth hitting each other, felt the reverberation throughout his skull, and he knew he was finished, that his life was over. He felt himself falling straight back, and as he did, he looked up and saw the ceiling of this dingy tavern, warped, spotted, and he had one final thought: *if only I could have had one more pint of ale.*

CHAPTER TWELVE

Erec stood at the bow of the ship, Alistair beside him, Strom at his other side, hundreds of his men behind him, working the ship, lowering the sails, and beside them his fleet, a half dozen ships, all sailing together for Boulder Isle. Erec looked out, straight ahead, at the fast approaching isle, the sound of ocean waves crashing all around him, and he wondered.

It was a sheer wall of rock, this island, like a giant boulder dropped down into the sea, rising a hundred feet high and a good mile in diameter. There was no shore of any sort, no way to land, to disembark. To the casual passerby it might not even seem like an isle—just a giant rock in the sea. But Erec knew better. As he looked closely he saw the entrance, camouflaged in the rock, a single, huge arch, carved right into the rock, and behind it an iron portcullis. It was like an island built into a carved-out mountain.

Standing before the entrance, on a narrow stone ledge, stood a dozen archers with crossbows at the ready, aimed at the ship, faces serious, visors down. In their center stood their commander, a hardened man Erec knew well: Krov. He stood there proudly, a stocky man with a stark bald head, covered in battle scars, a face weathered from the sun and salt air, and a too-long beard, and he stared sternly down at Erec as if he had never met him once in his life.

Erec's ship approached the entrance, and Erec stood there and looked up at Krov, wondering at the hostile reception.

Both armies faced each other in the tense silence, the only sound that of the crashing of the waves into the boulders.

"Would you aim arrows at a friend?" Erec called out, over the crashing of the ocean.

Krov smirked back.

"And since when are you a friend to me?" Krov answered coldly, hands on hips.

Erec was caught off guard by his response.

"Do you know who I am? I am Erec, son of the late King of the Southern Isles, friend and allies to you and your fathers for four generations."

"Aye, I know who you are," he replied coldly. "All too well. *Allies* is a stretch."

Erec stared back, puzzled.

"You fought with my father, you shed blood for my father," Erec called out. "Our cause has always been your cause. I fought beside you myself in one too many battles at sea. And we have saved you more than once from capture by the Empire. Why do you keep your arrows trained at us?"

Krov reached up and scratched his bald head.

"Those are all half-truths," he called back. "My father helped yours more than once. And I think you have received the better end of the bargain."

He glanced over Erec's ships.

"You don't arrive here as a friend," Krov called out. "You arrive with combat ships. Perhaps you are coming to take the island."

Erec shook his head.

"And why would I want this hunk of garbage you call an island?"

Krov stared back, seeming shocked, then slowly, he broke into a wide grin.

Suddenly, Krov threw back his head in robust laughter, and the tension broke on both sides. His men lowered their arrows, and Erec's men lowered theirs.

"Erec, you old bastard!" Krov called out, jovial. "It warms my heart to see you again!"

Krov reached out, threw a huge metal grappling hook through the air, and the cord unraveled as it sailed in an arc and landed aboard Erec's stern.

"What are you waiting for?" Krov scolded his men. "You heard the man! He's a friend! Pull them in!"

Krov's men dropped their crossbows and they all rushed forward, yanking the ropes hand over hand, pulling Erec's ship in. Krov then jumped down onto the stone ledge, and as Erec disembarked, he rushed forward and embraced him in a great bear hug. Erec, as always, was caught off guard by Krov's unpredictable ways; he seemed as if he would just as easily kill you as hug you. Part pirate, part mercenary and part soldier—Erec, as his father, never quite knew where to place Krov and his isle of Boulder men.

Krov leaned back and studied Erec's face.

"I have seen your father rarely and you less," Krov said. "You have aged. You are a man now. You and your brother," Krov said, nodding to Strom as he disembarked, too, and nodded back. "Why haven't you come to see me sooner?"

Erec studied him, too, and saw he'd aged over the years. His beard was now streaked with gray, his cheeks had reddened, his bald head was lined, and he had grown a small belly. Yet he was still as strong as Erec remembered, his grip like iron with his calloused sea hands.

"Our father is dead," Strom announced.

Krov looked to Erec for confirmation, and Erec nodded. Krov's eyes glazed over with sadness.

"A shame," he said. "He was a good man. A good king. Hard as a rock, but fair. I loved the old bastard."

"Thank you," Erec said. "So did we."

"And who is this?" Krov asked.

Erec followed his gaze and he turned and saw Alistair approaching, and they all stepped aside for her as Erec took her hand and helped her step up to the stone ledge.

"My beloved," Erec replied. "My wife. Alistair."

Krov took her hand and kissed it.

"You have good taste," Krov said, then turned to her. "But what are you doing with an ugly old bastard like this?" he asked her with a wink and a smile.

Alistair smiled.

"He is neither," she replied, "and even if he were ugly and old, I would still love him dearly."

Krov smiled.

"A classy woman," he said to Erec with a smile. "I am surprised she is with you."

"And why wouldn't she be?" Strom asked. "Erec is King now."

Krov raised his eyebrows.

"King, are you?" he said. "I suppose you would be," he said. "And a fine king you shall make," he said, clasping his shoulder firmly.

Krov suddenly wheeled and yelled to his men.

"Well, what are you waiting for!?" he scolded. "Open the gate! You heard the man—a King has arrived!"

The heavy iron portcullis was raised, with a loud creaking noise, revealing the city behind it, a massive city that looked like a stadium.

They all followed Krov as he led them beneath the arc and across the threshold to the city, and as they did, Krov stepped up, took Alistair's hand, and led her off to the side.

"My lady, stand here if you would."

"But why?" she asked, confused.

"Because I don't want you to get killed, too."

Erec, confused, suddenly looked up as he crossed the threshold into the city, and out of the corner of his eye spotted a knight on horseback, wielding a lance, charging down at him.

Erec, his reflexes kicking in, jumped out of the way at the last second, and the lance cut through the air, barely missing him. At the same moment, a knight charged Strom from the other direction, and Strom, too, reacted, rolling and jumping out of the way just before he was struck.

Erec was shocked to find himself standing in the courtyard entrance to the city, a stadium of sorts, several knights in armor on horseback, all charging for him.

He looked over at Krov, who stood several feet away, grinning back devilishly.

"How soon you forget the ways of Bouldermen," he said. "No one enters here unless they earn it. This is no isle of pansies, like your Southern Isles. It is an isle of warriors! You fight for entry here."

"And what of a horse and a lance?" Strom called out, indignant.

Krov grinned.

"This is Boulder Isle," he said. "Here, you must earn those, too."

Erec jumped out of the way as yet another knight came charging for him, barely missing, and he rolled on the hard dirt. A dozen more knights charged and Erec looked at Strom and the two of them silently decided on a course of action.

As the next knight barreled down, Erec dodged, grabbed his lance, and in one smooth motion yanked it from his hands, sending the knight jerking forward and flying off his horse.

Erec immediately grabbed the reins and mounted the knight's horse and, wielding his lance, kicked and raced off at a gallop.

Erec rode at full speed, aiming for a knight about to catch Strom unaware from the side. Erec reached him in time, jabbed him in his ribs with the blunt-edged lance, clearly used for sparring. The knight flew off and Strom, wasting no time, mounted his horse, snatching the knight's lance.

Finally on equal footing, Erec did what he knew best, lowering his lance and preparing to joust with the opposing knights. He raced right for them, not waiting, weaving in and out and taking down one after the other, leaving a trail of clanging armor behind them as each of them hit the ground. These Bouldermen might all be hardened warriors, but none had the skill to match Erec, the champion of the Southern Islanders and a knight with no peer in the kingdoms.

Beside him, Strom was doing equal damage, leaving his own trail in his wake.

Erec heard a sudden rumbling behind him, and he glanced back to see another knight charging him from behind, wielding a wooden flail, about to strike him in the head; before Erec could react, Strom charged sideways, wielding his lance and knocking the knight backwards off his horse before he could finish swinging the flail.

"Now we are even!" Strom called out to Erec.

Erec and Strom raced past each other, turning in broad circles, and then charged together, heading toward the remaining knights charging their way. Erec lowered his visor and lance, and knocked a knight off his horse at the same time Strom did. Together they parted the group, picking them off one at a time, circling again and again until they finished them off.

The growing crowd surrounding the courtyard roared in delight. Erec and Strom faced them all, raising their visors and lances in a final lap, victorious.

Krov stepped forward to greet them, a broad smile on his face, and Erec did not know whether to thank him or kill him.

"That's the Erec I remember!" Krov called out, and the crowd cheered again. "You've earned your stay here—both of you."

Krov turned and waved to the next arched gate, and slowly a massive portcullis was raised, revealing a city courtyard behind it.

"Welcome, my friends, to Boulder Isle!"

CHAPTER THIRTEEN

Darius galloped through the desert, racing beneath the suns, joined by Raj, Desmond, Kaz, Luzi and dozens more of his brothers in arms, the sound of their zertas rumbling in the midday silence. They tore across the barren landscape, using the zertas they had plundered from the Empire battle, wielding weapons they had scavenged from the Empire soldiers, and led hundreds of villagers, who ran behind them on foot. It was a chaotic group of warriors, all brought together in common cause, all out for blood, for freedom, and all united only by Darius's leadership, his sacrifice, his example. Darius was determined not to sit back anymore, but to bring the fight to the Empire's doorstep—and his people were determined to follow.

Darius did not know if he had energized them all by his leadership or if his people simply had nothing left to lose. Perhaps it had finally hit home that the Empire would surround and destroy them; perhaps they finally realized that they could no longer wait passively, to be slaughtered or maimed. Backed into a corner, they were forced to attack. Finally, Darius and his people saw eye to eye: finally, they were, like he, ready and happy to go down on their feet, fighting.

Lead by Darius's example, finally, they had all taken back their manhood, had claimed it for themselves. Finally they had all come to see that your manhood could not be taken from you—but neither could it be given. It was something that had to be claimed, that had to be insisted upon, that had to be demanded, and that had to be taken with your own two hands.

Each of them were emboldened and empowered, too, to have real weapons of steel, to hold the cold steel in their hands for the first time in their lives, to feel what real weight felt like—not the weight of bamboo. They were emboldened, too, by the thunder and speed of the zertas, magnificent war animals that made one feel as a true warrior should. They charged and they charged, following Darius blindly into the desert. Darius felt he could lead them anywhere.

But not all of them. There was still a faction of his village, led by Zirk, who blamed Darius, envied him, and did not approve of his course of action. These people, too, followed him now, having no choice, as they did not want to be left behind. As much as they might disagree with him, or be immersed in a power struggle with him, nonetheless, they had been slaves, too, and they, like all of them, were enjoying their first taste of freedom.

Darius kicked his zerta and they all charged faster, sweat running down Darius's back, stinging his wounds, as he held on for dear life, squinting into the horizon. It felt so liberating just to be out there, on his own, free to do whatever he wished, to go wherever he wished, during the daytime, that he barely felt his injuries. Every other day of his life, Darius had had to report to duty, had only had free time after the sun had fallen. And every other day, he certainly would not have dared venture outside of his village limits.

He was *free*—truly free. That word would have been unimaginable just days ago.

Darius charged and charged until finally he spotted, in the distance, what he'd been waiting for. It was his first objective: the slave fields of their neighboring village, perhaps a dozen miles away. All of the surrounding slave villages, separated by desert, were interconnected dots on the landscape, all under the thumb of the Empire, all circling the perimeter of Volusia. None of them, of course, were allowed to gather, to unite, to see each other. That was all about to change.

Darius sensed that other slaves would feel as he did. He sensed that when other slaves saw him and his people, free, liberated, attacking, they, too, would join the cause. And village to village, one man at a time, he could build an army.

Darius also knew he could not attack Volusia directly, not with his small numbers and their great army and vast fortifications. He knew, if he had any chance of winning, he had to attack the Empire army at its weakest, most vulnerable, points, where they least expected it: out in the fields, piecemeal, one village a time, where the taskmasters were scarce, spread out, unaware. Each slave field, Darius knew, had but a few dozen taskmasters to watch over hundreds of slaves. In the past, they had been kept down in their place, and no one had dared revolt, and so a few men could watch over many.

But that, if Darius could help it, was all about to change. Now these brutal taskmasters were about to learn the power of the common man.

Darius knew they could win—especially if they came upon them quickly, unaware, and if they liberated slaves and converted them into their growing ragtag army.

As they approached, Darius let out a loud cry, kicked his zerta, and charged faster, closing in on the slave fields. He could see from here, dotting the landscape, hundreds of slaves, all shackled, smashing rock, none of them expecting their arrival. Standing over them, interspersed throughout, walking up and down the rows, were Empire taskmasters, raising their whips, lashing them beneath the morning sun. Darius winced at the sight, the pain still fresh in his own back from the lashing, the sight bringing up fresh memories, a fresh desire for vengeance,

Darius scowled and kicked and charged even faster. All around him his men did the same, seeing the same view, feeling as he, needing no prodding to set wrongs right.

As Darius reached them, he saw the first row of slaves turn and look up at him, bearing down on his zerta, and he watched as their eyes widened in shock. Clearly, these slaves had never seen freed slaves riding zertas, wielding weapons of steel—had never seen anyone like them, with their color skin, riding, riding free, triumphant, beneath the sun.

Darius focused in on one particularly large taskmaster, who was whipping a young boy, and he raised a short spear he'd salvaged from the Empire, took aim, and hurled it.

The taskmaster finally turned at the sound of the zertas thundering toward them, and Darius watched in satisfaction as his eyes, too, widened in surprise—and then in agony, as the spear pierced his heart.

The taskmaster grabbed it with both hands, as if trying to pull it out, and looked up at Darius in confusion, before collapsing down on his back. Dead.

Darius and the others let out a great cheer, and their battle cry rose to the heavens as they thundered into the fields, row to row, a great wall of destruction kicking up a spreading wave of dust. Villagers stood there, frozen in fear, rooted to place, as Darius and his men raced by them, killing taskmasters left and right.

Darius and the others stopped before a group of slaves, who stood there, cowering.

The slaves looked up at them in wonder, still not moving. A large slave with dark skin and eyes wide with fear, sweat pouring down his forehead, set down his hammer and looked down at Darius.

"What have you done?" the man asked, panic in his eyes. "You have killed the masters! Now we will all die! All of us slaves shall die!"

Darius shook his head, came forward and raised his sword, and the slave cringed. Darius swung it down and severed the slave's shackles.

The slave looked down in shock. One a time, all of Darius's brothers in arms, Raj, Desmond, Kaz, Luzi and others came forward, raised their swords, and slashed away the slaves' shackles. The satisfying clink of broken chains hitting the desert floor rose up all around them.

They all looked up at Darius in amazement, too shocked to move.

"Do not call yourself *slaves* again," Darius replied.

"But our chains!" another slave cried. "You must put them back, quickly! We will all die for this!"

Darius shook his head, hardly believing how conditioned these poor men had become.

"You don't understand," Raj replied. "The days of fearing the Empire are over. It is we who now are bringing the fear to them."

"You can die fighting with us," Darius called out, to the growing crowd of freed slaves, "or you can die here in the fields, cowering as cowards! Who among you wishes to die a slave—and who among you wishes to die a free man?"

There came a cheer amongst the crowd of slaves, as they all began to realize that freedom had arrived.

"I cannot give you your freedom, my brothers!" Darius called out. "You must fight for it! Each and every one of you—join us now!"

A horn sounded, and Darius turned to see the dozens of Empire soldiers rallying, charging them. Suddenly, there came another shout from behind Darius, and he glanced back to see hundreds of his villagers, on foot, appearing over the horizon, charging to back him up, catching up.

The Empire soldiers suddenly spotted them, too, and as they did, they stopped in their tracks. No longer were they facing a dozen freed slaves—now they were facing several hundred. They stared at the horizon with shock and fear—and suddenly, for the first time in his life, Darius saw the Empire men turn and flee.

Darius let out a battle cry and led the charge, and this time, all of the freed slaves, as one, joined in. He led his growing army, charging through the fields, chasing after the Empire soldiers. They soon caught up to them as they fled, slashing down, slaughtering them left and right. Darius felt particular satisfaction as he watched a taskmaster drop his whip to run faster, as Raj hurled a spear right through his back.

Darius remounted his zerta and charged, rushing to meet the half dozen taskmasters who had regrouped and charged toward him. His brothers in arms remounted beside him. Behind them, all the slaves fell in line, rushing to join them.

The freed slaves joined in the fight, pouncing on the taskmasters, tackling them to the ground, piling on top of them and pummeling them to their deaths.

"That is for my boy!" one of them yelled out.

More slaves rushed forward and, using their shackles, still dangling from their wrists, jumped on soldiers from behind and wrapped their dangling chains around their necks, again and again, choking them to their deaths.

Finally, a group of a dozen Empire soldiers, realizing they were outnumbered and would die if they continued to flee, stopped, turned, banded together in a professional wall, and made a stand. They were an imposing bunch, large warriors, towering over the slaves, with thick, professional armor and weapons and with a brutal mindset to kill anything in their path.

Darius threw a spear down at them, and they blocked it easily with their shields, fighting as one, and he knew this would not be easy.

Darius rode up to them and dismounted, Raj, Desmond, Kaz, and Luzi following, along with several of his brothers in arms. He leapt down wildly, raising his sword high, and as he did, brought it down on a soldier's shoulder, finding the kinks in his armor, felling him.

The other soldiers immediately attacked.

Darius went blow for blow with them, surprised at their speed and strength, their swords clanging and sparking beneath the midday sun as they fought, pushing each other back and forth. Beside him, Raj and Desmond were immersed in heated battles, too, none of them able to gain an advantage. His other men and villagers began to catch up, to join them, and Darius heard their cries as they were cut down by these professional soldiers.

Darius went blow for blow with a skilled soldier, swords clanging, most of his blows defected by his massive, copper shield. Another Empire soldier rushed over and smashed Darius in the side of the head with his shield, dropping him to one knee.

Darius, not missing a beat, spun around, even with his head ringing, and slashed the Empire soldier at the knee; with a cry he fell forward to the ground.

Darius rolled out of the way as the other soldier slashed down for his back, trying to chop him in half.

Darius regained his feet and blocked a blow—but he could not turn in time as he saw another sword slash coming for his back.

Darius heard the sudden sound of shackles swinging through the air and saw one of the freed slaves reaching up, wrapping his shackle around the soldier's wrist and yanking it back, saving Darius from the deadly blow.

Darius turned and stabbed the soldier just before he could free himself and attack the slave.

Two more soldiers rushed Darius, and Darius ducked out of the way as his zerta rushed forward, stomping them, knocking them down.

More and more freed slaves joined them, charging forward, swinging their chains, lashing the Empire soldiers, retaliating for being whipped themselves. Indeed some slaves salvaged the whips from the desert floor and used them as fierce weapons, lashing Empire soldiers left and right. Many blows were blocked by the shields, but over time, as enough villagers arrived and enough chains and whips descended, enough blows got through. The Empire line began to weaken.

Soon there remained but one Empire soldier standing, who threw down his weapons, his shield, and faced them, raising his hands.

"Mercy!" he called out, as all the villagers surrounded him. "Let me live, and I will speak to the Empire for you! I will ask for mercy on your account!"

The crowd grew quiet as Darius stepped forward, breathing hard, gripping the hilt of his sword as he approached, scowling.

"What you fail to understand," Darius seethed back, "is that we don't need to ask for mercy. We are not slaves anymore. What we need, we take by force."

Darius stepped forward and stabbed the soldier in the heart, watching him die as he collapsed at his feet, staining the desert floor red.

"There is your mercy," Darius said. "The same mercy you extended to all of us."

All around Darius the air suddenly filled with the joyful, victorious shouts of his people, freed slaves, all of them jubilant, rallying to him, hundreds of them, his army already doubled. Darius raised his sword high, turning and facing them all, and they all, as one, cheered and chanted his name.

"Darius!" they called out. "Darius! Darius!"

CHAPTER FOURTEEN

Indra sat with the others inside Ragon's golden castle, in awe at her surroundings, wondering if all of this were real. They all sat on piles of luxurious furs, on a floor which was smooth and shiny, nearly translucent, before an enormous, ornate fireplace, its mantle made of shiny white marble, rising twenty feet high, framing a roaring fire. Beside her sat Elden on one side and Selese on the other, beside her Reece, then Thorgrin, O'Connor, and Matus. They all sat in a semicircle, spread out before the fire, all relaxed with each other's company, a comfortable silence falling over them.

Indra stared into the flames, losing track of time as night fell outside. She looked out through the open-aired arched windows and through them she could see twilight spreading, see the stars high up in the sky, twinkling red. She felt the gentle ocean breezes, heard the crashing of the waves in the distance, and she knew the ocean lay somewhere below.

Indra looked about and saw her friends were the most relaxed she'd ever seen them; for the first time in as long as she could remember, they kept their guard down, and she felt she could do the same. She gently released her grip on her new spear, not even realizing she was still clutching it out of reflex, and laid it down beside her, a part of her not wanting to let it go, the weapon already feeling like an extension of her. She leaned back into the furs, beside Elden, and looked into the flames. Elden tried to drape an arm around her, to come in close, but she pushed him away; she did not like people too close to her.

"Is it heavy?" came a voice.

Indra turned and saw Selese sitting beside her, eyeing her spear. She did not know what to think of Selese. On the one hand, she was the only other girl in this group, on this journey with them, and in that sense, they had bonded; yet at the same time, Indra had to admit that she was a bit wary of Selese, given that she had just emerged from the land of the dead, from the other side of death. She did not quite know what to make of her. Was she alive? Was she still dead? She seemed real to her, as real as anyone else. And in a way, Indra had to admit, that creeped her out.

Additionally, Indra did not really understand Selese, and never had. The two of them were such different people, cut from such different cloths. Indra was a warrior, and Selese was a healer, and more feminine than Indra would ever want to be. Indra could not understand any woman who did not want to wield a weapon.

"No," Indra finally replied. "It is surprisingly light."

They fell into a silence, and Indra felt she should return the courtesy; after all, Selese had tried to start a conversation.

"And your sand?" Indra asked. "Do you like having it?"

Selese smiled sweetly and nodded.

"I like anything that can help me heal others," she replied. "I could want no better gift."

"Then you are a better person than I," Indra replied. "I enjoy killing people—not healing them."

"There is a time for both," Selese replied, "and I consider myself no better than anyone. In fact, I admire you."

"Me!?" Indra asked, surprised. It was the last thing she had expected to come from Selese's mouth.

Selese nodded.

"Yes. I can hardly believe that you can wield a weapon like that. Any weapon really."

Indra, defensive as always, at first wondered if Selese were mocking her. But then she studied her soft, compassionate eyes, and she softened, realizing she was genuine. She realized that she had been judging Selese too harshly, just because she was unlike her. She had been cold, keeping her at a distance, not welcoming her into her back. She realized now, seeing what a good, genuine person Selese was, that she had been wrong. That was just her way, she knew, the way she had always been, too defensive with everyone. It was a defense mechanism, she realized, to help her survive in a cruel and taunting world—especially as a woman wielding arms.

"It's not so hard, really," Indra replied. "I could teach you."

Selese smiled and raised a hand.

"I thank you," she said, "but I am content with my healing potions."

"You are good at healing men," Indra observed. "And I am good at killing them."

Selese laughed.

"I suppose, then, that we shall make a good team."

Indra smiled back, feeling surprisingly at home with Selese.

"I must admit," Selese said, "at first I was afraid of you. A woman who can fight the way you do, who is unafraid of men."

"And what is there to fear?" Indra replied. "Either you kill a man, or they kill you. Fear won't make a difference."

Indra shook her head.

"I must admit," she added, "that I was afraid of you, too."

"You—afraid of *me*!?" Selese asked, shocked.

Indra nodded.

"After all, it was you who emerged from the land of the dead. From the other side. It was you who had not only faced death, but knew it. And by your own hand, no less. I fear death. I try to make myself afraid of no one. But I do fear death. And I fear anyone who has been too close to it."

Selese's face grew serious, and she drew a long breath as she stared into the flames, as if remembering.

"What was it like?" Indra asked, unable to resist. She knew she should not ask, should not press her, but she had to know. "Is it unbearable down there?"

As a long silence followed, a part of Indra hoped she would not reply, did not want to hear the answer. Yet another part was dying to know.

Selese finally sighed.

"It's hard to describe," she said. "It is not like entering another place. It is like entering another part of yourself—a deep, and sometimes dark, part of yourself. Everything comes back to the surface, back in your face, everything you did in life—everyone you loved, everyone you hated, everything you did and did not do. Love given and love lost. It all comes bubbling up before you, as if all happening once again. It is an odd state, a review of your life that never ends. It is a place of memories and dreams and hopes. A place, most of all, of unfulfilled desire."

Selese sighed.

"For me, more than most, because I took my own life, I was sent to a different place below. It was a place I was sent to reflect, to understand what I did and why. Memories play on repeat, and never end. On the one hand, it was cathartic; on the other hand, it was torturous. Because of the way my life ended, everything felt incomplete. I felt myself burning for one more chance, just one more chance to fix mistakes, to get it right."

Indra could see how deeply Selese felt it all, reliving it in her eyes, lost in another place. She felt that there was a translucent quality to Selese, as if a part of her were here, and another part still down below.

Selese turned and set her eyes on her.

"And what of you?" Selese asked. "What has driven you here? Was your life perfect?"

Indra thought long and hard about the question; she had never considered it before.

Indra shook her head.

"A far cry from perfect," she said. "It was anything but. I was raised in the Empire. In the Empire, one lives life as a slave. I lived inside a great slave city, and slaveship was my life. I witnessed everyone I love and knew be killed."

Indra sighed, feeling sick at the thought, it all rushing back to her as if it were yesterday.

"I could live with the bondage," she said. "I could live with the labor. I could live with the beatings. But what I could not live with was watching my family in bondage, watching them being slaves. That was too much."

Indra fell quiet, thinking of them, remembering her parents and sisters and brothers.

"And where are they now?" Selese asked. "What became of them?"

There came a long silence, nothing but the crackling of the fire, as Indra felt all of the others listening, watching her for a response.

Indra shook her head as she lowered it, feeling her eyes well with tears. She could not bring herself to say the words, so she just remained silent.

Selese reached up and laid a reassuring hand on her shoulder.

Finally, after a long while, Indra caught her breath.

"I watched them die," she said, the words sticking in her throat. "Each and every one of them. And there was nothing I could do. I was shackled to the others. I was helpless."

She sighed.

"I vowed to survive. I vowed to become a fighter. I vowed vengeance. The need for vengeance is a very powerful thing, more powerful, even than the need for food, for water, the need to live. It is what sustained me. It is what kept me going. I vowed to do whatever I had to to kill all those who took my family from me."

Elden came close, sliding over, and draped an arm around her.

"I am so sorry," he said. It was the first time he had spoken in a while, and the first time in as long as she could remember that he, always so silent, expressed his emotions.

But Indra shrugged off his arm, and despite herself, felt annoyed. She could not help it—it was the defensive part of her overwhelming her.

"I don't want your sympathy," she snapped, her voice dark, filled with anger. "I don't want anyone's sympathy."

Indra suddenly stood, crossed the chamber, and sat on the far side of the room, turning her back to all of them, bringing her spear with her. She sat there, facing the wall, looking out the window into the night, and held up her spear beneath the moonlight. She brushed away a tear, quickly, so that none of the others would see her like this, and she raised the shaft to the light, examining it. She watched all its diamonds sparkle, and she took comfort in her new weapon. She would kill them all, every last Empire.

If it was the last thing she did, she would kill each and every one of them.

*

Thor dreamt fast, troubled dreams. He saw himself sailing on the bow of a beautiful, long ship, brand-new canvas sails above him, rippling, the ocean glistening beneath him as they cut through the water like fish. They headed, he and his Legion brothers, toward a small island up ahead, an island marked by three distinct cliffs, like camel humps, yet white as snow. It was a visual that Thor could never forget.

As they sailed closer, up above, on the highest cliff, something caught his eye, reflected in the sun. He narrowed his eyes and made out a small, shining bassinet. He knew, he just knew, that inside it lay a baby.

His baby.

Guwayne.

The tides carried them so fast it nearly took Thor's breath away, and as they approached, sailing as if on the wings of the wind, Thor was filled with a joy and excitement he'd never known. He stood at the rail, ready to pounce, to run up the cliffs, the moment their boat touched the sand.

They suddenly touched down and Thor jumped gracefully over the rail, dropping twenty feet below and landing easily on the sand. He hit the ground running, and sprinted into the dense tropical jungle that bordered the island.

Thor ran and ran, branches scratching against him, until he finally reached a clearing. And there inside, high up atop a boulder, sat the golden bassinet.

A baby's cries filled the jungle air, and Thor rushed forward, scrambled up the boulder, and stopped at its plateau, excited to see Guwayne.

Guwayne, Thor was elated to see, was there. He was really there. He reached up for him, crying, and Thor reached down and grabbed him, weeping. He held his baby to him, clutching him to his chest, rocking him, and tears of joy fell down his face.

Father, he heard Guwayne say, the voice resonating somehow inside his head. *Find me. Save me, Father*.

Thor woke with a start, sitting bolt upright, heart beating wildly, and looked frantically around him. He did not know where he was, reaching out, reaching for Guwayne, not understanding where he could be. It took several moments for him to realize he was not there, but somewhere else. Inside.

In a castle. Ragon's castle.

Disoriented, Thor looked about and saw the others were all fast asleep by the fireplace. He looked out through the high arched windows, and saw dawn just beginning to break in the night sky. He shook his head, rubbing his eyes, realizing it had all been but a dream. He had not seen Guwayne. He had not been at sea.

And yet it had all felt so real. It had felt like more than a dream: it had felt like a message. A message meant just for him. Guwayne, he suddenly felt certain, was waiting for him on an island, a place with three white cliffs, close to here. Thor had to save him. He could not wait.

Thor suddenly jumped to his feet and roused each of his brothers, prodding them from their slumber.

They all jumped to their feet, clutching their weapons, on alert.

"We must go!" Thorgrin said. "Now!"

"Go where?" O'Connor asked.

"Guwayne," Thorgrin said. "I saw him. I know where he is. We must go to him at once!"

They still stared at him, confused.

"Are you mad?" Reece asked. "Leave now!? It is not yet dawn."

"What about Ragon?" Indra asked. "We can't just run out!"

Thor shook his head.

"You don't understand. I *saw* him. We have no time. My son awaits. I know where he is. We must go at once!"

There felt a sudden urgency overcome him, an urgency greater than any he'd ever felt in his life. He felt he had no choice.

Thor suddenly turned, unable to wait any longer, and ran from the room.

He burst down the corridors of the castle, down the stairs, and out the front door, sprinting alone through the fields, beneath the breaking light of dawn, one of the moons still high in the sky.

"Wait!" called out a voice.

Thor glanced back to see the others, all chasing after him.

"Have you gone mad?" Matus cried. "What's come over you?"

But Thor had no time to respond. He ran and ran until his lungs nearly burst, not thinking clearly, just knowing he had to reach his ship.

He soon reached the cliffs, and as he did, he stopped and stood there, looking down.

Their boat was still there, visible beneath the moonlight, looking exactly as it had when they'd left it. The seven ropes were there, too, still dangling over the edge.

Thor turned, grabbed hold of a rope, and began the descent. He looked over and saw the others descending beside him, all of them hastily leaving this place. He did not understand what was happening to him—and he did not care.

Soon, he would be with his son.

*

Ragon emerged from his castle, awakened by an unusual sensation in the breaking dawn, and he marched across the hills, perturbed, using his staff, and studied the horizon. Up above, Lycoples shrieked, flying in broad circles.

Ragon reached the edge of the cliffs and he looked out at the ocean, glistening in the dawn. As he studied the waters, he began to make out a shape: down below, far off, Ragon could see Thor's ship, sailing off, the currents already carrying it far away.

Ragon, anguished, raised his staff and tried to control the current to bring it back. He was shocked to realize he could not. For the first time in his life, he was helpless to control it, was up against a power greater than his own.

Baffled, Ragon studied the skies, and as he did, he noticed, for the first time, a shape. A shadow. He heard an unearthly screech, a screech that had no place being sounded anywhere above ground, and he felt a chill run down his spine. The shadow disappeared into the clouds just as quickly, and Ragon stood there, frozen, realizing what it was: a demon. Unleashed from hell.

Suddenly, Ragon understood. A demon had crossed over his island, had cast a spell of confusion over its occupants, had lured Thorgrin away under its spell. God only knew what it had made Thor believe, Ragon wondered, as he watched his ship sail away, getting smaller and smaller, away from Guwayne, away from his only son—and toward a danger far greater, surely, than Ragon could ever imagine.

CHAPTER FIFTEEN

Gwendolyn marched across the Great Waste beneath the relentless two suns of the desert sky, Krohn at her side, as she had been doing day after day, putting one foot before the other, stirring up dust, her legs aching with the endless monotony of marching. They had not stopped marching ever since they had left Darius's people, all of them determined to cross this desert, to find the Second Ring, to find help.

Yet as she looked up ahead, as she had for days, all she saw before her was more monotony, an empty landscape, nothing on the horizon, just more of this red waste. The hard desert floor was cracked, stiff, stretching forever to nothing, and nothing to break up the monotony except the occasional passing dust cloud or thorn bush rolling in the wind. It was the emptiest landscape she'd ever seen, a hopeless, barren place. She felt as if she were marching to the very ends of the world.

Krohn panted heavily, whining, and as she marched, her apprehensions deepening, Gwendolyn wondered what she had gotten her people into. They had been trekking for days now, already running low on provisions, especially water, and there was no hope in sight. There was no shelter in sight, either, and she did not know how many more nights she could have her people sleep out in the open, exposed, on the desert floor, with the freezing, whipping sand winds and the endless critters crawling on them at night. She was already covered in bites, awake every hour, swatting away exotic bugs that swarmed near her ear. Last night one of her men had died from a scorpion bite—and this morning Gwen had herself crushed the largest spider she'd ever seen, right before she put on her boot. It was a landscape of poisons and hidden death, a treacherous place, home only to reptiles and scorpions—and the bones of others who had been foolish enough to try to cross it.

"Did she really think this would lead us somewhere?" came a voice.

Gwen heard a murmuring, and she turned and saw her ragtag collection of people, what was left of the Ring, hundreds of survivors of the Ring, and she felt for them. They had endured so much—battles, voyages, sickness, hunger, the loss of loved ones, of their possessions, of their homeland—their suffering never seemed to end—and here they were, on yet another trek, to yet another destination that might not ever come to be. They were exhausted, cynical, and beginning to lose hope. She could hardly blame them. Her heart broke most of all for the baby, crying, its shrill cry always with them as Illepra carried her carefully, wrapped up to protect her from the sun, never failing her duties for her. Gwen wished she could give her water, shade, a comfortable place to sleep.

"If this Great Waste actually led somewhere," another person replied, "don't you think the slaves would've tried it already? Don't you think they would have tried to make their escape?"

"That's because it leads nowhere," the other said, "and they know it. They were not foolish enough to attempt to cross it."

Gwendolyn saw the faces of her people, angry, sunburnt, parched, desperate—and as they looked up and glared at her, their eyes filled with hatred, crazed from the relentless sun—she had to look away. Despite all their harsh words, she could not stand to see them suffering like that.

She also recognized the face of the one who was instigating it all—Aslin; he had been one of the instigators behind the rebellion back in the cave. She thought he had been humbled, but apparently not. She had been merciful to let him live back there; perhaps, she realized, that had been a mistake.

"Where is it that you think this waste will take us anyway?" she heard Aslin suddenly call out, in a loud voice rising above the din.

Gwendolyn was surprised to hear him so emboldened, as if gaining momentum, calling out in open rebellion.

"You really pretend to believe that there exists a Second Ring?" he added. "Why don't you just call this what it is: you're leading us to our graves."

There came a rumbling from some of her people, starting to warm up to him, and Gwendolyn felt her hair stand on end, felt the tension rising in the air behind her. She felt pained to be condemned by them so harshly, especially after all she had sacrificed for them. Was that what it meant to be a queen?

Beside her, Krohn began to snarl.

"It's okay, Krohn," she said reassuringly.

"We never should have fought for those villagers!" another of her people yelled. "We never should have stayed there to begin with!"

There came another disgruntled rumbling.

"We never should have burned our ships!" another yelled.

"We never should have sailed to the Empire!" another yelled.

The mumbling grew louder, and it was followed by the distinctive sound of a sword being drawn, cutting through the air. Krohn turned, snarling, standing before Gwen.

The crowd suddenly stopped marching, and Gwen turned to see Steffen standing there, sword drawn, facing the rebellious people.

"If you wish to complain," he seethed, "then have the courage to face the Queen and complain directly to her. Stop snickering behind her back like scared little children. It is treason to incite others, and if you continue this line of talk, you will learn what real death means."

Gwen was impressed by Steffen's strength, by the authority in his voice, by his deep, unshakable loyalty to her, and she felt overwhelmed with gratitude for his presence. She realized she had felt too guilty for what had become of her people to stand up for herself.

Aslin glowered back at Steffen.

Beside Steffen, Kendrick turned and drew his sword, too.

"You will have to get through me, too," he added.

Krohn's snarling intensified, as he began to walk slowly toward Aslin, and Aslin looking from Krohn to Steffen to Kendrick then finally, finally lowered his head.

"I was just saying," he mumbled, backing down.

Gwendolyn stepped forward and laid a gentle hand on Steffen and Kendrick's swords, and they sheathed them. She gestured to Krohn, and he quieted and came back to her, as she turned and faced her people.

"I know this journey is hard," she said. "All worthwhile journeys are. I know our entire exile has not been easy. But we are the people of the Ring. We have suffered worse, and we shall get through this. We are of indomitable spirit. We fight not only for the slaves, but for ourselves, for we are all slaves to the Empire—we always have been, as everyone under the sky. We fight finally for real freedom, to throw off the yoke of the Empire, once and for all."

Gwendolyn took a deep breath, seeing her people hanging on her every word, riveted.

"I know you are scared," she called out. "I am scared, too. We are on a mission for our very lives, for our freedom, and for the freedom of others. No one said it would be easy—freedom has *never* been easy. And fighting amongst ourselves will not make it any easier.

"I promise you, a brighter future awaits us. We need to stay to the course, to be strong. I would not lead you anywhere I would not go myself—and if we are all going to die, I will be the first to fall."

Gwendolyn saw in the faces of her people that many of them were mollified by her words, and she turned back and resumed the march, Kendrick and Steffen falling in beside her.

"Fine words, my lady," Steffen said.

"Father could not have said them better," Kendrick said.

"Thank you," she said, reassured by their presence and still shaken by her people's behavior.

"They don't speak for everyone," Kendrick said. "Only the disgruntled few."

"And there will *always* be a disgruntled few," Steffen added. "No matter how great a queen you are."

"I thank you both for your loyalty," Gwen said. "But I must mind, and I understand their frustration. I fear our greatest danger may not lie ahead—but right here, amidst us."

"If it be so," Steffen said, tightening his grip on his sword, "then I shall be first to kill the offenders."

"There are other dangers, my lady," Aberthol chimed in weakly, marching beside them. "Chief among them, lack of food and water. We have not found a single water source, and if we do not find one soon, I fear the sun may be our worst opponent of all."

Gwen had been thinking the same things. She looked back to the horizon as they continued to march, hoping for a sign, anything. But there was nothing.

She turned and looked at Aberthol, marching beside her, using his staff, looking weaker than she'd ever seen him.

"You have studied all the histories," she said to him quietly. "You know not only the history of the Ring but also that of the Empire. You know all the legends, all the geography. Tell me," she said, turning to him, "is it true? Can a Second Ring exist?"

Aberthol sighed.

"I would say its chances of existence are as good as not," he replied. "The Second Ring was always held out in the literature as part myth, part fact. You'll find numerous references to it in the early histories of the Ring, but few in the later volumes. It is dropped altogether in the recent histories."

"Perhaps that is only because it was never found," Gwendolyn said hopefully.

Aberthol shrugged.

"Perhaps," he replied. "Or perhaps because it never existed."

She pondered his words as they marched in silence. Finally, he turned and looked at her.

"Have you considered, my lady," he questioned, looking at her meaningfully, "what you shall do if it does not exist? If this Great Waste leads us nowhere but to a hostile slave city? Or worse, to more waste?"

"I have," she replied. "Every moment. What choice do we have? A certain death awaits us back in the village. This is the path of hope. The toughest path is always the path of hope."

They fell back into a gloomy silence as they continued to march.

As she trekked, hour after hour, the sun getting hotter and hotter, Gwen wondered how her life had come to this, how this could be all that was left of the once great and awesome Ring. These few hundred men, with a few dozen Silver, all that represented the place and nation whom she loved. She thought back to the wedding she had been planning to Thor, to the baby she once held in her arms, to the endless bounties of the Ring—and she bit back tears. How had it all come to this?

What she wouldn't give now to hold Guwayne again; what she wouldn't give to see Thor again, to have him by her side. To have Ralibar and Mycoples back. She felt utterly alone, and wondered if things could get any worse.

She contemplated her family, not long ago all together, and splintered, fractured in so many ways. Her father and mother, dead; Luanda, dead; Gareth, dead; Godfrey, entering Volusia on a dead man's mission; Reece, with Thor halfway across the world, most likely dead; and Kendrick, her last remaining relative at her side, on a fool's march into the desert where he would likely soon be dead. She wondered why destiny had been determined to rend everyone apart.

A hot, dusty wind blew up in her face, and Gwen sheltered her eyes as another cloud of desert sand tore through. She choked on it, coughing with the others, trying to regain her vision.

This time, though, the wind did not pass through; on the contrary, the red dust felt as if it were clawing at her face, scratching it, and it became stronger and stronger. Gwen heard a sudden shriek, an odd noise that sent a chill up her spine, unlike anything she'd ever heard, and as she looked up into the dust, she was shocked to see before her, emerging from the dust cloud, a pack of creatures.

The exotic creatures were tall and thin and twirled in the dust cloud, their bodies red, the same color of the dust, with long jaws and stretched-out ghoulish faces. There were dozens of them, carried by the wind, twirling inside the cloud of dust, and they let out a horrific wailing noise as they appeared, spinning amidst the dust, and suddenly attacking all her people.

"Dust Walkers!" Sandara yelled out. "Defend yourselves!"

Kendrick, Steffen, Brandt, Atme and all the others drew their swords, and Gwendolyn drew hers and spun along with them, as the Dust Walkers descended upon them from all directions. Gwen slashed and missed, and a Dust Walker scraped the side of Gwendolyn's face, scratching her with its claw. She screamed out in pain as her face was scratched, its palm as rough as sandpaper.

Another came at her and sliced her arm with its three claws, making her again cry out in pain.

Another came at her—and another, Gwen feeling as if she were tumbling in a field of thorns.

Steffen stepped forward and slashed wildly, as did Kendrick and the others—and they all missed. The Dust Walkers were just too fast.

The Dust Walkers darted in and out of the crowd, scratching and slashing, the cries of Gwen's people calling out as they inflicted a thousand small cuts.

Gwen, desperate, grabbed a dagger from her waist, spun, and slashed one right in the throat. It dropped to the ground, screeching, disappearing in a pile of dust.

"Get down!" Sandara called out. "Drop to your knees! Cover your heads!"

Gwen heard a baby's cry rip through the air and she looked over to see Illepra clutching the baby, both of them getting attacked. She dropped her dagger and rushed forward, protecting them, covering the baby with her body, and dropping them down to the ground.

Gwen lay on top of them, covering up the baby with her hands and arms and elbows, feeling the scrapes and scratches all over her as the cloud continue to blow through. She felt as if she were being scratched to death, and did not know how much more she could withstand. At least, though, she was protecting the baby.

Gwen knelt that way, as did the others, for what felt like an eternity, the horrific buzzing and howling and wailing of these creatures filling her ears.

Finally, the cloud began to recede, blowing through the desert, right past them, until the scratches grew lighter, the noise quieted, then it all stopped.

The desert was suddenly still, quiet, just as it had been before they'd arrived, and Gwen knelt and looked back and watched the cloud blow on through, disappearing into the horizon.

Shaking, Gwen got to her hands and knees and surveyed her people. They were all still on the ground, scraped and cut, looking traumatized. She turned the other way and looked out at the great expanse still waiting before them, and she wondered: what other horrors lay before them?

CHAPTER SIXTEEN

Godfrey opened his eyes with a start, clutching his belly, as he was kicked by someone twice his size in the jail cell. Lying on the muddy ground of the cell, he looked up to see a tall, unshaven cretin with a big belly, going prisoner to prisoner and kicking each one, apparently just for fun. As Godfrey stumbled to his feet, he did not know what was worse: this man's elbows in his ribs, or his body odor.

This entire jail cell, in fact, was stinking to hell, and as Godfrey looked around at its collection of losers, he could not believe he had wound up in a place like this. All about him were men of every race and color, from every corner of the Empire, all slaves to the Empire, none of the Empire race. They were all crammed into this cell, perhaps fifty feet wide, all of them sulking or pacing, knowing that nothing good lay in store for them.

Godfrey looked over to see Akorth, Fulton, Merek, and Ario, all awake, some pacing, some sitting, none of them looking too pleased. What a quick turn their fate had taken. It had not been long ago that they were all up on the streets of Volusia, all laden with riches and about to strike a deal to save his people. Now, here they all were, common prisoners, unable to even sleep on a muddy floor without being assaulted.

Godfrey scratched his arms and saw the red marks and realized he'd been bitten up by some sort of insect on the muddy floor. He scratched and scratched, annoyed. Probably fleas, he thought. Or perhaps bedbugs.

Akorth and Fulton looked even more disconcerted than he, their hair a mess, unshaven, dark rings beneath their eyes, both of them looking as if they could badly use a drink. Merek and Ario, though, despite their smaller size and younger age, despite being surrounded by such hardened criminals, appeared calm and fearless, resolute, as if they were taking it all in stride and preparing their next move. In fact, they looked much more composed than Akorth and Fulton.

"Don't get in my way again, boy," suddenly came a harsh, guttural voice.

Godfrey turned to see that same cretin, having finished his rounds, now facing him, with the largest belly he'd ever seen, getting close and scowling down at him.

"I wasn't in your way!" Godfrey protested. "I was sleeping! You are the one who kicked me!"

"What did you say?" The man glowered and began to walk threateningly toward him.

Godfrey began to back up, and as he did, he slipped on the mud and landed on his rear—to the laughter of all the other prisoners in the cell.

"Kill him!" one yelled out, egging on the cretin.

Godfrey's heart pounded wildly as he saw the cretin grinning and getting closer, as if ready to devour his prey. He knew that if he did not do something soon the man would crush him with his weight alone.

Godfrey scooted back on the mud, sliding, breathing hard, trying to distance himself from him.

But the cretin suddenly groaned and charged, and Godfrey could see he was going to pounce on him, land on him, and crush him with all his weight. Godfrey tried to back up more, but bumped his head into a stone wall. There was nowhere left to go.

Suddenly, Ario stepped forward, stuck out a foot, and tripped the cretin.

The man fell flat on his face in the mud, and Godfrey spun out of the way before he did, sparing himself from being crushed.

All the prisoners in the room now turned and watched, hollering, laughing uproariously. The cretin spun around, wiped the mud from his face, and locked eyes on Ario with a look of death.

Ario stood there, staring back, unflinching, calm and fearless. Godfrey, incredibly grateful to Ario, could not believe how calm he was, given that the cretin was five times his size and that he had nowhere to run.

"You little punk," the cretin said. "You're finished. Before I kill you, I'm going to tear you apart limb from limb. I'm going to teach you what it means to be in a prison!"

The cretin began to regain his feet and charge Ario, when Merek suddenly took two steps forward, raised his elbow and cracked him across the jawline, catching him perfectly just as he was rising, and sending him down to the ground, unconscious.

"I spent most my life in a prison," Merek said to the unconscious man, "and I don't need you to teach me. Where I come from, they call that a hatchet job. It shuts up a big fat mouth like yours."

Merek spoke loudly enough for all the other prisoners to hear, and he looked around slowly at all of them, challenging them, daring them to come close.

"The Empire took away my dagger," he continued. "But I don't need it. I got my hands. With these thumbs and fingers I can do a lot more damage. Anyone else want to test it out?" he called out loudly.

He turned slowly, meeting each and every person's gaze, until finally, the others looked away and the tension dissipated. Clearly, they all got the idea: Merek and his friends were not to be messed with.

Ario walked up to Merek.

"I had him right where I wanted him," Ario said proudly. "I didn't need your help. Next time, don't get in my way."

Merek smirked and shook his head.

"I'm sure you did," he replied.

Godfrey looked up, watching it all unfold in astonishment, as Merek came over to him and held out a hand and helped him up.

"Where did you learn to fight like that?" Godfrey asked.

"Not the King's Legion," Merek said, smirking, "and not in some fancy knight's barracks. I fight dirty. I fight to hurt, to maim or to kill. I fight to win, not for honor. And I learned what I learned in the back alleys of King's Court."

"I owe you one," Godfrey said. He turned and looked at the big fat cretin, unconscious, unmoving, face-first in the dirt. "I hate to think what would have happened if he'd got me."

"You'd be a mud sandwich," Akorth chimed in, coming over with Fulton.

"Get us out of this city and back to our camp," Merek said, "and that's payment enough."

"Wishful thinking," Fulton said ominously.

Godfrey turned and saw the formidable Empire guards lined up outside the cell, saw the thick iron bars, and he knew they were right. They weren't going anywhere.

"Looks like your plan's going from bad to worse," Merek said. "Not that it was that great to begin with."

"I, for one, don't plan on ending my life in this cell," Ario said.

"Who said anything about ending your life?" Godfrey asked.

"I was watching them while you were passed out," Ario said. "They've taken three of them already. They open the cells every hour, take another one. They don't come back. And they're not taking them for tea."

Suddenly, a horn sounded and three Empire men strutted forward, keys rattling, unlocked the door, walked into the cell, and looked all around menacingly, as if trying to decide who to take. They wore imposing armor, visors down over their faces, and looked like messengers of death.

They settled on a prisoner slumped against the wall, yanked him to his feet, and dragged him out of the cell.

"No!" the man screamed, resisting. "All I did was steal a cabbage. I had nothing to eat. I don't deserve this!"

"Tell that to her goddess Volusia," the guard muttered darkly. "I'm sure she would love to hear that."

"No!" he yelled, his voice fading as the cell door slammed behind him and they dragged him away.

Godfrey and his men exchanged a nervous look.

"We haven't much time," Merek said.

"What's your plan now?" he asked Godfrey. "You got us into this mess—now you get us out of it."

Godfrey stood there, pulling his hair, trying to collect his thoughts. It was all too much at once, had all been too fast for him to process. Even he, who always had found a way out of everything, was stumped. He looked at the iron bars, at the solid stone walls, and he did not see any way out. He decided to try what he knew he was best at: talking his way out of it.

Godfrey walked up to the cell bars and motioned for a guard, standing close by, to come close. He whispered loud enough to be heard.

"You want to be rich?" Godfrey asked, heart pounding, praying that he would go for it.

But the guard continued to stand there with his back to him, ignoring him.

"Not just rich," Godfrey added, "but rich beyond your wildest dreams. I have gold—more than you can dream. Get myself and my friends out of here, and you'll be rich enough to be King yourself."

The guard sneered back at him through his visor.

"And why would a criminal like you have so much gold?"

Godfrey reached into his waist pocket, and from deep inside, where it was hidden, he pulled out a small gold coin. It glistened in the light. It was the last coin he had on him, one he'd kept for emergency purposes. If this was not an emergency, he did not know what was.

Godfrey placed the coin in the guard's yellow, meaty palm.

The guard held it up and examined it, looking impressed.

"I'm not your typical prisoner," Godfrey said. "I am the son of a King. I have enough gold to make you a rich man. All you have to do is let me and my friends out of here."

The guard suddenly lifted his visor, turned and smiled at Godfrey.

"So you have more gold?" he asked, his greedy smile more like a sneer on his grotesque face.

Godfrey nodded enthusiastically.

"Will you lead me to it?" the guard asked.

Godfrey nodded.

"Yes! Just let us out of here."

The guard nodded, satisfied.

"Okay, turn around."

Godfrey turned around, heart pounding with excitement, expecting the guard to release him from the cell.

Suddenly, Godfrey felt a hand on the back of his shirt, felt the guard grabbing him roughly, then, in one quick motion, yanking him back with all his might.

Godfrey felt the back of his head slam into the iron bars, heard a loud thud, and suddenly, his whole world went spinning. He felt light-headed and dropped to his knees.

Before he collapsed on the mud floor, he saw the guard, looking down, laughing a cruel, guttural laugh.

"Thanks for the gold," he said. "Now piss off."

CHAPTER SEVENTEEN

Volusia walked slowly through the city of Dansk against the backdrop of a magnificent scarlet red sunset, fires still roaring on all sides of her as she canvassed the city, lighting up the early night. She felt victorious. She passed all her boulders which she had catapulted into the city, still ablaze, passed piles of rubble, of ruin, city walls which had held for centuries now nothing but remnants. She passed piles corpses, people still stuck in their death throes, others still clinging to life, moaning, still burning alive. She passed scores of soldiers, nothing but charred corpses, their weapons melted to their hands.

And she smiled wide.

Volusia's sack of this city had been merciless, cruel even by her standards. She had sent the flaming boulders over its walls endlessly, indiscriminately killing soldier and citizen, man and woman, knight and child. After killing their leadership, she had unleashed a sudden and intense barrage on them, too fast for them to prepare, to do anything but suffer. The city had been foolish to try to resist her, to think that their immense walls could keep her out, could stop her from getting what she wanted. How foolish the city had been to think that she would not use every means at her disposal to kill every man, woman, and child—anyone and everything in her way. Then again, she mused, even if they hadn't resisted, she probably would have slaughtered them all anyway. It was more helpful, she realized, to instill her reputation for cruelty than to have a city of prisoners.

All around her, lining up perfectly along the city walls, standing at attention, stood her hundreds of thousands of soldiers, in perfect formations, all of them awaiting her slightest command, her signal for what to do next. Here it was, her first city, her first test, razed to its knees in but a few hours. Here it was, the first proof of her power unleashed.

"Here they are, my Goddess," came the voice.

Soku walked beside her, amidst her huge entourage of soldiers and advisors, gesturing before her.

Volusia stopped and looked ahead, her entourage stopping behind her, and she saw rows of prisoners, alive, wounded, faces black with soot, coughing and chained to each other.

"What's left of their army," Soku said. "Five thousand men. They have surrendered the city and wish to join our ranks."

Volusia looked them over carefully, an endless sea of faces, extending all the way back to the city walls, and saw them all staring back at her hopefully.

"And did these men try to resist?" she asked.

Soku shook his head.

"No, Goddess," he replied. "These are the soldiers who surrendered without killing any of our men. There is no blood of ours on their hands."

Volusia looked over the rows and rows of fine soldiers, honorable men, who had only made the one mistake of getting in her path.

"A pity," she said, and turned to Soku.

"Kill them all."

Soku stared back at her, shocked.

"Goddess?" he asked.

"I will not keep anyone who did not try to kill me first."

Soku stared at her, trying to understand, and opened his mouth as if to object—but then closed it, clearly seeing the look in her eye. He, like the others, knew better than to question her command.

He turned to his commanders.

"You heard the Goddess," he said. "Kill them all."

Volusia watched with satisfaction as her thousands of men marched forward, spears held high, and charged into the fray of the city's captives—all of whom, shackled, defenseless, raised hands to their shocked faces.

"NO!" they shrieked.

But it was too late. One man at a time, Volusia's men hacked them down, slaughtering them left and right.

Volusia stood there and watched the butchery, her smile growing wider. Blood sprayed on her as the sun began to sink below the horizon, and she relished every drop, thinking:

What a perfect day this has turned out to be.

*

As night began to fall, Volusia marched farther and farther from the outskirts of Dansk, flanked by her entourage, and with her army marching a bit behind them. Beneath the two moons rising, the twinkling red starts emerging in the sky, she made her way along the desert floor towards the Path of the Circles. It was a moment she had been looking forward to for as long as she could remember.

The Path of the Circles was, indeed, the very reason she had decided to sack Dansk first. Despite their numbers and their fortifications, Volusia did not in fact care so much for the army, or its people, or even its city. The real jewel, the real conquest, was what lay just beyond it: this sacred site of power, a vast circle carved into the hard desert floor. No one knew for sure of its origin, or the source of its power, yet Volusia had heard all her life of the living gods and goddesses who had been anointed here. It was a rite of passage. If she wanted her people to view her as a true God, she knew, there would be no greater stamp of legitimacy than her initiation into the circle.

Just as important, Volusia wanted to make a pact with the protectors of the circle, the desert village of Voks. A taboo race of small green men, more creatures than men, practicing an ancient sect of sorcery so dark and forbidden that it was even outlawed in the time of her mother's mother, Volusia knew there was no tribe in the Empire to match their pure evil. Other sorcerers had limits to what they would do—but the Voks had no bounds to their ruthlessness.

Of course, there was a reason that the power of the Voks and their sacred circle had not been harnessed by all the rulers before her: they were considered too dangerous, too untrustworthy, their sorcery too volatile, too difficult to control. All those who had attempted it, Volusia knew from the history books, had died trying.

But she was different. She was Volusia, goddess of the city of Volusia, Empress-to-be of the Kingdom, and it was her *destiny*, she knew, to rule. No one and nothing could stand in her way. Her provincial generals cared only for numbers, weaponry, armor. They thought an army won based on the figures.

But Volusia knew numbers were but a small part of conquest. She knew she could defeat the Empire's millions with far fewer men. What she really needed was the Voks—and the ancient sorcery that they guarded.

"Goddess," Soku said, marched alongside her. "Can I persuade you to turn around? This is a bad idea."

Volusia sighed, annoyed. Soku had been in her ear ever since they had left the city, second-guessing everything she did.

"Your killing those captive soldiers back there, too, Goddess, was a mistake, if I may speak frankly," he added. "We needed those men. We need every man we can get. Those were five thousand good men. Now they are dead, and for no reason at all. They did not even resist us."

"That is precisely why I killed them," she replied.

He sighed.

"Sometimes I feel as if I don't understand you at all," he said, clearly leaving out the *Goddess*. "You are young still. You should learn from the ways of a hardened commander such as myself."

Volusia stopped abruptly, having enough, and faced him.

"You are the very same commander who allowed my mother to be assassinated, are you not?"

He swallowed, looking caught off guard.

"It was *you* who killed your mother," he replied. "I could not have foreseen that."

"Then perhaps I should find myself a commander who would have," she said.

He stared back, looking upset and uncertain.

"And if I killed my own mother, do you think I would have any qualms about killing my commander?" she added.

He looked down, humbled, and she turned and began marching again.

"Goddess," Aksan said, coming up along her other side, "he speaks the truth. This meeting with the Voks is a terrible idea. They are untrustworthy. Their sorcery cannot be contained or controlled. They might have a power—but it certainly no power you can control. They have been shunned by every race and every ruler in the Empire, and for good reason. They are outcasts."

"Speak to me again," she said, not even bothering to turn to him as she continued marching straight ahead, "and I'll have your tongue cut out."

He stopped speaking, panic in his eyes.

Volusia finally rounded the hill, and as she did, she stopped, in awe at the breathtaking sight before her: there, spread out below in the desert valley, was the circle she had always heard of. She could mistake it for no other. Perhaps a hundred yards in diameter, it was clear from the way it was etched, its perfect shape, its labyrinth of circles, etched in a maze within each other, that it was created by something other than mankind. She could feel the energy throbbing off the desert floor, even from here. It was a place that felt alive, more alive than any place she had ever been.

Standing guard around the circle, equally awe-inspiring, were the Voks—hundreds of them, hunched over in their green cloaks and hoods and emitting a soft chatter, audible even from hear, an eerie sound, like crab legs skitting across the desert floor. She could see from what was revealed beneath their cloaks that they were small, green men, a slimy hue to their skin. They huddled around the circle as if they were one with it.

As one, the Voks all turned toward her and looked up at her men. Without waiting, they immediately started walking toward her, like a million crabs emerging from the ocean.

Volusia hurried down the mountain slope to meet them halfway, anxious to meet them, to be infused with the power of the circle. Assuming they let her enter.

One of the Voks, slightly smaller than the others, clearly their leader, old, walking with a small, emerald staff, walked out in front of them and stopped before her.

Standing but a few feet away, he slowly looked up at her, his eyes completely white. Vokin. She knew of him—he was legendary. He seemed to be examining her, and it was a profoundly uncomfortable feeling. She could understand already why others did not want to interact with them. Just by his looking at her, she felt as if he were stealing her soul.

Yet Volusia forced herself to stare back at his all-white eyes and not look away. She was determined to show fear to no one.

"So," Vokin finally said, his voice sounding like old, cracking wood, "the Goddess has arrived."

Volusia's eyes widened at his words, wondering how much he knew.

"I have come for—" she began,

"I know why you've come," he interrupted. "The question is— are you worthy?"

Volusia stared back at him, shocked; no one had ever spoken to her that way before.

"I am the great Goddess Volusia," she replied, haughty, lifting her chin. "I am worthy of conquering cities. I am worthy of the entire Empire."

Vokin stared back silently.

"I have seen your future," he replied. "There lies much death and destruction in it. Much power. You are far greater than your mother. Far greater than any Empire ruler who has come before you, even Andronicus, even Romulus. But you cannot have power without us. And there will be a price to your power."

"A price?" she said, indignant yet encouraged by his prophecy. "I am already giving you a great gift. I am sparing you your life. Look behind me: have you not seen my men, filling the horizon?"

Vokin laughed heartily, not even bothering to look, his voice cutting through the air, setting her on edge. It had no fear in it whatsoever.

"Do you think all the men in the world stand any chance against our ancient art?"

Volusia thought hard and realized he was right; he was not a simple military commander that she could win over by fear or threats.

"Name your price," she finally said, determined. "Whatever it is, you shall have it."

"We will be partners," he said. "We will rule the Empire together. You shall rule, but we shall always be in the background, and whenever we call upon you, you shall give us what we ask for."

"Agreed," she said, eager to get on with it and assume power.

"The Voks will no longer be outcasts," he added. "We will become part of the mainstream class of the Empire. You will give us back the honor and respect we once had as a race. There will be a Vok circle in every city. Other races will defer to us."

"Agreed," she said, not caring, as long as she had power.

He studied her as the desert wind whipped through, clearly hesitating.

"There is one more thing," he said.

She studied him, wondering how greedy he was, wondering when this would end. She did not trust him already.

"Name it and be done with it."

"I am not going to tell you what it is on this day," he said. "But one day I will call on you for this special request. And you will have to give it to me. Whatever it is."

Volusia thought long and hard, wondering.

"Will it be my life you ask for?" she asked.

He shook his head and laughed.

"No, my dear," he said. "It will be something for more precious than that."

More precious? she wondered. She did not care, as long as she could ascend power. Once she was in power anyway, she could do what she wanted; there was no way they could stop her.

"And I shall enter the circle?" she asked. "And become a Goddess?"

He nodded back.

"A Goddess as there has never been," he replied.

She nodded.

"Done," she said. "Whatever it is, you shall have it."

He nodded back in satisfaction, and she saw something like a smile beneath his hood, as his face crumpled up in a grotesque way.

Volusia reached out to shake his hand and seal their pact, and he reached out and clasped her hand, three long, slimy green claws wrapping around her wrist and forearm. She wanted to pull her hand away, but she knew she could not.

Finally, mercifully, he pulled his hand away.

"Night thickens and the circle awaits," he said. "Follow me."

Volusia followed him as he turned and passed through the ranks of Voks, all parting way for him. The Voks created a passageway, just wide enough for her to pass, and she followed him, her men behind her, walking single file, as they entered the nation of Voks. Their clamoring intensified as she went, and she felt as if she were entering a kingdom of crabs. She could feel the evil energy coming off of them as they crowded around her, watching her pass. They made the strange chattering noises as she went, and they rolled their eyes up in their heads, the whites of them glowing in the night. She could not walk through them fast enough.

Volusia finally entered the circle, following the leader, just the two of them, leaving all the others behind. He walked the circles in a strange pattern, around and around, twisting and turning, following a path which only he knew. It was labyrinthine, and she felt as if it would never end.

Yet she also felt charged with a strange power as she went; the more she walked, the more she felt her legs, burning, felt a heat rising through her body. She felt as if she were changing, as if they circle were changing her.

Volusia finally reached the center of the circle, and as she did, he stepped aside and guided her to where she should stand. Then he turned and walked out of the circle, leaving her in the center alone.

Volusia stood there, alone, facing all her men, her army stretching to the horizon, all of them crowding around the circle, watching her.

"Volusia!" the Vok called out, his voice booming, magically loud, loud enough for all to hear, echoing off the desert floor, off the hills and valleys. "Stand here and be infused with more power than any man has on this earth. Stand here and receive the title of Supreme Empress of the Empire. Stand here and from this day, and forever more, be known as the Goddess Volusia, the great Goddess of the Empire, Queen of the six horns and Destroyer of Cities. Today, a Goddess has been born. Today, a Goddess stands amongst us!"

The Voks stepped forward with their torches, touched them to the desert floor, and as they did, suddenly a fire spread, its flames filling the circle, slowly spreading, twisting around the pattern. The fire licked its way around the circles, faster and faster, and as all the circles around her lit up, hundreds of circles in every shape and size, the desert night was as bright as day.

Volusia stood in the center of it all, and she felt glorious. She held out her palms to her sides, raising her arms, and she felt the heat of it—yet she did not burn. She felt herself infused with an energy, a power she could hardly understand. She felt invincible.

She felt like a Goddess.

Volusia threw back her head, raised her arms high to the sky, and shrieked out to every power she ever knew.

All around her, in every direction, her men fell to their faces, bowing down low to her as she light up the night.

"Volusia!" they cried, chanting her name again and again. "Volusia! Volusia!"

131

CHAPTER EIGHTEEN

Erec sat at the long banquet table, Alistair on one side, Strom on the other, and his hundreds of men of the Southern Isles filling the benches, facing, on the opposite side of the tables, Krov and his hundreds of Bouldermen. It had been a long day of feasting and it had morphed into a rowdy banquet hall here inside Krov's castle, perched high up on this cliff at the edge of the sea. One entire wall was carved out with tall, arched windows, facing the ocean, light streaming in, flooding the hall with fresh ocean air, and the sound of waves crashing far below. It was unlike any other castle Erec had ever been in, all other castles usually built with few or no windows for fear of attack. But here, on Boulder Isle, there was no fear of attack: perched high up on insurmountable cliffs in the midst of a desolate and rough ocean, no enemy could reach this castle without scaling cliffs for days or somehow walking right through the mountain. They could afford the luxury here of light and air; no one could attack them from this high up.

It made for a relaxing day and afternoon, as Erec and his men finally began to unwind, to find some respite here, taken in by Krov's hospitality, feasting on his fine meat and endlessly flowing sacks of wine. Erec was relieved to see all his men in good spirits after their long voyage, and pleased he had taken the chance to land here. He knew he had made the right choice, as unpredictable as Krov and his men could be. He reached over and held Alistair's hands, happy to see her relaxed, too, and she smiled back at him, love in her eyes.

Erec was pleased and yet he was not a man to waste idle time, and he still hadn't achieved his main purpose in coming here: to enlist Krov and his armies to his cause, to convince them to join them in crossing the sea and liberating Gwendolyn and the others from the Empire's grip. Erec had tried to broach the topic many times, but Krov had been too busy feasting in this increasingly noisy hall. Indeed, while Erec wanted his men to blow off steam, he was becoming anxious that this hall was becoming too rowdy, too drunk; he could detect that special tension in the air that came as men went from one sack of wine to one too many. It left bored, idle men looking for some way to vent, and too often that meant violence.

There came another shout, and Erec turned to see several of Krov's men wrestling good-naturedly in the center of the stone hall, grappling left and right on the floor between the tables. All the men turned and watched, egging them on, slamming their mugs on the wood, cheering. As Erec surveyed their faces, he could see that Krov's men were less refined than his own; most were unshaven, missing too many teeth, with small bellies, and had drunk far too much wine. They were elbowed each other too roughly, laughed too loud, and every other man had a naked woman on his lap. Most also wore jewels—no doubt loot they had stolen on the seas—draped around their necks.

These men were no knights, no professional warriors that stuck to a strict code of ethics, as his men were. They were mercenaries. Erec knew he should not be surprised: after all, these Bouldermen were pirates, and had been for generations.

"I don't like them," Alistair whispered into Erec's ear, reaching down and squeezing his hand beneath the table.

He glanced at her and could see the worry in her face.

"Nobody likes them," he whispered back, "but everyone deals with them at one time or another. They have men and they have ships, and they know these seas like no one else. There is a reason the Empire has not been able to contain them in a thousand years. They were crucial allies to our father when he needed them."

"They are a means to an end," Strom chimed in softly, leaning over. "Our father called upon the many times."

"It is true," Erec said "Our father called upon them many times, but our father never trusted them."

"How could you partner with someone you do not trust?" Alistair asked back. "What if they betray you?"

Erec looked carefully around the room, looked across at Krov, laughing, watching the wrestling match, a naked girl in each arm, a sack of wine in both hands.

"Trust is a strong word," he replied. "Sometimes those you don't trust help you most—and sometimes those you do betray you. In my experience, a man content with food and wine and riches has much to lose, and little to gain by treachery."

A group of musicians passed by, filling the hall with the music of harps, lyres, and drums, to the cheers of the men, who broke out into a song Erec didn't recognize—then passed just as quickly.

As they could hear themselves again, Erec noticed Krov turn and face him.

"Erec!" Krov called out, turning his full attention to him. "Why no drink?"

"I do drink, my lord," Erec replied, raising a wine sack.

Krov broke out into coarse laughter.

"Lord!" he called out. "I am no *lord*! Unlike yourself, I am lord of nothing. God forbid I should be a lord! I'd lose what little class I had left!"

Krov's men laughed along with him, until Krov finally turned his attention back to Erec.

"Yet why no drink?" he asked again. "You drink from one hand only. Both hands should be full!"

Erec smiled back.

"One hand will suffice, my lord," he called back. "I like to keep one hand free. After all, you never know when one of your men might cut my throat."

Krov stared back, then broke into hysterical laughter, slapping the table with his palm.

"You're good," he said. "You haven't lost your edge. I like what I saw here today—just like the boy I remember. Except, you're too serious. Far too much time wasted on the battlefield. You should drink more, enjoy the women."

"He *has* a woman," Alistair corrected sharply, glaring at him, clearly displeased.

Krov chuckled and nodded to her and raised his sack.

"As you say, my lady," he said. "But I have a woman, too. And here I am!" he said, grabbing the breasts of each of the naked women on his lap.

"Then I am so sorry for you," Alistair replied, "and sorry for your wife. Those are base pleasures. You will never know the true pleasure of loyalty and devotion."

Krov shook his head, laughing.

"Don't be sorry for me," he said. "Or for her. At least she's protected here—not free to be sold like all these other women."

His men laughed as they grabbed hold of the women on their laps, and Alistair looked away, disgusted.

Krov settled his gaze on Erec, and finally Erec could see his expression grow serious, if clouded by his red-rimmed eyes, overflowing with drink.

"I suppose you have not come all this way just to see me," Krov said to Erec, "or to discuss women!"

Erec shook his head.

"Alas, my friend," he replied, "I have not."

Krov nodded.

"I understand. No one ever comes to see Krov casually, as a friend. Krov, King of the Bouldermen, the man no one cares for, the man no one wants to consort with, the man everyone thinks they are too good for—until they need him. I do wish I had friends who would care to stop by and see me just for the sake of our friendship. But my friendships always seem to have a purpose. It is sad, yet it is my fate."

Erec reddened, realizing Krov's sensitivity and wanting to tread carefully.

"You were friends with our father," Strom chimed in.

Krov turned to him.

"Your father," Krov replied. "Now there was a good man. A fine man. An even better King. All of the Southern Islands loved him. I don't know if I loved him," he said, scratching his beard, seeming to contemplate it. "I respected him. He was a good warrior, had a fine mind. But again, he was no friend to me. Just like my other friends, he

135

called upon me only when he needed me. How many times was I invited to one of your glorious weddings in the Southern Isles? To any of your royal feasts? To any of your holidays? You Southern Islanders always thought you were too good for us. That is not being a friend."

Erec blushed, realizing he spoke some truth. He also wished Strom would be silent, and he gestured to him to stop, but Strom continued.

"Our father paid you well," Strom added.

Krov's expression darkened.

"Yes, he paid me well," he replied. "But it was not money that I wanted or needed. He never paid me with friendship. Like everyone else, he wanted me at a distance, at arm's length."

"He let you patrol our waters," Strom said. "Fish from our seas."

"Aye, he did. But he never invited me into his banquet hall. Why do you think that is?"

Erec remained silent. He knew the reason. It was because Krov was a pirate, a murdering and thieving and raping pirate with no loyalty and no morals. He knew his father did not respect him. He'd use him when he needed to, and that was all.

Suddenly, Krov, his mood changing like a lightning storm, unexpectedly slammed his palm down on the wooden table. His face glowered, and as it did, the music in the hall fell silent.

A thick tension fell over the room as all eyes fell to him.

"I said why do you think that is?" he shouted, throwing the naked women off his lap, standing in place, his voice rising, glaring down at Erec. "ANSWER ME!"

Everyone in the room stopped and stared, watching the heated exchange, on edge.

Erec met Krov's eyes firmly, remaining calm, not showing his emotions, as his father had always taught him, and realizing fully just how unpredictable Krov was.

"My father," Erec said back calmly, "never spoke an ill word of you."

"Nor did he speak a kind word of me, either."

"My father held no hard feelings toward you," Erec repeated. "He considered you a partner."

"A partner but not a friend. I ask again: why was that?"

Krov's anger seemed to deepen, as did the tension in the room, and Erec knew that he needed to make a quick decision on how to respond. If he did not respond correctly, he sensed the room would soon erupt into bloodshed.

"Do you want the honest answer?" Erec asked, deciding.

"I won't ask for it again," Krov said, his voice hard and cold, now clutching the hilt of his sword. As he did, Erec noticed several of his men did, too.

Erec cleared his throat, let go of Alistair's hand, and slowly stood and faced Krov, standing proud and erect, unflinching.

"My father honored chivalry above all else," he said, his voice loud and clear, dignified, honest. "He honored *honor*, and all those who strived for it. He did not condone thievery, or taking women who did not choose to be with you, or killing men for a price or for what their ship contained below. My father lived for honor. If you want the honest answer, I will give it to you: in his eyes, you lacked honor. And he did not want to associate with those who lacked honor."

Krov stared him, his eyes flaring, cold and dark, staring right through him, and Erec could see them shifting, see the restlessness behind them, see that he was debating whether to kill him.

Erec reached down casually, and slowly rested his own hand on the hilt of his sword, just in case Krov lunged for him.

Suddenly, to Erec's surprise, Krov's face relaxed, and then broke into a smile.

"Honor!" he called out, and laughed. "And what is honor? Where has all your honor gotten you? Look at all the honor that they had in the Ring. Where has it gotten them? Where did it get the Ring? Now it is destroyed. Now it is no more. All by a dishonorable army. Sold out by those without honor. I would choose life over honor any day—and I would choose wine and women over your dour faces, your solemn life, your code of chivalry."

Krov suddenly reached down and grabbed a mug, smiling.

"You gave me an honest answer," he said. "No other man would be brave enough to. That, sir, is honor!"

He raised his mug.

"TO HONOR!"

All his men in the hall stood and raised their mugs and cheered with him.

"TO HONOR!" they cheered.

Krov laughed, as did the others, as he took a long swig of his sack, and all the tension in the room dissipated.

Erec, still on edge, still wary, nodded slowly back, drank from his mug, and sat down, too.

"You are a fearless man," Krov said to Erec, "and that is what I love about you. I might even love you more than your father. It remains to be seen if we shall be friends, but I think we just might."

"I can always use new friends," Erec said, nodding back respectfully.

"Now tell me," Krov, said, serious, getting down to business, "why have you come here?"

Erec sighed.

"I need your help. *We* need your help. What remains of my people, the exiles from the Ring, led by Gwendolyn, have found refuge in the Empire."

"The *Empire*!?" Krov asked, clearly shocked. "Why would they flee there?"

Erec shrugged.

"Perhaps it seemed the most counterintuitive place to go. After all, would your enemy seek you in their own backyard?"

Krov nodded, slowly warming to it.

"That Gwendolyn," he said. "Always too smart for her own good. Like her father. I'm amazed to hear she's still alive—that any of them are still alive—after what Romulus did to them. She must be a better Queen than anyone expected."

Erec nodded.

"I received a falcon," he said. "They need our help, and I wish to liberate them. My fleet, as you know, will be up against far greater numbers. No one knows these waters better than you. I need you to join us, help us in our war against the Empire."

Krov shook his head.

"Always the idealist," he said. "Just like your father. I've spent my entire life dodging the Empire, and now you would ask me to battle them head on." He slowly shook his head. "Mad. To battle the Empire would be suicide."

"You need not battle them," Erec said. "Just navigate for us, help us get to where we need to go. Accompany us through these waters, and through the Dragon's Spine."

Krov looked up at him, and Erec could see his face frozen in fear at the words.

"The Dragon's Spine?" he asked. "Don't tell me you mean to pass through it," he said, real fear in his voice.

Erec nodded back calmly.

"It is the most direct route," Erec said, "and the least likely for detection. We haven't time for any other alternative."

Krov shook his head.

"Better to go around the Horn of Azul," Krov said.

"That would add moons to our journey," Erec said. "Like I said, there isn't time."

"Isn't time to die, you mean?" Krov said. "Better to take moons and be alive than take days and be dead. No one passes through the Dragon's Spine and lives."

"You have," Erec said, looking at him meaningfully.

Krov met his look and slowly sighed, his eyes glazing over in memory.

"That was years ago, when I was young and my hair was thick and blond," Krov said. "Now it is thin and bald, I have a belly, and I am not nearly as foolish I had once been. Now I like my life. I vowed I would never pass through it again—and I won't."

"You know the Spine better than anyone," Erec said. "Where the rocks lie, where the waves break, which way the currents run, where the Empire patrols—and where the monsters lurk. We are going through the Spine," he said, determined, strength and authority in his voice. "You can stay here and cower in fear and be poor, or you can join us and be rich."

Krov met his glance, his face serious, in business mode.

"How rich?" he asked.

Erec smiled, expecting this.

"A ship full of the finest gold," Strom chimed in. "And a renewed pact of our isles' loyalty."

Erec reddened, wishing Strom would not have interrupted. His younger brother was always speaking when he should listen.

"*Loyalty!?*" Krov repeated, his face souring. "And what am I to do with loyalty? Will it buy me whores? Will it buy me wine?"

"If you are attacked, we will come to your aid," Strom said. "That is worth your life."

Krov darkened, shaking his head.

"I don't need your aid, or your protection, boy," he said to Strom. "In case you haven't noticed, our people do just fine. Indeed, as I see it now, it seems to be you who needs our aid."

Strom reddened, and Erec finally held out a hand and gestured for him to be silent.

Erec looked at Krov.

"It is fine gold," he said to him softly, smiling, man to man, "and a bold mission. Just reckless enough for you to be unable to pass by."

Krov leaned back and rubbed his beard, turning his attention back to Erec. Finally, after a long silence, he chugged the rest of his sack of wine, wiped the back of his mouth, and threw it on the floor. He stood and faced Erec.

"Make it two ships of gold," he said. "And we set sail at first light, while I'm still stupid enough to say yes."

Erec stood, and smiled slowly.

"I had a feeling you'd say that," he said. "Which is why the two ships are already waiting."

Krov stared back at him, then slowly broke into a huge smile.

He came around the table, and embraced Erec.

He leaned back, held his shoulders, and looked him in the eye.

"You will make a fine King, Erec son of Nor," he said. "A fine King, indeed."

CHAPTER NINETEEN

Darius walked through the camp of his growing army, joined by Raj, Desmond, Kaz and Luzi as he went from man to man in the sprawl of villagers, checking on the wounded, meeting each new man face-to-face, helping to remove shackles, looking into their eyes and shaking their hand. He saw hope welling in each of their eyes as they looked to him, each shaking his head and not wanting to let go, each looking to him as if he were their savior.

No one had ever looked at Darius this way in his life, and it felt surreal. In his eyes, he was just a boy, just a boy who strived to be a warrior, just a boy who had a hidden power which he could never use, didn't want to use, and which he could never reveal to the others. That was all. Darius had never expected to become a leader of men, to become someone that others looked up to, someone whom they turned to for leadership and direction. His entire life, he had been told by others that he was going to amount to nothing, that he was the least important of the bunch; his grandfather had always kept him down, had told him he was not worth much, that that was why his father had left him. All of the village elders, all of his trainers, particularly Zirk, the commander of the boys' troop, had told him his skills were average, at best, and that his size was too small. They told him to never dream too big.

Darius had always known he was not the largest of the bunch, or the strongest. He knew he was not the best looking, that he didn't have any wealth, and that he didn't come from a noble and illustrious family. And yet Darius had always had heart, conviction, passion, and a determination, one which he felt was stronger than others. Somehow, he always felt that that would carry him through, and even enable him to rise above other boys and other men, even those supposedly better than he. He felt things more deeply, and he refused to see himself as others saw him. He had insisted in his mind on painting a strong mental image of himself, as a hero, as a leader of men, and on clinging to it, regardless of how others tried to keep him down. They could crush his body, but they could never crush his spirit—and they could never touch his imagination. And his imagination, he felt, was what was most precious of all. It was the ability to see himself as someone else, to see him rising above his position. And it was that very *sight*—not size, not strength, not wealth, not power—that enabled him to do it.

Now, as he walked through the ranks of his new and ever-growing army, Darius could see how they all looked at him, and it was like watching his own imagination come to life, unfold before his eyes. He knew, he just knew, that it was his tenaciously clinging to his imagination, his vision, that had caused this. It was his ability to drown out all the voice of negativity around him that had tried to keep him down, had insisted on telling him what he could never be. To rise to power, he knew, he felt, all depended on one thing: how strong you can block out the voices of others, block out the sea of negativity that tries to tell you who you are, tries to tell you what you can never do in this lifetime. It is a sea that pounds at you every day, from every angle, Darius realized, like fresh waves washing up on the sands. Those who could block it out, who could cling to their own visions of themselves, could, Darius knew, rise above anything.

As Darius walked through, looking at all the new faces, his own friends following him as a leader, he saw that it was important, for their sake, that they thought of him as a leader. They all needed and craved a leader, someone to navigate them through these uncertain times. He gave them hope, confidence, direction, however bleak the picture might seem. He knew he had to give it to them. He owed it to them, even if he didn't entirely feel it yet within himself.

"Thank you, Zambuti," one of the freed men said, rushing forward and grabbing Darius's hand with both of his. "You have freed us all. You have given us life."

Darius was shocked at the expression of reverence. *Zambuti* was only reserved for the highest possible respect, a term that meant *beloved leader*, of such endearment that even the village elder did not receive it.

As long as he had known, the slaves had had no real leader. Not a true one.

Darius shook his head.

"You gave *yourself* life," Darius said. "And I am not your Zambuti."

"You are," another freed man replied, rushing forward, shaking Darius's hand, too.

"It is a duty!" echoed another man, as more and more men gathered around him. "You are our leader now! The only true leader we've ever had. The only who has stood up to them. You've given us back our lives. Now it is up to you to lead us slaves!"

There came a cheer of approval.

"You are not slaves any longer!" Darius called out to the growing crowd. "Do not call yourself that again! You are free men. You have chosen your fate, you have chosen your freedom, and for that I am very proud of you. I shall lead you—if you shall lead yourselves!"

There came another cheer of approval.

There came a sudden commotion, the sound of men cheering, agitated, and Darius, curious, turned and walked through the crowd, thick with people, all parting ways for him.

As he reached the far end of the crowd, Darius spotted a small clearing, the center of the commotion, and inside he saw the village elders congregating, addressing the new slaves.

"We have won a victory here this day," an elder called out. "We have been graced by the gods. And yet, do not be emboldened to think this should lead to more victories. Now is not the time to fight more. Now is the time to try to negotiate peace with the Empire."

"There shall be no peace!" one of the villagers yelled out.

"The days for talking peace are over!" yelled another.

"How dare you defy your elders!" one of the village elders, a thin, stern man whom Darius recognized from his village, yelled back.

"You are not our elders!" yelled back a freed man from the new village. "We have not survived here today to listen to your commands. We have not thrown off one slave taskmaster to place on our heads a new one!"

The villagers cheered.

Zirk suddenly pushed through the circle, jumped up onto a large boulder in the center, and faced them all, demanding attention.

"I am commander of our forces!" Zirk yelled. "It is *I* who trained all the warriors here today! And I am the eldest among these warriors! It is *I* who will lead you to our next fight, wherever it shall be. You are now all under *my* command!"

Darius stood there, watching it all, irate. Zirk had always been threatened by him. And now here he was, the same man who had tried to keep him down, to stop the insurrection, claiming credit for it.

Darius watched as there came a tense silence among the crowd. He wanted to call out, to set wrongs right—but he realized it was not for him to seize power. It was up to these men to want him.

Slowly, the silence broke as a group of slaves stepped forward into the center, and pointedly ignored Zirk, turning their backs to him. Instead, they turned and faced Darius.

Darius was shocked to see them all looking his way, pointing right at him.

"You are not our leader," they said to Zirk. "Darius is."

There came a cheer amidst the villagers.

"Darius is the one who led the battle here today. Darius is the one who freed us, and our families. It is to Darius that we owe our allegiance. Zambuti!"

"Zambuti!" the others echoed.

Darius felt a rush of gratitude as he stood there—but suddenly, Zirk, indignant, jumped down from the boulder and rushed between them.

"You cannot take him as leader!" Zirk yelled, desperate, looking at Darius with envy and jealousy. "He's just a boy. A boy who *I* trained. He is not even the greatest of our fighters. He can lead no one."

One of the villagers stepped forward and shook his head.

"It is not the age of a man that makes a leader," the man replied, "but the heart within him. It is he who shall lead us."

The villagers erupted into a great cheer.

"ZAMBUTI!" they cried, again and again.

Zirk, outraged, scowled and stormed away, pushing his way through the crowd and disappearing.

Several slaves rushed forward, grabbed Darius, and to his surprise, placed him atop the boulder. As they did, all the other slaves cheered, and they all looked up at him, rejoicing.

Darius looked out at the sea of faces, all looking up to him in adulation, and realized how much he meant to them. How much they needed him. How much they needed someone to believe in. Someone to lead them. He could see in all their eyes that they would go anywhere in the world he would lead them.

"It was the honor of my life to fight by your side today," Darius called out. "It was an honor to witness your bravery. You are free men now and the choices are yours. If you wish to join me, I cannot promise you life—but I can promise you freedom. If you wish to join me, we will not sit here and cower in fear in the desert, but, come what may, we will carry this fight all the way to the Empire cities!"

The men cheered wildly, rushing forward and embracing him, pulling him down off the rock, and Darius knew the great war was just beginning. He knew that he now had his army.

"ZAMBUTI!" they cried. "ZAMBUTI!"

*

Darius walked through the camp, concerned, as he was being led by Loti. She held his hand as she weaved in and out of the camp, and he could not stop thinking of the news she had just given him.

"Is he dying?" Darius asked her.

Loti shook her head sadly.

"I don't know, my love," she said. "But it's best to hurry."

Darius's heart pounded as they weaved in and out of the camp, wondering if this was it. His grandfather, she had informed him, lay gravely wounded. He had been injured in the last skirmish, even though he did not fight, a random spear thrown through his spine, and he lay unmoving. Loti had stumbled upon him, tending to him as she had made her rounds of the wounded, and had come right to Darius.

Darius's emotions swirled with mixed feelings as they marched toward him. He thought of how his grandfather had treated him so harshly his whole life, recalled all the resentment he had against him. Yet at the same time, he was also his grandfather, had been present when his father was absent, had raised him and given him a place to live. He was also his only living relative, aside from Sandara. That counted for something. As upset as he was with his grandfather, he had to admit he had some love for him too, this fixture in his life. And Darius could not help but feel as if his being injured in the skirmish were all his fault.

They finally reached a clearing, filled with the wounded and the sick, and Darius's heart fell as he spotted his grandfather amongst the bodies, lying there, a large wound through his spine and into his stomach, covered in bandages, already seeping blood. His grandfather looked weaker than he'd ever seen him. He looked to be on death's door.

Darius felt overwhelmed with grief, and he did not want Loti to see him like this.

"I would like to see him alone," Darius said.

Loti nodded, seeming sad but also seeming to understand, and she turned and walked away, giving them their privacy.

Darius hurried over to his grandfather, knelt down, and held his hand.

"Potti," Darius said, using the affectionate term he had always used for his grandfather.

His grandfather opened his eyes weakly and looked up at Darius. Darius could see the light in them fading.

"Darius," he said, with a weak smile. Darius could see how much it meant to him that he was there.

"I waited for you," his grandfather continued, weakly, his voice hoarse. "I waited for you before I die."

Darius squeezed his hand, fighting back tears as he clutched it, hating the idea of his dying. There had been so much tension between them all their lives, such a battle for control—and yet there had also, Darius had to admit, been so much love. His grandfather was a stern man, but at least he had been dependable, always there for him. He felt overwhelmed with guilt, feeling that perhaps he, regardless of how he had been treated, should have been more respectful toward him, less defiant.

"I'm sorry," Darius said. "I'm sorry I was not here to receive this blow for you. I am sorry that you lay dying."

His grandfather slowly shook his head, eyes welling with tears.

"You have done nothing to be sorry for," he finally replied, his breathing shallow. "You are like a son to me. You have always been like a son to me. I was harsh with you because I wanted you to be strong. I wanted you to learn. I didn't want you to rely on anyone but yourself."

Darius brushed back tears.

"I know, Potti," he said. "I have always known."

"I did not want you to end up like your father," he said. "And yet, deep down, I knew it was your destiny."

Darius stared down at him, confused.

"What do you mean?" he asked.

His grandfather coughed, blood coming up, and Darius could feel him dying in his arms. He was burning to know what he meant, what he had to say about his father. His father's disappearance had been a mystery that had been gnawing at him his entire life. He was dying to know who he was, when he had left, where he had gone, and what had become of him. But his grandfather had always refused to speak of it.

His grandfather shook his head and fell silent for a long time, so long that Darius did not think he would reply.

Finally, though, he spoke, his voice hoarse.

"Your father was no common slave," he said, his voice nearly a whisper. "He was not like the others. He took after my father."

"*Your* father?" Darius asked, confused.

He nodded.

"A great warrior," he said. "The man after whom you were named."

Darius's heart stopped at the news.

"A warrior?"

His grandfather nodded.

"And much more. He was not only a warrior. You see, the blood in you—"

He suddenly erupted into a long coughing fit, unable to speak. Darius watched, tortured to know more, feeling as though all the mysteries of his life were finally opening up.

Finally, he stopped coughing, and this time, his voice was even weaker.

"Your father, he will tell you all," he whispered, gasping. "He lives. You must find him."

"He *lives*!?" Darius asked, shocked. He had always been certain he was dead. "But where? Find him where!?"

His grandfather suddenly closed his eyes and let go of his hand, and Darius sensed him leaving.

"Potti!" Darius cried out.

But there was nothing more Darius could do. He knelt there and watched his head fall back limply, watched him die, so many unanswered questions still swirling in his mind, feeling his destiny hanging before him for the first time in his life.

He leaned back and cried a wail of grief.

"Potti!"

*

Loti stood on the far side of the clearing and watched Darius at his grandfather's side, holding his hand, crying, and she turned away, unable to bear the sight. She could not stand to see Darius so overcome with grief, and she wanted to give him his privacy. She watched Darius's expression change as his grandfather spoke and she was, of course, burning with curiosity to know what he was telling him, to know what could be affecting him so much. As far as she knew, they had never really gotten along.

As Loti thought of Darius, she realized she had come to love him with all her heart—and even more, to respect him. She still could not comprehend how he had saved her, how he had sacrificed himself for her like that, how he had taken all those lashes on her behalf, had been prepared to submit himself to awful torture and death for her. In some ways she felt that this entire war had started as a result of her actions, of killing that taskmaster who had lashed her brother, and while she was proud of her actions, she felt a sense of guilt. She also felt intense gratitude: she knew that if it hadn't been for Darius she would be dead by now, as would her people, and she felt more love for him than she could possibly express.

"There you are," came a voice.

Loti turned to see Loc coming up beside her, a smile on his face.

She looked down and saw the wound on his arm, and her face flashed with concern.

"Do not worry," he said, "it is just a scratch."

She examined the slash in his left bicep, his good arm, bulging with muscles and now, covered in dried blood.

"How did you get this?" she asked.

He smiled.

"I might be lame," he replied, "but I can fight too, sister. I may not be not as fast or as strong as the others, but my one good arm is far stronger than a lot of people's regular arms. With the proper spear or mace or flail, I can reach an enemy ten paces away. More than one taskmaster lies dead in the field today because of this lame man—and I have just paid a small price for it."

Loti, so proud of him, was nonetheless concerned at the wound, which seemed deep; she quickly took out a spare bandage from her waist and wrapped his arm, again and again.

"You are brave," she said. "I don't know anyone else in your condition that would risk going into battle."

He smiled.

"I have no condition, sister," he said. "I am as happy and as free as any man on this earth. Conditions and limitations exist in the mind only. And they do not exist in my mind. I am proud of the state I was born into."

She smiled back, so uplifted by him, as always.

"Of course," she said. "I am proud of you, too. I didn't mean to say—"

He raised a reassuring hand.

"I know, my sister. I know what you meant. You always mean well for me. You always have. You could never offend me."

"LOTI!" shrieked a voice.

Loti flinched at the strident sound, a voice she knew well, one that sent a chill up her spine, so disapproving, so scolding. She did not need to turn to know it was her mother fast approaching.

She reached them and glared disapprovingly back and forth between her daughter and son.

"Stop this nonsense, whatever it is you are doing, and come with me at once," she demanded. "Your people need you."

She looked back at her, confused.

"My people need me?" she echoed. "What does that mean?"

Her mother glared back at her; she hated being questioned.

"Don't you question your mother!" she snapped. "Come with me at once—both of you."

Loti and Loc shared a puzzled look.

"Come with you where?" Loc asked.

Her mother placed her hands on her hips and heaved a great sigh.

"A great group of slaves turned warriors, from another village, might wish to join our cause. They only wish to speak to you, as you are the famed one in their eyes, the one that started it all, that killed the first taskmaster. They will not join us otherwise. Come now, quickly, and do your people a service."

Loti looked back at her mother, confused.

"And why would you care so much about our cause?" she asked her. "You, who are opposed to fighting?"

Her mother seethed, taking a step closer.

"It is because of *you* that this war started," she scolded. "We never would be fighting otherwise. But now that we are fighting it, we

151

must win. And if you can help, then so be it. Now are you coming or not?"

Their mother stood there, glaring down at both of them, and Loti could see she would not take no for an answer. The last thing she wanted to do was go with her mother anywhere; but for Darius, for the cause, for her people, she would do anything.

Her mother turned and stormed off, and they fell in behind her, weaving in and out of the crowd, following her as she led them God only knew where.

CHAPTER TWENTY

Gwendolyn lay curled up in a ball on the hard desert floor of the Great Waste, awake, as she had most of the night, and looked out into another desert morning. The sky broke in a scarlet red, the first of the suns rising, impossibly large, seeming to fill the entire universe. It cast a somber light onto everything, this desolate place, and already she felt the heat beginning to rise.

Krohn, curled up in her lap, shifted and whined, snuggling against her, sleeping contentedly, the only thing that had kept her warm during the freezing night. Gwen shifted, too, but was in pain as she did, her body still scratched up from their encounter with the Dust Walkers.

Nearby on the desert floor, slept Steffen and Arliss, Kendrick and Sandara, Illepra and the baby—everyone, it seemed, had someone to lie with but her. At moments like this she missed Thor more than anything, would give her life to be able to hold Guwayne. But everything good in the world, she felt, had been stripped away from her.

Gwen opened her eyes, wiping the red dust caked to her eyelids, yet she hadn't really slept. She'd lay awake all night, as she had most nights here in the Waste, tossing and turning with worry for her people, worry for Thorgrin, for Guwayne. She blinked back tears, wiping them away quickly so no one would see them, even though most of her people were asleep. It was at moments like these, in the stillness of dawn, that she allowed herself to cry, to mourn for everything that she had lost, for the bleak future that seemed to lie ahead. Out of sight of the others, she could allow herself to reflect on all that she had and to feel sorry for herself.

Yet Gwen only allowed it for a moment; she quickly wiped it away and sat up, knowing that self-pity was only harmful and would not change anything. She had to be strong; if not for herself, than for others.

Gwen looked about, at all her hundreds of people sprawled out around her, among them Kendrick, Steffen, Brandt and Atme carrying Argon, Illepra carrying her baby, Aberthol, Stara, and dozens of Silver, and she wondered how many days they had been out here. She had lost track of time. She had been warned that the Great Waste had a way of doing that to you.

It had been one endless march, trekking deeper and deeper into a desert with no landmarks in sight. It had been a cruel monotony. Her provisions were running even lower, if possible, and her people were getting weaker, sicker by the moment—and even more disgruntled. Just the day before—or was it two days? Gwen could not remember anymore—they lost their first victim, an older man who had simply stopped walking and collapsed at his feet. They had all tried to rouse him, but he lay there, already dead. Nobody knew if he had died of the heat, of illness, starvation, of dehydration, of a heart attack, of an insect bite, or of some other unknown malady out here.

Gwendolyn heard a crawling noise, and she, still sitting there, looked up to see a large, black insect with an armored back, a long tail, and an even longer head, crawling up to her. It stopped, raised its front legs, and hissed.

Frozen in fear, Gwen sat perfectly still. It craned its neck, its glowing eyes fixed on her, and a long tongue slipped from its mouth. She sensed it was about to strike. She had seen one of her people die of one of these before, and it wasn't pretty. If she were standing, she could crush it with her boots—but it had caught her here, in the early morning, sitting, vulnerable. And now she had nowhere to go.

Gwen looked around and saw the others were all asleep, and she began to sweat, thinking what awful way this would be to die. She slowly backed away, but as she did, it crawled closer and closer to her. Suddenly, she saw its armor plates rise up, and she knew it was about to launch.

There came a snarling noise, a scrambling of paws, and as the creature leapt into the air, Krohn, apparently watching and waiting the entire time, suddenly leapt forward, snarling, and caught the insect run in midair in its jaws, just inches before it reached Gwendolyn. The creature wiggled in its mouth until Krohn clamped down on it. With a high-pitched cry, it finally died, green ooze leaking from its body, falling limp in Krohn's mouth.

Krohn dropped the limp carcass down to the ground, and Gwendolyn rushed forward and hugged him, stroking him and kissing him on the head. Krohn whined, rubbing his head against her.

"I owe you, Krohn," she said, hugging him, so grateful for him. "I owe you my life."

Gwen heard a baby cry, and she looked over and saw Illepra sitting up with the baby girl Gwen had rescued from the Upper Isles. Illepra looked over and smiled tiredly back to Gwendolyn.

"And I thought I was the only one awake," Illepra said, smiling.

Gwen shook her head.

"She's kept me up," Illepra added, looking down at the baby. "She's not sleeping. Poor thing—she's so hungry. It breaks my heart."

Gwen examined the baby, the small girl she had rescued from the Upper Isles, and she felt anguished, overwhelmed with guilt.

"I would give her my food," Gwen said. "If I had any."

"I know, my Queen," Illepra said. "Yet there is still something you can give her."

Gwen looked back, surprised.

"A name," Illepra added.

Gwendolyn nodded, her eyes lighting up. She had thought of naming her many times, and yet each time she had been unable to settle on one.

"May I hold her?" Gwen asked.

Illepra smiled, stepped forward, and placed the baby in Gwen's arms as Gwen stood. Gwen held her tight, rocking her. As she did, the baby finally fell quiet, looking up into Gwen's eyes with her large beautiful blue eyes. She seemed to find a sense of peace, and Gwen, too, felt a sense of peace holding her; she almost felt as if she were holding Guwayne. They were nearly the same age.

It made her cry—and she quickly turned and wiped away her tears.

Gwen wanted so badly to name her, but as she stared into her eyes, she came up blank. Try as she did, it would not come to her.

She handed the child, sadly, back to Illepra.

"When the time is right," Illepra said, understanding.

"One day," Gwen said to the baby, before she let her go, "when we are done with all this, we shall have much time together. You will know my son Guwayne. You shall be raised together. You shall be inseparable."

In Gwen's mind, she quietly resolved to raise this child as if she were her own; yet deep down, she knew they might not even survive for that day.

Gwen wished she could give the baby food, milk, water—anything. But she had nothing left to give. All of her people were slowly wasting away, and she herself had not had a good meal in days, giving most of her rations to the baby and to Krohn. She wondered if her people would even have the energy to march through another day. She had a sinking feeling that they would not.

The sun rose higher and all her men began to scramble to their feet, her camp soon alive and awake, preparing to face another day. She led the way wordlessly, wasting no more time as the heat grew by the minute, the ragtag procession all beginning to fall back into place, to march, all heading deeper into the nothingness.

"And where to now, my lady?" called out Aslin, in a loud, taunting voice, emboldened once again, loud enough for all the others to hear. "What great destination do you have in store for today?"

Steffen, beside her, darkened and lay a hand on his sword as he turned and faced Aslin.

"You best mind your tongue," he snapped. "It is your Queen you speak to."

Aslin scoffed.

"She is no Queen of mine," he spat. "Not any longer. A Queen leads a people, and she has led us nowhere but to death."

Steffen moved to draw his sword, but Gwen reached out and laid a reassuring hand on his wrist.

"Save your effort," she said softly to him, and he grudgingly released his grip and continued marching with her.

"Never mind them, my lady," Kendrick said, coming up beside her. "You are a far greater Queen than they could ever hope for. A far greater Queen than they deserve."

"I thank you," Gwendolyn said. "But they are right. I have led them nowhere. I don't know if Father foresaw this when he chose me to succeed him."

"It was exactly for times like this that Father chose you," Kendrick insisted. "There has never been a time like this, and he knew you would have the steady to hand to guide your people through. Look at how far you've taken us already. You have already saved us all from a sure death on the Ring. It was only because of your foresight that we escape. We are all living on borrowed time. Time we were not supposed to have. Time we only have because of you."

Gwen loved him for his words, which as always set her at peace, and she laid an appreciative hand on his wrist, then took it away.

They marched and marched, all of them deeper and deeper into the Great Waste, the suns creeping higher overhead, Gwen already feeling herself covered in sweat. She trembled, shaking as she went, and she no longer knew if it was from the violent change in temperature, the exhaustion, or the lack of food and water. Her mouth was so parched, it was hard to swallow; even speaking was becoming an effort.

Hour after hour passed, deeper into the Great Waste, and Gwen found herself looking down, tracing the lines in the desert floor, losing all sense of space and time. She was beginning to feel dizzy.

"UP AHEAD!" a voice suddenly cried.

Gwendolyn, yanked from her thoughts, stopped and looked up, hearing the frantic tone of the voice and knowing it must be real. As she did, she was shocked by the sight before her.

There, in the distance, something was emerging on the horizon, and at first she wondered if it were a mirage. It looked like a large mound, perhaps a hundred feet tall, with nothing else around it. It was the first object they had encountered in this endlessly empty desert.

They all picked up the pace as they walked faster and faster, encouraged, approaching the mound. They marched as one, with a renewed energy, the bickering finally stopped, Gwen's heart pounding with excitement as they neared the structure. It rose into the sky, a dark brown color, made of a strange material Gwen could not quite understand. At first she thought it was an immense boulder, but as she got closer realized it was not. It looked as if it were made of clay.

They marched closer, till they were hardly twenty yards away.

"What do you think?" Kendrick asked, just beside her.

Gwen examined it, unsure.

"It is not a rock formation," Aberthol chimed in. "Nor is it a structure."

"Sandara?" Gwen asked, as she walked beside her. "This is your homeland. What is this?"

Sandara squinted, and slowly shook her head.

"I wish I knew, my lady. I've never been this far into the Great Waste. None of my people have. I have seen or heard nothing of this before. It is nothing I recognize."

"Food!" one of her people yelled out.

Suddenly, there was a rush of people, all of them stampeding for the huge mound. Led by Aslin, they rushed to the mound and as they got closer, Gwen saw what they were looking at: a sap-like material oozed from it, ran down its sides, collected in a puddle at its base.

"It's sweet!" Aslin yelled, reaching out and licking the sap with his fingers. "It tastes like honey!"

Gwen salivated at the thought, but something about this did not feel right.

"I don't know what that mound is!" Gwen cried out, over the din. "It may not be safe! All of you, get back here! Step away until we've examined it closely!"

To Gwen's surprise, though, none of her people, already convened at the mound, listened to her. Only her entourage and the Silver remained behind, obeying her.

"And why should we listen to you?" Aslin called out. "We are done listening to you and your advice!"

The crowd cheered, to Gwen's dismay, and they continued eating, grabbing the sap hand over fist and stuffing their mouths.

"It is a mountain of honey!" another person yelled out. "We are saved!"

Gwen watched them, looking up into the sun and examining the mound, with a deep sense of foreboding.

"My lady?" Kendrick asked, turning to her. "It seems safe enough. Shall we eat?"

Gwendolyn remained where she was, a good thirty yards away, examining the mound, unsure. It all felt too good to be true. She sensed something was just not right.

Gwen began to feel a slight trembling on the desert floor beneath her feet, and began to hear a soft buzzing noise.

"Do you hear that?" she asked.

"Hear what?" Steffen asked.

"That sound…"

Suddenly, Gwen's eyes opened wide in fear, as she realized what was happening.

"GET BACK!" she shrieked. "ALL OF YOU!" Back away from the mound NOW!"

Suddenly, before any of her people could react, the walls of the mound exploded, sending its clay everywhere, and inside it there appeared an enormous monster, bursting out of its shell.

Gwendolyn looked up, shocked to see an enormous creature, a hundred feet tall, with aqua skin, rippling muscles, and impossibly long arms. It had a face like an ox, yet with long sharp teeth, and jagged horns all up and down its jaw. Horns protruded all over it, in every direction, like a porcupine. It looked ferocious, enraged—as if awakened from a deep slumber.

It leaned back and let out a roar, and all of Gwendolyn's people, now standing at its feet, stopped, frozen, honey dripping from their hands, all too terrified to move.

There was no time for them to react anyway. The creature suddenly swiped down with its claws, faster than Gwen imagined, and in one swipe, it killed dozens of her people. They went flying up into the air, shrieking, and fell down with a splat on the desert floor, their necks broken. It then stepped forward and stomped them to death.

"ARROWS!" Gwen commanded.

The soldiers and Silver who had remained behind with her immediately obeyed her command, stepping forward, drawing their bows and releasing their arrows, all firing for the creature's head, Steffen and Kendrick unleashing more than the others.

Dozens of arrows pierced the creature's face and head, and it shrieked, then reached up and tore them right out of its skin, as if they were all merely an annoyance. The monster then lunged forward, raised one arm high, made a fist, and brought it straight down like a hammer on a dozen more of Gwen's people, the spikes on its arms impaling them on the spot.

Kendrick, Brandt, Atme, and Steffen formed a protective circle around Gwen, along with dozens of Silver, all raising their swords, bracing themselves as the creature came close.

Gwendolyn knew she had to take some dramatic action; if she didn't do something, all of her people, she knew, would be dead within moments. She turned and looked everywhere, desperate for some solution, and she suddenly had an idea: she spotted Argon, still motionless, carried on the shoulders of healers on a stretcher, and desperate, she ran over to him.

"ARGON!" she cried out, shaking him again and again.

She was sure he would rouse, find some way to help her; he had always been there for her in times of crises.

But even he did not respond.

Gwen felt crushed, hopeless, as the beast tore through her people, killing them like ants, their screams filling her ears. This time, she was truly on her own.

"My lady!" came a frantic voice.

Gwen turned and saw Sandara standing beside her, panic in her eyes.

"I know this beast," she said. "It has attacked my people before. It is a Mound Hatcher. There is only one way it will die: by the blood of a ruler."

"I will do it," Gwendolyn said, without hesitating. "I will give up my life to save my people."

Sandara shook her head.

"You do not understand," she said. "It does need your life. Just your blood. Give me your hand."

Gwen reached out and opened her palm, and Sandara sliced it quickly with her dagger. Gwen cried out in pain, the cut fast and sharp, and felt the hot blood rushing from her palm.

Sandara quickly reached down and caught it in an empty vial. She then handed it to Gwen.

"It is for you to do, my lady. You must douse the beast!"

Gwendolyn grabbed the vial of blood, capping it with her thumb, and ran, rushing through all her people, avoiding the monster's feat and spikes. The ground shook as the beast roared and stamped his foot, crushing people all around her.

"HERE!" Gwen shrieked up to it, waving her arms, trying to get its attention.

The monster finally turned and set its sight on her, lowered its head, looking her in the face as if examining her.

"Take *me*!" Gwendolyn yelled.

The monster snarled, opened its mouth wide, and came rushing down at her, as if to swallow her whole.

Gwen reached back and hurled the vial of blood with all her might; she watched with wonder as it landed inside the creature's open mouth.

The monster stopped in midair right before it could reach her, and froze. It began to ossify, turning to stone from top to bottom, cracking as it went.

There came an explosion, and the Mound Hatcher shattered, showering down all around her, small fragments of rock and dust.

Suddenly, all was still. Gwen looked around in the chaos, the bloodshed, and saw that some of her people, at least, had survived. One more horror of this desert, at least, was behind them.

CHAPTER TWENTY ONE

Soku, commander of Volusia's armies, could not believe the twists and turns that fate had taken. But a moon ago, he had been in command of only a few thousand soldiers, guarding the well-fortified city of Volusia, with little for him to do. It was a steady and safe position that had not changed much ever since even the time of her mother.

How much, and how quickly, things changed. Now, since Volusia's capture of Maltolis, her gaining of two hundred thousand soldiers, the men under his command had grown far beyond what he could have expected. Their missions had grown increasingly bold, their conquests increasingly greater. At every turn Volusia had proven him wrong, had surprised him, had shown more cunning and ruthlessness than any general he had ever known.

And yet, he also was not pleased with the current state of affairs. Volusia was too unpredictable, too reckless, too fearless; he did not know what she would do moment to moment, and he did not like to take orders from people he did not understand. She had won thus far, and yet it may have all been by chance.

Most dangerous of all, she believed too much in herself, was too drunk with her own power. At first he had thought that her claiming herself to be a goddess was merely a plot, a cunning ploy to keep power over the masses. He had admired it.

Yet now, the more time he spent with her, the more he came to see that she really believed it. She really considered herself a goddess. She was growing dangerously out of touch with reality each day.

And now it had come to this: a pact with the Voks, the darkest, nastiest, least trustworthy race of all. It had been, in his view, a terrible and fateful choice. She had gone from being megalomaniacal to being delusional: she really believed that she and her two hundred thousand men could capture the capital and conquer the Empire's millions.

Soku knew it was only a matter of time until her downfall—and he did not plan on being on the wrong side of it.

"And which path do you advise?" Volusia asked him.

Soku snapped out of it, looked up and saw Volusia staring back at him. He stood there with her large entourage of men around her, Aksan, her personal assassin, and most unnerving, Koolian, her sorcerer, who gaped back at her with his wart-lined face and glowing green eyes. She was also joined by her other commanding generals, all of them going around and around, as they had been for hours, debating the best strategy.

Soku looked down at the crude drawings etched into the desert floor at their feet, three diverging paths, each leading to three different circles, each representing a different Empire division. They'd all been debating which one to attack first. Soku knew that the best approach would be to attack the circle to the far right, the Empire's second flank. That path led over mountains, would give them the high ground, and give them the advantage of surprise. If they took that route, they might even gain enough momentum to continue on to the capital.

But Soku did not want Volusia to win. He did not want to advise her in her best interests; he wanted this war over. He wanted her out of power. And he wanted power for himself.

Volusia did not know it yet, but Soku had already struck a deal with the Empire. He had sold her out, and he would be given power in her place. He had coordinated exactly where their armies would meet, had coordinated the truce procession that would lead to her death. All he had to do now was to sell her on it—and his path to victory would be complete. She had always trusted him; that had always been her weak point. Just like her mother before her. Volusia would be ambushed, surrounded, and vanquished, and he would be given the position of command of the Empire's millions.

Soku cleared his throat and put on his most earnest expression.

"Goddess," he said. "If you wish to win, there is but one path to take. Straight down the middle," he said, outlining the path in the dirt with a stick as he spoke. "You must strike approach the capitol unashamedly, in the Valley of Skulls."

"A foolish idea!" Aksan said.

"Suicide!" a general added. "No one else advises such counsel. It is the most obvious route."

"Let him speak!" Volusia said, authority in her voice.

The others fell silent as she turned to him.

"Why do you counsel this, Soku?" she asked.

"Because it is the path the Empire would least expect," he lied. "They have greater numbers, and they would never expect us to attack them head on. They will put all their strength on their flanks. You will catch them unaware, and divide their flanks. More importantly, if you approach their city head-on, they will see you coming. They will send messengers. They will send offers for a truce. You must give them a chance for a truce, Goddess. After all, there remains now no Supreme Commander of the Empire. They need a commander. They might voluntarily choose one in you. Why fight for a victory when one might be handed to you?"

Soku was impressed with his performance; he'd said it with such authority, he nearly believed it himself.

"A reckless proposition," another general countered. "The Valley of Skulls is where the Empire is strongest. It is the very front door of the capital. It would leave us vulnerable to ambush. And the Empire will never negotiate a truce."

"All the more reason the Empire would not expect it," Soku replied. "And all the more reason they might offer it. When you approach from a position of strength, Goddess, they will be more inclined to embrace you as their ruler."

She met his eyes, and she stared at him long and hard, as if gauging him; he felt his palms sweating, wondering if she was seeing through his charade. If she knew he was lying, he knew she would have him executed on the spot.

He stood there, his heart pounding in the thick silence, waiting.

Finally, Volusia nodded, and he could see in her eyes that she trusted him completely.

"It is a bold plan, Commander Soku," she said. "And I admire courage. I will follow it. Prepare the troops."

She turned to go and as one all her advisors bowed.

Soku, elated, turned to leave and as he did, he felt a cold hand on his shoulder.

He turned to see Volusia standing there, staring back at him, her eyes glistening as if filled with fire.

"Deliver me victory, Commander," she said. "I trust in victory. And I do not forgive defeat."

Volusia turned and walked away, and as he stood there, watching her go, he felt a pit in his stomach. She felt all powerful, untouchable.

Would he really be able to topple her?

CHAPTER TWENTY TWO

Godfrey felt himself being smothered by a pile of bodies, one atop the other, as he lay face up at the bottom of a pit. One Empire corpse after another was being hurled into the pit, landing on top of him, smothering him until he could no longer see the sky.

Godfrey woke with a start, unable to catch his breath. He felt as if all of his ribs were being crushed, and he opened his eyes in the blackness, confused. He found himself truly being smothered, and it took him a moment to realize he was no longer dreaming. He was lying on the muddy prison floor, on his back, and he could not make sense of the picture before him: staring him in the face, a few inches away, was the huge, grotesque face of that obese prisoner, the bully, the one who had attacked him earlier. He was scowling in Godfrey's face, their noses touching, and Godfrey finally realized what was happening: the man was lying on top of him. He must have jumped on top of him while he was sleeping. He had him in a bear hug and was trying to crush him to death.

The man's weight was more than Godfrey could bear—he must have weighed five hundred pounds—and he grabbed hold of Godfrey and squeezed and squeezed, wrapping his arms around Godfrey, his legs around Godfrey, clearly trying to crush every bone in his body. Godfrey felt his bones beginning to break, felt himself gasping for breath, and knew that in moments, he would be dead.

What an awful way to die, he thought. *Smothered by an obese man on a floor of mud, in a stinking prison cell halfway across the world in the depths of the Empire.*

Even for him, used to base places, it was more than he could bear. He had never imagined dying like this. He had always thought he would meet his end in a tavern fight, or in a brothel bed, or from drinking one too many drinks. All of which he could accept. He had not expected a warrior's noble death, had not expected the bards to sing songs for him, or royal banners to be flown at his funeral.

But he did not want to die like this. Not with his face in an obese man's stinking armpit, his ribs crushed like he was a common animal.

"Say good night, little man," the man hissed in his ears as he squeezed harder.

And harder.

Godfrey had been called many things in his life, but with his tall frame and big belly, he'd never been called "little." Somehow, that shocked him even more than being smothered to death. Then again, he realized, everything was relative: this man was a monster, a giant.

Godfrey's eyes bulged in his head. He gasped for air, and felt he couldn't last one more second. He writhed, trying to break free, but it was useless. He was beginning to see stars.

Suddenly, the man froze on top of him, releasing his grip. His eyes opened wide, his tongue stuck out, and for some reason, he stopped squeezing. In fact, he grew limp, his eyes crossing in agony, gasping for breath himself.

Then suddenly he slumped down, dead.

Godfrey immediately scrambled to shove the man's dead weight off of him, even heavier now than when he was alive. With one great heave, he managed to roll out from under him.

Godfrey got to his hands and knees, coughing, heaving and gasping, trying to catch his breath. As he did, he looked over, still on guard, staring at the dead man and not understanding what had happened.

Then Godfrey spotted something flashing out of the corner of his eye; he looked up and saw Ario, holding a small dagger, wiping blood off its tip.

Ario stood there, a calm, expressionless boy, and matter-of-factly tucked the dagger back in his waist. Godfrey stared at him, amazed that such a small boy could kill such a huge man—and even more amazed that he looked so calm, as if he hadn't done a thing.

"Thank you," Godfrey heaved, feeling a rush of gratitude for him. "You saved my life. I would have been dead."

Ario shrugged.

"I liked that man a whole lot less than you."

Godfrey quickly surveyed the cell and saw Akorth and Fulton asleep with all the other prisoners, leaning back against the wall, snoring. Godfrey looked at them, annoyed. They were useless. If it hadn't been for this boy, a fraction of their age and size, he would be crushed to death.

"Psst!"

A sudden hiss ripped through the air, and Godfrey looked across the dim cell, still dark in the night, lit only by a single torch, and he barely made out Merek's figure as he stood by the cell door, alone.

Godfrey looked past Merek and saw only one guard outside, sitting slumped against the bars, asleep. The torches were dim, barely flickering, barely enough light to see by.

Godfrey heard a clanking of a key, and he watched, shocked, as Merek unlocked the cell discreetly. As he did, Merek beckoned to them frantically.

Godfrey and Ario rushed over and kicked Akorth and Fulton, covering their mouths as they did to keep them from making a noise. They then dragged them to their feet and pulled them toward Merek.

They quickly joined Merek as he swung open the cell and led them outside, locking it behind him. Godfrey saw the guard still sitting there, slumped against the bars—and he realized now, as he looked carefully, that he was not asleep, but dead. His throat slashed ear to ear.

Godfrey looked up at Merek, and realized what he must have done.

"But how did you get his keys?" Godfrey asked.

Merek only smiled.

"You ask that to a thief?" Merek replied with a grin.

Godfrey was thrilled that Merek had joined them on this mission; he was worth more than a hundred warriors. He realized he would take a thief over a knight any day.

They followed Merek as he took off, darting in and out of the corridors, weaving this way and that.

"I hope you know where you're going," Godfrey called out in a whisper.

"I've been in one prison or another almost my whole life," he said. "I have a sixth sense for these things."

As they followed him in a dizzying fashion, Godfrey continually checking back over his shoulder for fear of being caught, Godfrey finally looked forward and was surprised to see them all emerging from the dungeons. Merek led them down a long ramp and to a final cell door. Beyond that, Godfrey could see the shining streets of Volusia, glistening in the night.

Merek took out the key ring, immediately found the right one, and unlocked it. He opened the final door and stepped aside with a coy smile.

Godfrey stared back, amazed.

"It is not only warriors who win wars," Merek said.

Godfrey clasped Merek on the shoulder, proud of him as they stood there looking at their freedom.

"You hold more value than a million knights, my friend," he said. "I will never go to jail again without you."

Merek smiled and bolted out the door, as Godfrey and all the others followed.

They all burst out onto the empty, nighttime streets of Volusia, Godfrey surprised at the contrast, the quiet, given how noisy and bustling it had been during the day. He looked down, surprised, its golden streets quite a contrast from the mud floors of the prison. Godfrey marveled at how pristine the city looked even at night. It was deserted, yet serene. Torches lined the streets, reflecting the gold, and the streets were immaculate, not filled with vagrants, as were the back alleys of all the cities Godfrey had ever visited. Godfrey didn't even see any Empire guards; he assumed there was no need for patrols, as this city was so safe.

Before them, reflecting the torchlight, Godfrey could see all the waterways interlacing the streets of Volusia, the gentle lapping of them adding to the tranquility.

"Where now?" Ario asked.

"To the gold," Godfrey replied. "We must get it back and get out of here."

They all followed Godfrey as he took off down the streets; at first he was disoriented, but he soon recognized some intersections, landmarks, statues, and found his way. If there was one thing he could never lose track of, it was his gold.

Godfrey finally reached the spot he recognized, saw, a block away, the statue of the golden ox beside the water.

He stopped and ducked behind a wall, examining it from the down the street.

"What are we waiting for?" Fulton asked, clearly anxious to go on.

Godfrey hesitated, standing there, catching his breath.

"I'm not sure," he said.

All seemed clear, yet Godfrey was hesitant to go out into the open and retrieve it.

"I want to make sure no one's watching," he added.

"You mean, like Empire soldiers?" came a dark, ominous voice.

The hairs on Godfrey's neck stood on end as he turned slowly, with the others, and saw standing over them, in the corner of the dark alleyway, an Empire soldier.

He walked out of the shadows, but a few feet away, a sword in his hand, a dark smile on his face.

"Did you really think you were smart enough to not be followed?" he asked. "Did you really think I was stupid enough to allow you to escape?"

They all stared back, speechless.

"You let us escape," Ario said, realizing. "You made us think we had done it on our own. But you were watching all along. It was a trap."

The soldier smiled wide.

"The only way for you to lead me to the gold," he said. "Without your lying. Now I know where it is, for sure, and now I'll gladly take it. Then I'll take your lives. There's no rush, see? What did it hurt to let you live an extra hour?"

His expression darkened.

"Now move!" he commanded.

Godfrey marched with the others down the street, exchanging a troubled look with Merek and Ario, and knowing there was little he could do. He felt the tip of the Empire soldier's sword in the back of his neck, prodding him along, and he sweated with each step as they walked toward the waterway. He hoped Merek and Ario didn't try anything stupid. This was no convict; this was a professional Empire soldier, twice their size, with real armor, real weaponry, and an obvious desire to kill. As they went, Godfrey racked his brain for a way out of this one, for any idea, but he could come up with nothing. They had been outsmarted.

Godfrey was driven by the soldier's sword all the way to the water's edge and he stood there, beneath the statue of the ox, and debated what to do. He knew his options were limited. The soldier was huge, the sword was at his neck, and if any of them moved too hastily, they would surely be killed.

"Why have you stopped?" the soldier demanded.

"The gold lies in the water, my lord," Godfrey said.

"Then you better get swimming," he demanded. "ALL OF YOU!" he said, turning to the others.

Godfrey gulped, not knowing what else to do, as he went to the water's edge and dropped to his hands and knees.

"Any of your friends tries anything," he added, "and you get my sword first. And if one of you comes up without any gold, you won't be coming up at all."

One at a time, the others got to their knees, too. They all looked at Godfrey, and he could see the hesitation in their expressions. He nodded for them to go in, not knowing what else to do. This was no time for heroics.

Godfrey slipped into the water, and it was cold, giving him a shock. He submerged beneath, and thought hard.

Godfrey grabbed the gold, relieved it was still where he left it, and the others did, too, each grabbing a sack. He surfaced, gasping for air, dripping wet, and plopped it down on the street with a clank. All the others did, too.

The soldier looked down, impressed. Godfrey could see the greed in his eyes.

"Open it!" the officer commanded.

Godfrey began to climb out of the water, but the man held the sword tip at his throat.

"I didn't say get out," he said.

Godfrey, still in the water, reached over and untied the sack of gold. There, gleaming beneath the torchlight, was enough gold to hire an army.

The Empire soldier's eyes opened wide. Godfrey knew his time was running out; he thought quickly.

"There's more," he said. "Far more."

The soldier looked at him, surprised.

"Then what are you waiting for? Get swimming!"

Godfrey nodded to the others, and they all sank down again beneath the water; this time, though, he had a plan: he deliberately reached for a smaller sack of gold, one big enough to hold in his palm.

Godfrey surfaced, and as the others each brought up a large sack, this time Godfrey lingered at the water's edge, pretending to struggle.

"I need help, my lord," Godfrey said. "It's too heavy. I cannot pull it up."

The soldier scowled back at him.

"I'm not stupid," the soldier replied. "Get it up yourself, or die where you are."

Godfrey gulped, realizing this man was no fool.

"OK, my lord," he said. "I will. But in that case, please allow me to just crawl up on the stone so that I can have leverage to hoist it."

The soldier hesitated.

"OK, crawl up," he said. "Stay on your hands and knees and keep your back to me as you bend over to retrieve it. And this better be the biggest sack of gold of your life, or else you're going to sink with it."

Godfrey, heart pounding, praying that his scheme worked, scrambled up onto the stone. He turned around, his back to the soldier, on his hands and knees, and he bent over into the water and grabbed the small sack of gold. He made a great effort of straining and struggling as he bent over, reaching for it. He grabbed it firmly, closing his eyes, sweating and gulping, praying. He knew he had only one shot at this.

Please God. I know I have been a terrible person. I know I'm probably beyond redemption. But I'm sure this soldier's a lot worse. At least I've never harmed anyone, at least not anyone who didn't deserve it. Let this work. Let me win. Just this once.

Godfrey knew it was now or never.

He took a deep breath, reached down, grabbed the sack, and held onto it tight. He felt the soldier's sword jab him in the back.

"Let's go!" he prodded.

"Here it is, my lord!" Godfrey called out.

Godfrey waited until he felt the soldier lower his sword, then he suddenly hoisted the sack and spun around in the same motion, aiming for the soldier's sword.

He spun, his momentum carrying him, and the sack of gold swung through the air, and to his amazement, it was a perfect strike. The sack connected with the soldier's sword, knocking it from his hand and sending it clattering down to the ground.

In the same motion, Godfrey jumped to his feet, stepped forward, and using two hands, swung the bag of gold at the soldier's face. It all happened too fast for the stunned soldier to react, and the bag connected with his jawbone—again, a perfect strike. The weight of all those coins smacked him across the face, sending him staggered backwards, falling to his hands and knees.

Before he could get up, Godfrey rushed forward and brought the sack of gold down on his face, smashed his nose, breaking it. Emboldened, he smashed him again and again, so hard that the sack finally broke.

Gold coins went flying everywhere, rolling up and down the streets. Godfrey, enraged, feeling good to finally have vengeance on the Empire, stepped forward with all his might, and kicked the man between the legs, finally knocking him out.

Godfrey stood holding the empty sack, trembling, shocked at what he had just managed to do. He didn't know what had overcome him—and he didn't realize that he had it in him.

The others all stared at him in amazement.

"Didn't know you had it in you," Merek said, clearly impressed.

Godfrey shrugged.

"I didn't either."

"See what not having a few drinks can do to a man?" Akorth chimed in, patting him on the shoulder.

"Looks like we lost a perfectly good sack of gold," Fulton said, gesturing to the scattered coins.

Fulton shrugged.

"I guess it was worth Godfrey's life," he said.

Godfrey stood there, dripping wet, shaken from the whole ordeal, hardly believing what had just happened, what he had just done. He looked at his friends standing there, all equally in shock, dripping wet, the sacks of gold sitting by their feet.

Godfrey turned and eyed the loose coins, some of them still rolling in the streets, still settling down with a clinking noise.

"Let's get our gold and get out of here," he said.

He began to go but was stopped by a sinister voice, cutting through the night.

"I don't think you'll be going anywhere."

Godfrey wheeled, hairs on edge, and was shocked to see a group of Finians a few feet away, standing there silently, patiently, in their red cloaks, their hoods pulled down, their fiery red hair glowing beneath the torchlight. They were humans, but too pale, too thin, hollowed-out faces, and they stared back at Godfrey, smiling as if they had all the time in the world.

"You are dressed in our clothes," one of them said, stepping forward, clearly their leader, "and yet you wear them poorly. Next time you rob from Finians, you should be more discreet."

He smiled wide, examining them, shaking his head, and Godfrey stared back, not knowing what to say. He exchanged a puzzled look with the others, but they seemed to be dumbfounded, too.

"A sorry lot you are," the leader continued. "You'll be coming with us now. Along with your gold. Not that we need it. But I'd like to hear your story. And remember: we are not as stupid as the Empire soldiers. If you look closely at my friends you'll see small crossbows aimed at you. Make one move and you'll all be dead and floating in the water."

Godfrey looked over and saw the other Finians indeed holding small crossbows beneath their cloaks, all aimed right for them. He gulped.

"In fact, I have a mind to just kill you right now," the leader added. "But I am first curious to hear how a sorry lot like you got inside Volusia, how you got our cloaks, how you have so much gold. Then I might kill you. Or maybe not—depending on how good your story is."

He smiled wide.

"You've had your battle of swords," the leader added. "Now you will have your joust of words. Are you smart enough to outwit us?"

Godfrey looked back at them, dreading the idea of another imprisonment, yet knowing he had no choice. There was something about these people he didn't like, didn't trust. They seemed so calm, so friendly, yet deep down, beneath their smiles, he had a feeling that they were even more deadly than the Empire.

They prodded him, and he began marching with the others, all with hands raised high above their heads, being led by the Finians down unfamiliar streets, to God only knew where.

CHAPTER TWENTY THREE

Thor stood at the bow of the small sailing vessel as they sailed away from Ragon's isle in the breaking dawn and toward the horizon, the direction in which his dream compelled him to go, the direction in which he felt certain Guwayne was awaiting him. The dream had felt so real, it had felt as if he had truly experienced it. He felt with certainly that Guwayne lay just up ahead, that he needed him urgently. Thor stood at the edge peered into the mist, anxious for it to lift, to reveal the location his son; he watched the currents, and willed them to carry his boat faster.

Your child awaits you on the island.

The voice from Thor's dream echoed in his head, again and again; Thor looked out and squeezed the rail, giddy with anticipation. He could hardly wait to hold Guwayne again; he felt terrible for letting him go, and this time he would let nothing stand in his way until he found his boy.

"Are you certain we sail in the right direction?" Matus asked skeptically, coming up beside him.

Thor tuned and saw all the others—Reece, Selese, Elden, Indra, O'Connor—all standing there, dressed in their new armor, wielding their new weapons, shining in the light—and all looking back at him skeptically.

"This is the direction in which my dream has led me," he replied.

"And if your dream is wrong?" O'Connor asked.

Thor shook his head.

"It can't be," he said. "You don't understand. It was more than a dream: it was a vision. I *saw* it. I saw my boy."

Reece sighed.

"We were all comfortable on Ragon's isle," he said. "We had provision, shelter—we finally had a break from our travails. We left so abruptly."

"And it seemed Ragon was about to reveal to us another surprise—perhaps more weapons, or something else important," Elden chimed in.

Thor could see the disappointment in their eyes, and he considered their words; he, too, had felt a strong connection with Ragon, had felt the great power of the man, and had been comfortable on that isle. His island had truly been a magical place, an idyllic place, and he, too, had wanted to spend more time there.

He reflected, furrowing his brow, and could not quite understand why he had left so quickly. Were they all right? Had he been wrong to leave? Thor felt confused.

Yet the vision of that dream would not leave his mind, as if it were right in front of him, pulling him away from the isle and toward the horizon.

"I can't quite explain it," Thorgrin said. "It was unlike any dream I'd ever had. It was like a command. It showed me Guwayne in danger, urgently needing me. I just could not allow myself to sit there for one more second."

Selese sighed.

"I have been a healer all my life," Selese chimed in, her voice soft and sweet, yet demanding attention. "I know most everything about the human body. Yet I know little about dreams. I don't know from where they come, or whether they come to help or confuse us. I don't know if they come from inside us or from someplace else."

The boat fell silent, and Thor contemplated her words. Could his dream have been sent to confuse him? To trick him? But why? And how?

"I don't think anyone knows that, my lady," O'Connor said. "And anyone who professes to know is a liar."

"One thing I do know," Reece chimed in. "We're getting awfully close to the Dragon's Spine—and that's one place we do not want to be."

O'Connor turned and pointed off into the horizon, and they all turned and followed his gaze. In the distant horizon, partially obscured by the mist, were a pair of sharp cliffs, jagged, like a spine, rising hundreds of feet into the air, with perhaps a few hundred yards between them. Treacherous rocks stretched out alongside them, forcing all ships to sail in the narrow waterway between them.

"What do you know of it?" Thor asked.

"It is a place of legend," Reece added, his voice filled with awe. "Growing up I was drilled on it. The most dangerous spot in the Southern Seas. A place of awful storms, beasts—a place few pass through alive."

"Up ahead we have the fork," Elden said. "See the currents? If we wish to avoid it, now is our chance."

Thor stood there, hands on his hips, staring at the ocean, wondering. Reece came up beside him.

"Which way, old friend?" he asked. "Do we fork north, for an empty ocean, or south, for the Dragon's Spine? We will follow you any way you choose."

Thor closed his eyes and tried to tune in, to allow his senses to guide him. He stood there, quiet, listening to the wind, the lapping of the waves against the boat, then suddenly felt a sense of certainty.

"We fork north, my brother," Thor said, turning to Reece. "Away from the Spine."

Reece looked much relieved, as did all the others.

They all broke into action, immediately adjusting the sails, grabbing the oars, Thor helping them. Thor grabbed an oar and rowed with the others, pulling them through heavy waves, their boat lifting lower and higher, spray splashing him in the face.

Finally, they finished rowing over the conflicting currents of the fork, and the new current grabbed their boat and pulled them in a new direction. They began to relax on the oars, and let the sails do the work.

There suddenly came a great shriek, from high up in the sky, and Thor looked up and his heart lifted to see Lycoples, circling high. Lycoples flapped his wings furiously, circling low, as if trying to signal something to Thorgrin. He dove down, right by Thorgrin's face, forcing him and the others to duck, and Thor was wondering what he was trying to tell him.

179

Lycoples kept circling back toward the island from where he'd come, almost as if he were trying to urge them all to turn back around to Ragon's isle.

"What do you think he's trying to tell us?" Indra asked.

"It looks like he wants us to turn back," Elden replied.

"But why?" Matus asked.

Thor studied the skies, unsure. After many attempts, Lycoples finally gave up, turned, and flew back to where he came.

Thor looked to the skies, puzzled, as he had always been, by the way of dragons. Why would Lycoples want them to turn back around, when Guwayne lay somewhere on the seas ahead?

Hour after hour passed, all of them falling into silence, embraced by the mist. Thor found himself lost in his thoughts, as he thought of Gwendolyn, of what she must be going through. His heart broke for her, and it anguished him that he could not be by her side.

He also found himself thinking of Lycoples, of his son up ahead, and he was filled with a renewed sense of hope. Thor craned his neck and scanned the skies, and wondered: would he ever see Gwendolyn again? He could picture himself returning to her with her son, with a new dragon, starting life all over again. Was it too late? he wondered with a sense of dread. Was she even still alive?

Thor began to hear a faint sound, one that pulled him from his reverie. It was a sound of waves splashing on rocks, against a distant shore. He was certain of it.

Thor looked over and saw the others, too, standing, staring into the mist. They must have heard it, too. They all looked at each other with a questioning look, their eyes all holding the same question: *land?*

As Thor peered into the mist, slowly, a wind arose, and it began to lift, revealing what lay beyond. The sound of the waves crashing against rocks grew louder, and as Thor looked out, he was surprised to see an unusual island coming into view.

This small island was bordered by a white beach, the brightest white Thor had ever seen, and all the rocks around it—everything— was white. Its trees were all white, too, a dense jungle that stretched nearly all the way to the shoreline, all glowing white. Even the ocean water, as they came closer to the isle, turned entirely white.

Above the isle flew scores of white birds, squawking, circling, unusual birds that Thor did not recognize, of every shape and size.

Selese stepped forward before Thor, and looked out and gasped.

"The Isle of the Lepers," she said, her voice low with reverence.

"You know it?" he asked.

"Only what I've heard," she said. "It is a place known by all healers. It is a refuge for all those who are afflicted. A place where lepers can live freely. A place for those with no hope of healing. A place to stay far away from—unless you want to catch the disease."

Thor felt a sense of dread. Could Guwayne be in such a place?

He closed his eyes and as he did, he sensed that this isle was where he needed to go—that this was where his child was.

Thor opened his eyes and shook his head slowly.

"I don't understand," he said. "I sense it. This is where I'm being led. This is where my child is."

"If it is," Selese replied, "it would be a sad day for him. No one who visits here can escape untouched. It is an affliction for which there is no cure."

"We must turn around!" Reece said. "We cannot touch down there, lest the rest of us catch it. Do you not see? Even the water is infected."

Thor examined the isle as they sailed ever close, now hardly a hundred yards away, their boat rising and falling with the waves crashing in his ear.

"I would not risk harming any of you," he said. "This is a trek for me to take, and me alone. You can all stay on the boat. I will find him and bring him back."

"You will come back a leper," Matus said gravely.

Thor shrugged.

"I have been to hell and back for my son," he said. "Do you think I would let a fatal disease stand in my way?"

They all looked away, silent, none able to offer a response.

The waves picked up and carried them closer to shore, the spray hitting Thor in the face. The closer they got, the more his heart pounded. He could feel his destiny rushing toward him. He knew that his child was out there.

Their boat beached on the shore, and the second it touched down, Thor disembarked, his boots crunching on white gravel.

He stood there and looked out at the island before him in wonder, squinting against the glare. Everything was caked in white, as if washed by salt. Even the mist in the air hung with a white tinge to it. The air smelled a bit different here, too; it smelled not only of ocean, but also of death.

This island, Thor sensed, had a solemn, abandoned feel to it, as if it were a place forgotten by others, a place of great peace and solitude—yet also of sadness and tragedy. Thor studied the swaying white trees, the huge leaves shimmering in the wind, and he wondered if his dream was true. Could his child really be here?

Thor turned and saw the boys in the boat, and for the first time ever, he could see real fear in their faces. They had followed him into the Empire, across the seas, to hell and back, and had done so fearlessly. Yet this place of fatal disease had clearly stricken them all with terror. None of them wanted to die a slow, lifelong death.

They all sat in the boat, unmoving.

Thor nodded back to them solemnly. He could see in their eyes that they wanted to join him, but were afraid. He understood. After all, walking onto this island would be a death sentence.

Thor turned and began the march inland, toward the dense white jungle, his boots crunching on the gravel, taking one step at a time, the sound of the ocean waves fading. He entered the jungle, the large leaves brushing against him, a new feeling beneath his feet, leaving the shore behind him—and he knew he had crossed the tipping point:

There was no turning back now.

*

182

Thor marched through the jungle, scratched by branches and not caring, and he peered everywhere, trying to see through the dense canopy, looking for Guwayne. He let his senses guide him, turning left and right, allowing himself to be led through the thick foliage, to the place where his instincts brought him.

"Guwayne!" he called out, his voice echoing in this empty place. "Guwayne!"

Thor's cry was met by that of a strange bird, somewhere high above, calling down to him as if mocking him.

Thor marched deeper into the jungle, and he soon emerged as it gave way to a new landscape. Before him were rolling hills of white grass, large white trees swaying in the wind.

Thor did not waste any time leaving the jungle and embarking on the hills, looking all around him, everywhere for any sign of Guwayne.

But this island seemed deserted. There was no sign of anyone or anything—just the birds overhead, whose screeches punctuated the air.

Were there really lepers here? Thor wondered. Or was it all a myth?

Thor hiked and hiked, finally cresting a hill, and as he did, he looked down and saw a new landscape, and all of his questions were answered before him. There, sitting in a small valley, nestled amidst the hills and large trees, with a small river running by it, was a low, circular building made of all-white stone, looking ancient, as if it were one with the landscape. It was only perhaps a hundred yards in diameter, with a flat white roof, and no windows that he could see. It had but one door.

On the white landscape that surrounded it, Thor saw signs of life: there were cauldrons hanging over small bonfires, chickens wandering, signs of people living here—people who had no fear of leaving their livestock and food and cooking out in the open, who had no reason to be guarded. People who did not expect any visitors. Ever.

Thor took a deep breath and steeled himself as he marched down the hill, toward the building, not knowing what to expect. He had a strong feeling rising up within him, an inner voice telling him that his child was inside. How, he wondered, was that possible? How could Guwayne have gotten inside? Had someone abducted him?

Thor knew that, with each step he took, he was getting closer to his death sentence. He knew leprosy was an awful affliction and that he would certainly catch it; it would stay with him the rest of his life, turning his skin white, and eventually result in an early and weakened death. He would become an outcast, a person no one wanted to be near.

Yet he did not care. His son was all that mattered to him now. More than his own life.

Thor reached the door and hesitated before it. Finally, he passed the point of no return—he reached out and grabbed the handle, the same handle that all the lepers touched, an all-white skull and crossbones, and he turned it. He knew as he touched it that there was no turning back.

Thor stepped inside and immediately sensed a heavy feeling in the air: it felt of death. It was solemn in here, quiet. His eyes adjusted to the one long, dim room, yet it was not nearly as dim as he had expected. On the far wall were a series of arched, open-air windows lining the wall, letting in the refracted sunlight and ocean breezes, white drapes billowing in the wind.

Thor stopped and looked at the sight before him, his heart pounding, taking it all in, peering through the haze for any sign of his child. He saw a series of straw beds, each ten feet apart, lining the walls. On each bed lay a leper, their skin all white, some with bandages around their faces, some on other parts of their bodies. Most lay there, quiet and still, perhaps two dozen of them. Thor marveled that so many people could coexist in one room and not make any sound at all.

As he entered, they all suddenly turned and looked his way, and he could see the surprise in their faces. Clearly, they had never had a visitor before.

"I'm looking for my child," Thorgrin called out, as they all stared back. "Guwayne. An infant boy. I believe he is here."

They all looked at him silently, none of them moving, none of them saying a word. Thor wondered when the last time was any of them had even spoken to an outsider. He realized that this life of seclusion, of being outcasts, had probably worn away at their psyches.

Realizing after a long silence that no one was going to respond, Thor began slowly walking down the aisle between the beds. He checked their faces as he went, and they lay where they were and stared back with sad faces, faces that had lost hope long ago, and observed him in wonder.

Thor looked everywhere for signs of Guwayne, any evidence at all that a child had been here—yet he could find none. He did not hear a baby's cry; nor did he see any signs of a bed that could hold a baby.

Yet as Thor reached the final bed, a sensation arose within him, a burning feeling, and his heart pounded as he suddenly felt that his child was there, behind that curtain, in that final bed. He turned to look, pulling back the curtain, expecting to see Guwayne.

Instead, he was baffled to see a child lying there, staring back at him. She looked to be perhaps ten. She looked as surprise to see him as he was to see her. She had large, crystal blue eyes, the color of the sea, mesmerizing, eyes filled with love, with hope—with life. She had long blonde hair, beautiful, wild, looking as though if it had never been washed. The skin on her face was remarkably clear, free from any blemish, and Thor wondered if she was in the wrong place. She did not appear to have any sign of the disease.

Then Thor looked down and saw her right arm and shoulder, bright white, the skin eaten up by the disease.

She immediately sat up in bed, alert, filled with life and energy, unlike all the others. She appeared to be the only one of the bunch that had not been broken by this place.

Thor was perplexed. He had sensed his child was behind this curtain—and yet she was the only one here. Guwayne was nowhere to be found.

"Who are you?" the girl asked, her voice inquisitive, full of life and intelligence. "Why have you come here? Have you come to visit me? Are you my father? Do you know where my mother is? Do you know anything about my family? Why they have left me here? Where is my home? I want to go home. I hate this place. Please. Don't leave me here. I don't want to stay here anymore. Whoever you are, please, please, please take me with you."

Before Thor could respond, still trying to process it all, she suddenly jumped up from the bed and threw her arms around his legs, holding him tight.

Thor looked down at her in surprise, not knowing how to react. She knelt there, crying, clutching him, and his heart broke.

He reached down and gently laid his hand upon her hair.

She sobbed.

"Please," she said, between cries, "please don't go. Please don't leave me here. *Please*. I'll give you anything. I can't stay here another minute. I will die here!"

Thor stroked her hair, trying to console her as she wept.

"Shhh," he said, trying to calm her, but she would not stop crying.

"I'm so sorry," he finally said. "But I came here looking for my son. A baby. Have you seen him?"

She shook her head, clutching harder.

"There is no baby here. I would know it. There is no baby anywhere on this island."

Thor's stomach dropped as the words sunk in. Guwayne was not here. He had somehow been misled. For the first time in his life, his senses had led him astray.

And yet, why had he sensed his child in that bed, right before he drew the curtain? Who was this girl?

"I pray to God every night for someone to come and rescue me," she said between tears, her voice muffled against his leg. "To take me away from this place. I prayed for someone exactly like you. And then you arrived. Please. You can't abandon me here. You *can't*."

She hugged his legs, shaking, and Thor tried to process it all. He had not expected this, but as she clutched him, he could feel her distress, and his heart broke for her. After all, she had not asked for this affliction, and clearly, her parents had abandoned her here in this place. The thought of it angered him. What sort of parents would abandon their child, regardless of the affliction? Here he was, willing to cross the world, to enter hell, to take on any affliction for himself to find his own child.

It also tore him up because he, too, he realized, had been abandoned by his own parents. He hated things being abandoned. It struck deep into his heart.

"You don't want to come with me, child," Thorgrin said. "When I leave this place, I will be going on a dangerous quest. I don't know even where exactly I am going, but it won't be safe. I will be facing hostile enemies, foreign lands, heading into battle. I won't be able to do that and protect you. Your chances of living are greater here. Here, at least, you will be safe and cared for."

But she shook her head insistently, tears flowing from her eyes.

"This isn't living," she said. "Here there is no life. Only waiting for death. I would rather die while trying to live than live while waiting to die."

Thor looked into her eyes as she looked up, her crystal eyes glistening, and he could see the warrior spirit within her, shining back at him. He was overcome by her fierce will to live, to really live. To overcome her circumstance. He admired her spirit. It was a fighting spirit. He could see that she would be deterred by nothing. And it was a spirit that, try as he might, he just could not turn away from.

He knew he could make no other decision; his warrior's spirit would not allow it.

"Okay," he said to her.

She suddenly stopped crying, froze, and looked up at him, eyes wide in shock.

"Really?" she asked, dumbfounded.

Thor nodded, and he knelt down, looking her right in the eye.

"I will not leave you here," he said. "I cannot. Pack your things. We shall leave together."

She looked at him, her eyes filled with hope and joy, a joy greater than he had ever seen in anyone, a joy that made all of it, any risks he was taking, worth it. She leapt forward into his arms, wrapping her arms around him, hugging him so tight he could barely breathe.

"Thank you," she said, crying, weeping. "Thank you, thank you, thank you."

Thor hugged her back, and as he did, it felt like the right thing to do. It felt good to be able to hold and protect and nurture a child, even if it was not Guwayne. He knew that to hold her was infecting him, even now, and yet he knew he could make no other choice. After all, what was the purpose of life, if not to help those in need?

Thor turned to go, and she suddenly stopped and turned around and ran back to her bed, grabbing something before returning to him and taking his hand. He looked down to see her clutching a small white doll, a crude one, made from the sticks and leaves of the island, and wrapped with a piece of bandage.

She grabbed his hand and yanked him and led him quickly out of the place, to the amazed eyes of all the others lying there listlessly, watching them go.

They walked outside, exiting the building, and Thor was momentarily blinded by the glare. He held up one hand, and as his eyes adjusted, he was shocked by the sight before him.

Standing before him were all his brothers—Reece and Selese, Elden and Indra, O'Connor, Matus—all of them standing outside the building, waiting for him patiently, all dressed in their new armor, bearing their new weaponry. They had come after all. They had crossed the island, had risked their lives, for him.

Thor was touched beyond words, realizing what they had sacrificed for him.

"We took an oath," Reece said. "That first day we met, back in the Legion. All of us. It was a sacred oath. An oath of brothers. An oath stronger than family. It was an oath to watch each other's backs—*wherever we should go.*"

"*Wherever we should go,*" all the others repeated, as one.

Thor looked back at them all, each one, face to face, and his eyes welled up as he realized that these were his true brothers, blood thicker than family.

"We couldn't leave you," Matus said. "Not even for a place like this."

The girl stepped forward, looking up at them curiously, and all eyes turned to her, then questioningly to Thor.

"We have a new companion," Thorgrin said to them. "I would like you to meet…"

Thor, puzzled, realized he didn't know her name. He turned to her.

"What *is* your name?" he asked her.

"Here, we never knew our parents," she said. "We were all given up at birth. None of us know our names. Our real names. So we name each other. Here, they all call me Angel."

Thor nodded.

"Angel," he repeated. "That is a beautiful name. And you are indeed as pure as snow."

Thor turned to all of his brothers and sisters.

"Guwayne is not here," he announced. "But Angel will be joining us. I am taking her from this place."

They all looked at him, and he could see the uncertainty flashing through their eyes, could see what they were all thinking: to bring her would infect them all.

Yet, to their credit, not one of them objected. All of them, Thor could see, were willing to risk their lives for her.

"Angel," Selese said sweetly, smiling, stepping forward, addressing her. "That is a very fine name, for a very sweet girl."

She stroked her hair, and Angel smiled back broadly.

"No one's ever touched my hair before," Angel said back.

Selese smiled wide.

"Then you shall have to get used to it."

Thor stood there, wondering what this all meant. He had been certain Guwayne was here. He recalled his dream: *Your child awaits on the island.* He looked at Angel, smiling back at Selese so sweetly, so filled with life, with joy, and he wondered: is she my child? Maybe she was. Not in the literal sense of the word—but maybe he was meant to raise her, as his own. An adopted child?

Thor did not understand, yet he did know it was time to move on. Guwayne was still out there, and he had no time to lose.

As one, they all began to walk—Thor, Reece, Selese, Elden, Indra, Matus, O'Connor, and now Angel, holding Selese's hand—an unlikely group, yet somehow all fitting perfectly together. Thor did not where this could lead, and yet he knew that somehow, this all felt right.

CHAPTER TWENTY FOUR

Erec stood at the bow of the ship, hands on his hips, studying the sight before him in awe. There, rising up from the seas, were two ancient rock formations—the Dragon's Spine—serrated rocks that rose in a jagged formation, a hundred feet high, with rocky shores sprawled alongside them, forcing all ships to travel between them. Erec looked up at it looming before them as they sailed closer and closer, mouth agape at their immensity. He'd never seen anything quite like it. Two sets of red cliffs, rocks sharp, shaped to points, in rows, like the curved spine of a dragon. The currents raged, getting stronger with each moment, and they sucked the ship toward the center, like an angry beast sucking prey for its open mouth.

Making matters worse, the waves and tides were vicious here, growing ever more intense the closer they got, the winds stronger, the clouds darker. In the middle of the Spine, Erec could see, the waves rolled a good thirty feet high, then crashed down against the jagged rocks on either side, the entire channel between the spines like a violent whirlpool in a bathtub. It seemed like a sure death.

The Dragon's Spine lived up to its reputation; indeed, as they neared it, their ship bobbing wildly, Erec could begin to see the remains of dozens of other ships, washed up on its rocks, pieces of them still clinging to boulders as if clinging to life, a vestige of what once was. Those pieces, Erec knew, represented countless sailors' deaths. Even now, in death, waves crashed mercilessly against them, pounding the fragments to ever smaller pieces. It was a fierce testament to all the ships that had tried foolishly to broach the Spine.

Erec gripped the rail, his stomach dropping as their ship suddenly dropped twenty feet in a wave, and clung to Alistair's waist on his other side, to make sure she was okay. On his other side stood Strom, his face wet from the spray, slipping on the deck but hanging onto the rail.

"Did I not tell you to go below?" Erec pleaded with Alistair again, yelling over the wind to be heard.

Alistair shook her head, gripping the rail.

"I go where you go," she replied.

Erec looked back and saw his fleet behind him, and looked over and saw Krov's all-black ships sailing alongside him, flying the black flag of the Bouldermen. He spotted Krov, hands on his hips, standing at the bow, looking over at him, clearly unhappy. Krov, though, somehow managed to stand with steady legs, balancing on his boat even with the waves crashing all around him, looking unfazed, as if it were just another sunny day at sea.

He shook his head at Erec.

"You couldn't go around, could you?" he yelled out, annoyed.

Erec turned and looked straight ahead at the looming waves and rocks. He turned back and saw many of his men going below the decks.

He turned again to Alistair.

"Get down below," he said. "I beg you."

She shook her head.

"I shall not," she insisted. "Not for anything."

Erec turned and looked at Strom, who shrugged back as if to say: *I can't control her.*

"She is a wife fit for a King," Strom said. "What do you expect?"

A towering wave suddenly crashed over the deck, knocking them all back off their feet, sliding across it. Erec, his nose filling with salt water, was momentarily blinded, as the bow went entirely underwater, submerged.

Just as quickly the boat straightened, and they stopped sliding, each of them banging their backs into the rail.

"All the ships single file behind us!" Erec commanded, rushing to his feet. "NOW!"

Several of his soldiers rushed to do his bidding, shouting the orders up and down the ranks. Erec heard a horn sounding, and he looked back to see his fleet gathering single file. Erec knew this was their only chance of all making it, of threading the needle of the Dragon's Spine comfortably.

"STEER FOR THE MIDDLE!" Erec yelled. "Stay as far from the rocks as possible! The current's pulling left, so steer compensate right. Lower the sails, and get ready to drop anchors if need be!"

Men rushed about in every direction executing his commands, and Erec had barely finished giving the orders when he turned and looked up. He braced himself as he saw another immense wave crashing down.

Erec grabbed Alistair's wrist, hanging on to her as their boat was thrown left and right, rocking as well as plummeting. Alistair reached out and grabbed a thick rope, and as Erec slipped, it was she who held onto him, wrapping the rope around his wrist just before he fell overboard and another wave subsumed them. Because of that rope, he remained on board, in her grip.

They straightened and Erec, so grateful to Alistair, looked all about. They were now in the midst of the Spine, right between the two huge rocks, and their boat was being jerked in every direction. It veered suddenly as a strong current took it and almost smashed into a sharp rock on their left. At the last second, the current jerked the other way and somehow, by the grace of God, pulled them back away from disaster. But not unscathed: as they grazed the jagged shoreline, Erec heard a cracking noise that put a pit in his stomach and he looked over to watch half the rail of his ship taken out, swiped by the rocks. He swallowed hard, realizing what a close call it was, how they had been spared from far worse damage.

Halfway through the Dragon's Spine, Erec knew there was no turning back. The raging currents drove them through it, and up ahead in the distance, he could see the light. He saw where the Dragon's Spine ended. It was incredible. Perhaps two hundred yards before them, as one emerged from the Dragon's Spine, the ocean was perfectly calm, still, the sun shining, a perfectly beautiful day. It was surreal, like passing through a door.

All they had to do was make it the next two hundred yards. Yet, Erec realized, that was probably what dozens of other sailors, their ships smashed, lining the rocks, had thought too as they had tried to make it through.

Please, God, Erec thought. *Just two hundred yards.*

No sooner had he prayed than Erec heard a horrific noise, as if his prayer had been answered by a demon. He heard it rise up, even over the raging wind and crashing waves, and as his ship rose on a high wave, he looked up and was horrified to see the source of the noise.

There, rising up from the waters, guarding the exit to the Dragon's Spine, was an immense, primordial monster. With a neck longer than his ship, with fins and scales, and arms and legs, claws at the end of each of them, and a jaw larger than a dragon's, it was a green vision of death.

It turned right for his ship and opened its jaws and roared so loud, it split Erec's mast. Erec raised his hands to his ears, trying to drown out the noise, as the beast lifted his head high and began to bring it down low. It opened wide its jaw as if to swallow his ship in one bite, his face so wide it blocked out the sun, and Erec knew it was too late.

He knew, without a doubt, that this was how he was going to die.

CHAPTER TWENTY FIVE

Darius stood in the desert night, his face lit up by the torchlight, and looked out proudly at the sea of faces. There, spread out before him, stood thousands of former slaves, now free men, not just from his own village but from all the neighboring villages. In every direction, surrounding him, there were more faces than he could count, all looking back at him with hope. His revolution had spread like wildfire, from one slave village to the next, now out of his hands and spreading on its own. Now he could not even control it if he wanted to. Slaves freed slaves, villages freed villages, and these, in turn, freed others. They slaughtered taskmasters, rose up for their freedom, rallying more and more people to his cause They all sought him out, congregated before him, all forming a single army. They were short on weapons and short on armor—they had only what they managed to salvage from the Empire—yet they had spirit. All of their deep-seated resentment had finally been unleashed, something deep within their hearts and souls let loose, and Darius was elated that others felt as he did.

Darius stood there, Dray at his feet, close to him as always, chewing contentedly on a bone Darius had found for him—and snarling at anyone who came too close to Darius—and he studied the sea of new and unfamiliar faces. All of them had one thing in common: hope brimmed in their eyes. And they all had another thing in common: they all looked to him. They clearly all looked up to him as a leader, and he felt the weight of it on his shoulders, taking it very seriously. He did not want to make the wrong move.

"Zambuti," said a slave as he passed, bowing his head at Darius. It was a familiar refrain that Darius was hearing everywhere he turned these days, men gathering by the thousands just to see him. Some reached out and touched him, as if not believing he were real. Darius hardly knew what to make of it all. It was like a strange dream.

His people, Darius was thrilled to see, no longer had the fearful, cringing attitude they once did. Now they walked out in the open, proudly, chest out, shoulders back, as free men, as men with dignity. The entire desert night was filled with their torches, Darius turning and seeing torches as far as he could see, and more arriving by the second. Momentum was turning, Darius felt, perhaps even shifting to their side. There was a feeling in the air he'd never felt before, as if great, momentous things were happening, that all of their lives were about to change, and that he was right in the middle of it.

"You've started something big, my friend," Desmond said, coming up beside him, Raj on his other side, the three of them standing and looking out as the cool desert winds blew through the night. "Something that I believe not even you can control."

"Something that has become even bigger than you," Raj added proudly, looking out.

Darius nodded.

"That is good," he replied. "They are free men now. They should not be controlled by anyone. Free man should control themselves and their own destiny."

"And yet they look to you," Kaz added, joining them, "and all men must have a leader. What destiny will you lead them to?"

Darius stood there, looking out into the night, wondering the same thing. Leading men, he felt, was a sacred responsibility. He looked about him and saw an inner circle was forming around him, including Raj and Desmond and Kaz and Luzi and a dozen other boys he had trained with back in his village. They all crowded in close, along with many others, who looked intently at Darius, hanging on his every word.

"Name our next conquest!" called out a brave warrior from another village, "and we shall follow you anywhere!"

There came a cheer of approval.

"There is another village waiting to be liberated," one of them called out. "It is a day's ride north of here. We can reach it by sunrise, if we rise all night, and free several hundred more men!"

There came another small cheer of approval, and Darius looked off into the desert night, and pondered. There were so many villages out there to liberate; it was a task that could occupy a lifetime.

Darius took his sword and stepped forward into the group of men and began to draw on the sand. They quickly formed a circle around him, giving him space to draw and crowding around to see what he was doing.

"We are here," he said, marking the spot, scratching a line in the hard desert floor with the tip of his sword. He drew a broad circle around it, and from it he drew several paths, forking off in all different directions.

"We must forget all these directions," he said, his voice filled with authority. "We have already freed enough villages, rallied enough men. The longer we do, the longer it gives the Empire to summon the entire power of their army and counterattack. We can free a few hundred more men—perhaps even a few thousand—but it still will never give us greater numbers than they."

He took a deep breath.

"What we need now is not strength in numbers. What we need is speed. Surprise. I say that the time for liberating, the time for rallying, are through. Now, it is time to attack."

They all stared down at the desert floor, then looked back up at him, confused.

"Attack where, Zambuti?" one of them asked.

Darius met their gaze.

"Volkara," he said.

They all gasped at the words, and he was not surprised.

"Volkara!" one men called out. "The Volusian stronghold?"

Darius nodded back.

"Attack Volkara?" Zirk asked, indignant, stepping forward as he pushed his way through the crowd. He entered the circle, stepping on Darius's etching, and, hands on his hips, glared back at him. "Are you mad? Volkara is not some village, boy—it is an Empire stronghold. It is the main city guarding the outskirts of Volusia, and the only city between us and them. It is not a clay village but a real fort, with real walls, made of thick stone, and real soldiers, with real weapons. It is a city in and of itself, with at least two thousand slaves inside. Even if our army were three times the size, we could not take it."

Darius glared back at Zirk, infuriated that he would show up here and defy him at every turn. Before he could respond, others chimed in.

"Volkara is a cruel place," Desmond said. "It is well known that it is where they bring slaves to torture them."

"It is also very well-manned," Raj added. "At least a thousand Empire soldiers guard its walls. And those walls are so impregnable, they don't even have to put up a defense."

Darius looked out into the night, past the sparkling torches, into the blackness of the desert, knowing Volkara was somewhere out there.

"And that is exactly why we will attack it," he said, confidence rising within him even as he spoke the words.

All the men looked to him, baffled.

"They will never expect an attack," he continued. "They are not on guard for it. And even more important: if we win, we will show the Empire that they are vulnerable. We will rock their very foundation of confidence. They will begin to doubt themselves. They will began to fear us."

Darius looked about.

"And our men, in turn, will begin to believe in themselves—to know that anything is possible."

All the others looked at him in reverence, a thick silence in the air, even Zirk not responding.

"When, Zambuti?" one of them asked.

Darius turned and looked at him.

"Now," he replied.

"*Now!?*" Zirk asked.

"No one attacks at night!" one of the men called out. "It is not done!"

Darius nodded.

"Which is exactly why we're going to do it. Prepare yourselves," Darius commanded, turning to the others. "We attack tonight. By the time they know what happened, Volkara will be ours. And from there, we will be at the footsteps of Volusia, and ready to attack the city itself."

"Attack *Volusia*?" Zirk cried out. "You really are mad. This is a suicide mission, devoid of all reason."

"Wars are always one by men who ignored reason," Darius replied.

Zirk, in a huff, turned and faced the other men.

"Ignore what this boy says and follow me instead!" he called out. "I will lead you on a safer path. We will not take such risks!"

Darius braced himself as all the other villagers turned and looked at Zirk, a tense silence in the air; but without hesitation, they all suddenly ignored him, instead turning back to Darius.

"Zambuti is our leader now," one of them said, "and it is Zambuti we shall follow. Wherever he shall lead us."

Zirk, red-faced, turned and stormed off into the night.

The men were all silent, all looking at each other, and Darius could spot fear, uncertainty in their eyes.

"How will we get through those gates, past those walls?" Desmond asked. "We have no siege equipment of any kind."

"We won't get through the walls," Darius replied as the others crowded around and listed. "We will get over them."

"Over them?"

Darius nodded.

"We can climb," he said. "We will fashion our spear tips into grappling hooks, and fasten those to ropes. We will sneak up to the rear of the city, where nobody will be looking for us, and grapple our way over the wall. Once we slip inside, we will creep up on them and assassinate all of them. Silence and speed will be our friends, not strength. Sometimes surprise is more powerful than force."

Darius saw the uncertain look in the men's eyes, these brave men who had suffered their entire lives, who had watched relatives die, whose very lives depended on his strategy. He would understand if they said no.

Yet to his surprise, each man, one at a time, stepped forward, and clasped his hand.

"Our lives are yours now," one of them said. "It is you who have saved us. You who have given them to us."

"We would follow you anywhere," one of them said, "even to the very gates of death."

*

Darius sprinted through the night, hundreds of men behind him, Dray at his side, all of them following closely as they ran barefoot on the desert floor. Darius tried to be as silent as he could—all of them did—and they ran through the night, a silent, lethal army. All that could be heard was the light pitter patter of their feet as they glided across the desert floor, hundreds of men throwing their lives to the wind as they fought for their freedom in the blackness.

Darius's heart pounded in his throat as they approached the stronghold of Volkara, his palms sweating as he clutched his grappling hook and the bunch of rope draped over his shoulder. He ran for all he had, knees high in the air, his lungs about to burst, determined to make it there before they were discovered. Luckily there was no moon tonight and they had the cover of darkness on their side.

In the distance there finally began to emerge a faint glow, punctuating the desert night, and as they got closer, Darius saw a series of torches flickering, lighting up the entrance to the city. It was an imposing entrance, framed by an arched gate, fifty feet high—and it had the most unusual entrance Darius had ever seen. There was no road leading into the city, not even a door—instead, there was a waterway, beginning a hundred yards out into the desert. and flowing right through the main entranceway. There was no way to enter the city on foot or by horse—one had to travel this canal. Darius could see at once that this would make the city impregnable.

Additionally, rows of Empire soldiers stood outside it, and rows more inside.

Yet Darius was undeterred. He hadn't planned on entering through the front door to the city anyway, or even trying to enter on foot. They could have their canal. He would find his own way in, a way they could have never possibly anticipated.

Darius began to circle the city broadly, far enough to be out of sight of the guards, and this was the signal: behind him, his men forked, half following him and the other half skirting the city along the other side.

Darius ran right up alongside the city wall, staying in the deepest darkest shadows, and kept running right alongside it.

Darius eventually turned the corner sharply, running alongside the rear wall of the city. Built to withstand any attack, the rear wall of this city had no back windows or doors of any kind, which was perfect for Darius's purposes.

Still, as Darius turned a corner and ran, he saw guards standing there, looming up ahead.

"Go Dray!" Darius commanded.

Dray needed no prodding: he raced forward, ahead of the army, and made the first kill of the night, leaping up on a guard just as he turned around and clamping down on his throat with his mighty jaws.

Darius was close behind; without missing a beat, Darius drew a dagger from his waist and never slowed as he slashed the first guard's throat and stabbed the second in the heart. Beside him, Desmond and Raj each stabbed the other two, thus killing all four silently.

On the far side of the castle, Darius could see his men turning the other corner and slashing the other guards' throats, all of them falling quickly, before they realized what was happening. Both sides convened in the middle, as was the plan. Darius was encouraged: so far, so good. They had all made it undetected to the rear walls of the city, all the guards dead and no horns sounding to announce their arrival.

Darius immediately gave the signal, and without wasting any time all of his men grabbed their hooks, reached back, and hurled them up for the top of the city walls.

Darius watched all the ropes unfurling, rising a good fifty feet in a high arc, then wrapping around to the other side of the stone wall. He yanked his rope and felt his hook catch on the other side of the stone wall, as he had hoped. He looked up and down his ranks of men, and saw them doing the same.

Darius immediately pulled himself up, grabbing the rope with both hands and climbing, his feet flush against the wall, his heart pounding as he went as fast as his hands and feet could take him and prayed that they remained undetected. If Empire soldiers appeared at the top, there would be no way to defend.

The coarse rope burned his palms as Darius scaled the wall quickly, breathing hard, his bare feet scraping against the stone, knowing that his life depended on speed. All around him his men did the same, all scaling the walls for their lives, like a thousand ants scaling a city.

Dray remained behind, snarling, guarding the rear wall for them.

Finally, lungs burning, palms on fire, Darius reached the top with a final pull and collapsed on the wide stone landing. As he did he shook his rope, signaling the coast was clear and for the others to all climb up—as all his men did up and down the ranks. Down below his men, lined up, all grabbed the ropes and climbed, just a few feet behind one another, dozens using one rope at once.

Darius knelt and turned and looked out, looking down at Volkara, having a bird's eye view from here. He could see the entire fort spread out below him, lit dimly by torches lining the walls. It was an incredibly well-armed fort, hundreds of soldiers patrolling it.

And yet, as he looked carefully, Darius saw that the mood here was relaxed—too relaxed. Half of the soldiers appeared to be asleep on their shifts, while the rest lounged about and spoke to each other, or played games. And all of them faced the front of the city. None faced the rear. Clearly, none of these men, helmets and armor off, weapons a few feet away from them, expected any attack on this night.

After all, why would they? What foe was there who was crazy enough to attack the Empire? None.

Darius knew the time was right to give the signal. He took his spare grappling hook, leaned back, lit its rope aflame, and threw it high in the air, a good thirty feet overhead, letting it sail in an arc backwards, back into the desert, its fire apparent in the sky.

Immediately, on the horizon, he saw his men light a torch in return, the one he had commanded them to light.

"MOVE!" Darius whispered harshly.

As one, all of his men reversed their grapples and ropes and quickly rappelled down the other side of the walls. Darius wrapped a cloth around his palm and slid down so fast, he could feel it burning his palm even through the cloth. The world rushed by him as he nearly free-fell down to the ground, and within just seconds, he was touching down lightly, quietly on the ground, his bare feet hitting.

All around him, his men touched down, too.

Without missing a beat, Darius turned and sprinted into the city, all his men running with him, racing right for the closest group of soldiers. Darius ran up to an unsuspecting soldier and just as the soldier turned, just beginning to realize, Darius stabbed him in the heart with his dagger.

Darius went to another, held his mouth, and sliced his throat. Then another. And another.

They all spread out, weaving in and out, each choosing one man, as Darius had instructed. His men blanketed the city like ants, killing guards left and right, bodies piling up silently as the Empire didn't know what hit them. They still didn't even know they had an intruder in their midst.

Darius sprinted throughout the city, aiming for the front entrance, wanting to take control of it from rear to front. He signaled his men, and they all stopped and took hiding positions behind massive stone pillars, all awaiting his command before attacking the front.

Darius knelt there, breathing hard, looking out toward the front of the city. Hundreds of soldiers were spread out between here and there, and he wanted them all to be congregated, to be easier to kill, and to have their backs to him. He knelt there and watched, hoping, waiting for the sign, the final act of his plan.

Finally, Darius felt a rush of relief as he saw exactly what he'd hoped to: a small, floating vessel suddenly appeared floating down the waterway, through the city gates, aflame.

Darius watched all the guards rouse from their slumber, all of them gathering around, congregating near the front of the city, all watching it in wonder. They all convened on the entrance, and looked out curiously into the desert night, clearly wondering who was out there. He waited and waited, until the crowd was at its thickest.

"CHARGE!" Darius yelled.

As one, he and all his people charged, swords drawn, and attacked the unsuspecting Empire soldiers from behind, all of them distracted by the burning boat. They attacked from behind, slashing and stabbing them as they turned. They managed to kill dozens of them before they were alerted.

The remaining Empire soldiers all turned around, finally catching on to the invasion. Horns sounded throughout the city, and Darius's apprehension deepened as he knew the real battle had begun.

Hundreds of Empire soldiers, in full armor and professional weaponry, turned and fought back. Darius's men began to fall.

Darius ducked a sword slash, and another grazed his arm, and he cried out in pain, his sword knocked from his hand. But he quickly pulled out his dagger and stabbed the soldier in the throat as the man charged in to kill him.

Darius bent down and recovered his swords, and as he did, he spun around and slashed another soldier's throat. Two Empire soldiers attacked him, and Darius used his shield to block the blows. Finally, Desmond arrived and killed one of his attackers—and Darius used the shift in momentum to lunge forward, smash the other soldier in the head wish his shield, then stab him in the heart. He thought of all of his brethren the Empire had killed as he did it.

Many of Darius's people fell—yet Empire soldiers fell, too, and with bodies piling up on both sides, Darius felt as if he were gaining momentum. At least they were managing to truly attack an Empire city, and to hold their own with their forces—and that alone, he knew, was an amazing feat.

With the front of the city exposed, all of the Empire soldiers turned to fight Darius. Darius's third and final group of soldiers finally appeared, as planned, and attacked in the front. They all waded through the waters of the canal, splashing wildly, as they pulled themselves up to dry ground inside the city walls and attacked Empire soldiers from behind.

Now Empire soldiers found themselves sandwiched between Darius's forces on both sides—and as they did, the momentum shifted. Empire soldiers fell rapidly in all directions as Darius's men overwhelmed them with their speed and swiftness.

The fighting went on, swords clanging in Darius's ears, sparks lighting up the night, the sound of men crying piercing the fort. All around him, men fell. Yet still they fought and fought, constantly closing the gap.

Finally, Darius killed one Empire soldier, after a particularly brutal give and take of swords and shields, and as he did, he raised his sword and shield to kill the next one.

But to his shock, there was no one left behind him: the Empire soldiers were all dead.

Darius could hardly believe it as he stood near the front gates and turned and looked back, surveying the city. He saw all his men milling about, standing over the Empire bodies. He saw a city filled with fresh corpses, both his own people's and the Empire's, glistening beneath the moonlight. A city that had finally fallen silent.

The men all realized it, too. They suddenly broke out into a cheer of victory, raising their fists and torches high in the air.

They rushed forward and embraced Darius, hoisting him on their shoulders. Darius reveled in it, cheered with them, hardly believing it had really happened.

An Empire city was in their hands.

They had won. They had truly won.

CHAPTER TWENTY SIX

Gwendolyn marched through the Great Waste, weak with hunger, her legs shaking, her skin burnt under the relentless heat of the morning suns. It had been yet another day, somehow, of marching for hours, somehow clinging to life. Krohn limped along at her heels, too exhausted to whine, and those closest to her—Kendrick, Sandara, Steffen, Arliss, Brandt and Atme carrying Argon, Aberthol, Illepra, and Stara—all still marched, too. Yet many of her people—too many—had dropped along the way, their carcasses littering the desert floor, Gwen and the others too weak to bury them—too weak to even stop. Gwen flinched every time another one dropped, and the insects suddenly appeared, scurrying from who knew where, and covered the body within moments, devouring it down to the bone. It was as if this entire desert were just waiting for them all to drop.

Gwen looked up at the horizon, seeing the perpetual red dust lingering there, searching in every direction for any sign of anything.

There was nothing.

The most remorseless, cruelest thing in the world, she realized, was not the sight of an enemy, or a monster, or anything else—but the sight of nothing. Emptiness. Lack of life.

It was unforgiving. For her, it signified death. Death not just for her, but for all of her people, all of whom she had led here.

Gwendolyn kept marching, somehow forcing one foot after the next. She summoned a strength deeper than she ever knew she had and forced herself to march on, to be strong, out in front, leading her people, like a shepherd of a flock that she knew would never find a home. Their provisions had long ago vanished, their water skins dried up, and her throat was so parched, she could barely breathe. With nothing left on the horizon, she knew there remained no alternative to death.

Gwen knew that if she were alone out here, she may have long ago lay down and allowed herself to die. It would have been more merciful than this. But pride forced her to go on. She thought of the others, she thought of her father, and she forced herself to be strong. She thought of what her father would have done. What he would have expected of her.

As she marched and marched, she began to have visions. She had flashbacks to other times, other places. She blinked and came out of them confused, not even knowing what was real anymore, where she was. The images in her mind were beginning to become more real than what lay before her.

Gwen had a flashback of her father. She saw him sitting so proudly at the head of the dining table, young, at the height of his power, wearing his crown, his mantle, his beard still without gray, laughing that hearty laugh that always put her at ease. Around the table sat also her mother, at his right, healthy and happy, as Gwendolyn remembered her long before her sickness. Sitting there, also, were her brothers and sisters—Kendrick, Gareth, Godfrey, Reece, and Luanda—the six of them all still young, all still managing to get along, all around the table with their parents looking down at them.

"Here's to your beloved mother!" her father said, raising a cup, laughing, drinking his wine, her mother smiling, leaning in to kiss him.

"And here's to our six wonderful children—each and every one of them fit to rule the kingdom," her mother added.

"When will *I* be Queen?" Luanda asked.

Her father looked at Luanda, still a child, and he laughed.

"Just wait, my child. One day you will be Queen. You needn't rush!"

He then turned to Gwendolyn.

"And you, Gwendolyn?" he asked, looking at her.

Gwendolyn looked at him and blushed.

"I do not wish to be Queen, Father. I only wish to be your daughter."

Her father slowly lowered his cup as he looked back at her, and she could see in his eyes a look that she would never forget. She could see how touched he was, how much her words had meant to him, how they had gone right into his heart. He looked back at her with such love, loyalty, and admiration, and that look went right through her. It had sustained her, all her life.

"You have already accomplished that, my child. That and far more."

A hot blast of wind whipped Gwendolyn in the face and she blinked, snapping out of it, coughing, dust in her eyes and mouth. Her breathing raspy, she rubbed the dust from her eyes as it nearly sealed them shut, trying to pry it out. The wind brought no relief—but only more heat, if possible. Enough heat even to snap her out of a nicer place.

Gwen did not even want to look up, too afraid to see nothing, to be disappointed once again. But she forced herself to, hoping this time it would be different, that perhaps somehow a distant something would be on the horizon, a lake to drink from, a tree to shade them, even a cave.

She looked up, bracing herself, and wished she hadn't: there was nothing. Merciless, cruel nothing.

Yet something else caught her eye: she looked up, and saw a sudden shadow crossing overhead. It seemed to be the only cloud in a cloudless sky, and at first she was confused by it. Was she seeing things?

But she watched it pass by overhead, and was sure it was real, and she was even more confused. It was not a cloud, but a black shadow, flying through the air. It went by so fast, she could hardly tell its shape, but it swooped down toward her, then swooped up just as quickly, and as she blinked into the sun, she could have sworn it looked like a demon.

Like a demon released from hell.

Gwen turned to follow it with her eyes, but just as quickly, it flew away, disappearing quickly from sight.

Gwen felt a chill, felt it was an omen of something terrible to come. As it had flown close to her, she had the most awful feeling, as if she had been cursed by the creature.

"ENOUGH!" suddenly shouted a voice.

It was a violent shriek, a shriek of desperation. Gwen recognized it immediately as the shriek of a man who had lost his mind, who had nothing left to lose.

Gwendolyn turned, Krohn at her side, snarling protectively, and saw Aslin, leading a small mob of her people, and charging toward her, looking mad, delusional, touched by the sun.

"Better to have died in the Ring, in peace with our fathers, and be buried in good soil. Now we shall die here, and be buried nowhere. We shall become nothing but food for the scorpions and the spiders. If I am to die here, it won't be before I kill her first! Blood calls for blood!"

He drew his sword, the sound cutting into the air, raised it high.

"Kill the Queen!" he yelled, and let out a great shout.

To Gwendolyn's shock and horror, behind him several hundred of her people followed, drawing their swords, shouting in approval, joining him. More than half of her people rallied behind him, and all began to charge her.

Gwen didn't have the energy left to resist. She stood there and awaited her fate. If her people all wanted her dead, then so be it. She would give them what they wanted. Even this.

Gwendolyn was not so surprised that he wanted to kill her; she was more surprised that he still had that much energy left in him, could run so fast and reserve so much energy to hate her. He was hardly ten yards away and he moved so fast that the others, so lethargic, had no time to react. She could see in his eyes how much he hated her, how much he wanted her dead. It was like a knife in her heart to see that anyone could hate her that much in the world. What had she done so wrong? Hadn't she tried to be the best person to everyone that she could?

Gwen had thought she had been a good Queen; she had tried desperately to save her people, every step of the way. She had even sacrificed herself, back in Silesia, to Andronicus, so that the others could live. She had tried to do everything right.

And yet here she was, this was how she ended up: in the midst of the Empire, in the midst of a waste land, searching for a Second Ring that likely didn't even exist, torn apart from her husband, from her child. Most of her people hating her, wanting her dead.

Gwen stood there proudly, faced Aslin, and braced herself, unflinching, as he approached her with his deadly blow. He raised his sword high in both hands, but a few yards away, and began to plunge down, right for her heart.

Suddenly, there came a great clang. Gwen looked up to see Steffen stepping forward and blocking the blow, slashing the sword from Aslin's hands, cutting it in half, sending it to the ground. At the same moment, Kendrick appeared on her other side, and thrust his sword through Aslin's heart. Krohn, too, burst into action, leaping onto Aslin's chest and sinking his fangs into Aslin's throat, driving him down to the ground, killing him.

The three of them were all before here, all three rushing to kill anyone who got close to her.

Gwen stood there blinking, overwhelmed with love and gratitude for Steffen, Kendrick, and Krohn, all of whom had saved her life, yet again.

But the fight was just beginning. All around her, battle cries arose as the unruly mob of half of her people charged forward, even without Aslin, the momentum he started unable to be stopped. They all charged blindly for her, none thinking clearly, as if killing her could somehow change their plight.

Yet at the same time, the other half of her people, over a hundred strong, including Kendrick, Steffen, Brandt, Atme and a dozen Silver, all drew their swords to protect her and attack the mob.

Gwen's heart ripped in two as she witnessed vicious fighting erupting, man-to-man, soldier to soldier, former allies, former countrymen, men who were once as close as brothers, all turning on each other. They were all great warriors, all well matched, all going blow for blow. Swords clanged beneath the desert sky, as screams and cries arose and men killed each other brutally and the desert floor ran red with blood. They were all made mad by the sun, Gwen knew, and half of them probably did not even know anymore what they were fighting for. They just wanted to kill—and, more likely, be killed.

Steffen stepped forward and blocked the swords of two men on either side of Gwendolyn; he slashed one in the stomach then drew his dagger and stabbed the other in the heart.

Brandt stepped forward, wielding his mace with lightning speed, blocking a blow meant for Kendrick, while Atme came to his side, swung his ax and killed a man right before he thrust a sword into Brandt's back.

Krohn leapt on all attackers who came too close to Gwendolyn, killing more men than any other.

Kendrick turned and blocked two sword thrusts with his shield, then wheeled around and used his shield as a weapon, smashing one man in the face, then turning and kicking the other in the chest, sending him to his back. As they came back at him a second time, he sidestepped and dodged their blows, and at the same time slashed each one across the chest, killing them both.

A spear fell from a dead soldier's hand, rolling up against Gwendolyn's ankles. She looked up and saw a man charging Kendrick from behind, a man he couldn't see, and without thinking, she reacted: she picked up the spear and hurled it into the man's back. The man stumbled and fell, face-first, at Kendrick's feet.

Gwendolyn felt a pain in her stomach as she watched the man fall, one of her own people, killed by her own hand. He was a man she had known well, a local lord of King's Court, a man who had been loyal to her father in his day. It was a sad day, she knew, for her people. She could hardly believe that starvation and madness and hopelessness could drive men to such ruin. Gwen wanted to yell at them all to stop this madness, to be civil. But she knew nothing could make it stop. It was like watching some horrible nightmare unfold before, a nightmare she could not stop. Some great evil had been set in motion, and it wouldn't end until all these men were dead.

Men slaughtered each other left and right, the clanging never seeming to end, until finally, amidst the clouds of dust and light, there came a great stillness.

The world itself seemed to stop. Gwen looked out and saw the desert floor lined with the dead. She craved to see something moving, to see life, anything.

Instead, all she saw were corpses.

Gwendolyn looked around and was immensely relieved to see Kendrick and Steffen were still alive, along with Brandt, Atme, Aberthol, Illepra, Argon, Stara, Arliss, Sandara, and a half dozen members of the Silver. And, of course, Krohn.

But that was all. Several hundred of her people—all that remained of the exiles of the Ring—now lay dead. She and her dozen or so people were all that was left.

Gwen could hardly breathe. Her people, dead. Killed by their own hands.

What did that leave? she wondered. What was she Queen of now?

Gwen dropped to her knees, grabbing her hair, and wept.

How had things, she wondered, gone so horribly, horribly wrong?

CHAPTER TWENTY SEVEN

Thor sat in the small sailing vessel as they sailed into darkening skies and rising waves, looked over at the others and marveled at how much things had changed. In addition to his group of familiar faces—Reece and Selese, Elden and Indra, O'Connor and Matus—there now also sat with them a new face, staring back, filled with life: Angel. It was shocking to Thor to see her sitting there with them, to have a new member to their group—a young girl, no less, who sat there beaming, so filled with life and joy. It was a marked contrast to all of the others solemn, hardened faces.

Thor sat right beside her, did not try to keep his distance from her affliction—nor, he was proud to see, did any of the others. They all treated her like one of their own, as if she had been part of their group forever, as if she did not have a contagious disease. Thor himself felt overjoyed to have her there. He was inspired by her happiness, her joy for life, despite all she had suffered. She was a role model for him. She lived as if she had no affliction, as if nothing in the world were wrong with her, and was overflowing with a sense of freedom, clearly elated at being off the island. Thor was beginning to see the world through her eyes, and everything was beginning to feel new to him, too.

As they bobbed in the vast sea, the current pulling them to a blackening horizon, Thor could not help but feel a sense of aimlessness; for the first time, he had no idea where they were going. Always he had felt a driving sense of purpose, knowing exactly where he was going to find Guwayne. He had been certain he would find him on that island. How could he have been so wrong? Were his senses beginning to fail him?

But now, with Guwayne nowhere in sight and with no real leads, Thor had no idea where to look. As they drifted, he felt as if he were at the whim of God, wherever he should take him. And he began to have a sinking feeling that he might not ever find Guwayne again.

Thor saw the faces of his brothers, forlorn, shell-shocked, all of them having been through so much, and clearly looking as if they had no idea where to go next. Their people were far away, in a hostile Empire, if they were even still alive. Thor thought of Gwendolyn and felt a pit in his stomach. He wanted to return to her, to help her—but he was halfway across the world and he still had not found Guwayne.

Thor looked up and searched the skies for Lycoples, wondering if she could help. But all he saw were increasingly thickening clouds, no sign of the dragon in sight. The only sound he heard was the increasingly loud howl of the wind.

"A fish!" Angel screamed in delight and stood, watching the waters, clapping and pointing.

Thor followed her gaze and saw one of the many common white and blue fish they had seen following the boat all throughout their journeys, skimming the surface, then disappearing beneath the waves. Thor marveled that it would bring such delight to her, but then realized, having never been off that island, everything must seem new and exciting to her.

Angel scanned the ocean with delight.

"I've always wanted to go somewhere," she said. "Anywhere. I don't care where we go, as long as I never step foot on the island again. Every one of them—they were all just waiting to die."

"Well, we may not be waiting," Elden said, looking up at the horizon, "we might be dying pretty soon."

All of them turned and followed his gaze, and Thor's stomach dropped as he saw what lay ahead of them. The sky, sunny overhead, was completely black and frothing in the distance. He saw a solid wall of water coming right for them, impossibly fast. It was a downpour, a massive storm, and moment to moment Thor could feel the wind getting stronger, the boat rocking more forcefully.

"We need a bigger boat," Reece observed.

Thor knew they had to sail away from that storm, to get out of its path. With a sense of urgency, he jumped to his feet and began working the sails, and the others all jumped in along with him, some raising and lowering sails, others turning the rudder, and others rowing. They all worked as hard as they could, and they managed to turn the boat and catch the wind in the opposite direction, trying to get away from the storm. They no longer cared what direction they were going in—as long as it wasn't toward that blackness.

The wind picked up, sailing them faster than ever, the boat tilted sideways as white caps popped up all around them. And yet, even as fast as they were going, as Thor turned back and checked the horizon, he saw the storm bearing down on them. It was a futile endeavor. The clouds closed in on them, like a cheetah racing their way.

Even more ominous, Thor spotted rough seas traveling their way, enormous waves, big enough to crush their boat ten times over.

Thor gulped, having a bad feeling about this, and he looked straight ahead, hoping for any sign of shelter, another island perhaps, and saw where the wind was driving them: the destination ahead was even more ominous than the one behind them. The Dragon's Spine. It lay right in their path, and the wind was driving them right toward it, with frothing and churning seas.

Trapped between two deadly locations, Thor did not know which was worse. Either one could easily tear their boat to pieces. The others, too, seemed frozen in indecision, all of them in awe at the power of nature.

The wind picked up so loud, Thor could barely hear himself think, and he knew the inevitable was happening. They were caught up in something greater than themselves, and there was simply nothing they could do. Theirs was just a small sailing vessel, meant as an outship for Gwendolyn's greater ship—not meant to traverse the seas, and certainly not meant for a storm like this. Indeed, they were lucky they had made it as far as they had in this small vessel without a storm like this coming sooner. This, Thor realized, was their first real storm.

Thor watched as the angry storm narrowed the gap, but a hundred yards away. They began to get pelted with more wind, more rain, and the waters began to rise and fall, twenty-foot waves, then thirty, rising ever higher, then dropping just as quickly. Thor felt his stomach plummeting.

The wind raged even louder, tearing off their sail, and Thor watched it lift into the air and disappear. He realized they needed to prepare for impact.

"Get down!" Thor yelled. "Lie down on the deck! Grab hold of something and don't let go!"

They all followed his command, all jumping down to the deck. Only Angel continued to stand, staring out, fascinated by the sky, the most fearless of all of them. As the waves crashed around her, Thor saw her begin to slip, and knew she was about to go over the edge.

Thor leapt up, landing on top of her just as a wave crashed over the edge the boat. He pinned her down to the deck, not letting her go as the wave pushed them from one side of the boat to the other.

"Hold on to me!" he yelled over the wind.

Thor grabbed hold of her with all he had, wrapping an around her arm with leprosy, and not caring. With his other hand, he grabbed hold of a wooden pole secured to the deck.

After that last wave hit, her expression changed to one of fear.

"I'm scared," she said, shaking, as another wave crashed down on them.

"Don't be scared," he said. "It's all going to be okay. I've got you. Nothing will happen to you that won't happen to me first. I swear it. By all the gods I swear it," he said, meaning it more than he'd meant anything in his life.

She clutched his waist, her nails digging into his skin, and as she did, she screamed as an enormous wave came crashing down on them. The weight of it felt as if it were crushing Thor's ribs.

Thor suddenly felt them both underwater, tumbling, over and over, deep beneath the waves. He saw the faces of all his brothers in arms spinning upside down, again and again, in the water, as he felt himself plummeting, deeper and deeper, unable to surface.

He could think of nothing in all the chaos, as water filled his eyes and ears and nose, as the pressure bore down on him, nothing at all, save for one thing: *hold onto Angel. No matter what, hold on.*

CHAPTER TWENTY EIGHT

Alistair stood at the bow of the ship, Erec by her side, and looked up with all the others at the enormous monster bearing down on them all, screeching, its jaws open wide, revealing hundreds of rows of jagged teeth, and preparing to swallow them all. Alistair knew that this monster would destroy their ship, that one swipe of those clause would crack their ship in half, send it plummeting into the raging ocean and drown them all—if its teeth did not get them first. They had sailed right into the jaws of death—and there was no turning back.

Alistair knew that, if they were to survive, something had to be done quickly. She looked around at all the men, all paralyzed with fear, and she knew they would do little but meet their deaths. She could not blame them. Nothing could be done. They were staring destiny in the face, a monster against which no weapon could suffice.

Alistair did not want to die this way; even more so, she did not want Erec, who she loved more than herself, to die this way. The thought of losing him, of their not being together, of him dying here, on this ship, with this sea as his grave—and with their child in her belly—was more than she could bear.

Alistair closed her eyes, determined to change her destiny, determined to not accept this fate, and in that moment, she felt time freeze. She felt her entire body turning hot, prickling with the heat, the familiar energy welling up within her that arose in times of crisis—the power she did not understand and which she could not always control. She felt it overwhelming her, taking over her, a flush racing through her body that made her feel that she and her body were no longer one.

Please God, she prayed, feeling Him listening. *Grant me the power you have given me. Allow me to stop this creature from destroying us. Allow me to save all these people. Allow me to save Erec. Allow me to save our child.*

Alistair felt the heat passing through her palms, such a powerful heat she could barely control it, and suddenly, time came rushing back to full speed, as she opened her eyes and found herself back in this place and time, back in the present moment.

She looked up at the monster, unafraid, and raised her arms high above her head. She aimed her palms at the beast, and allowed her energy to come forth.

Alistair watched, amazed, as two orbs of light went flying from her palms, up toward the creature. It all happened so fast, in the blink of an eye, she had to brace herself, as the creature's claws came right for her and as the light impacted it with the sudden force of an explosion.

The orbs lit up the blackened skies, like lightning flashing through the storm, and Alistair watched as the creature's hand was suddenly turned sideways. Instead of destroying their ship, the monster swiped down and smacked the water to the side of the ship, just missing them. It was a blow that surely would have killed them all.

The creature hit the water with such strength and power that it caused a sudden wave to rise up, like a mountain in the water, setting off a tidal wave. The displaced water rose up, ever higher, in an enormous wave, lifting their boat.

Alistair felt their boat suddenly shoot high up in the air, a good fifty feet, before it came crashing down on the far side of the wave.

A horrific cracking noise tore through the air and Alistair looked over and watched one of the ships of their fleet go crashing down on the wrong side of that wave, on the jagged rocks of the Dragon's Spine. It smashed into pieces, its men screaming as they tumbled down through the air and into the raging sea. Alistair winced as hundreds of men met their deaths.

The monster, now in a rage, turned back and focused on Alistair. She could see the fury in its soulless eyes, see how determined it was to kill them. It raised its claws in hate and brought them down for her ship again.

"Alistair, get down!" Erec yelled, seeing the beast coming for her and trying to protect her.

But Alistair ignored him. She did not need his protection; she did not need anyone's protection. She had the power of God within her, and the power of God, she knew, had dominion over any creature in the world.

Again Alistair raised her arms at it, and aimed it at the creature as it swooped down for her.

Orbs of light shot forth, and this time she managed to divert the creature's claws to the other side of the ship, once again just missing and setting off another enormous wave.

The cracking of wood and men's screams filled the air yet again, and Alistair turned to see another ship sent over the waves and smashing into the Dragon's Spine, all its men crushed to death.

The creature wheeled, enraged, and this time it took aim on another one of Erec's ships, before Alistair realized what it was doing. In an instant it smashed it to bits, its claw coming down right on the center of it. It flattened the mast and the sails, flattened the deck, breaking it all into a million little pieces. Men shrieked, crushed beneath its weight, meeting a horrible death in the storm-swept seas of the Dragon's Spine.

Alistair examined the beast, turning back to her yet again; she had underestimated it. It was more powerful than she had realized, and while she'd been able to avert it, she hadn't been able to stop it completely. She felt those men's deaths were on her head. She had never encountered a power as strong as this.

The winds howled and the storm raged, as enormous waves kept rolling them up and down on the sea. The creature, infuriated, set its sights on Alistair, and this time, she could see the determination in its eyes. It clearly had never encountered a power such as hers, either.

The monster launched at her with the length and weight of its entire body, arms raised out, diving forward, as if aiming to land on their ship with the full weight of its belly. What remained of the light in the sky was blackened under the shade of the beast's shadow, as it came down with all its weight, right for them.

All the men on her ship shrieked and cowered, all putting their hands on their heads, cringing, ready to meet their deaths. All except Erec, who stood by her proudly.

Alistair though, did not cower, and did not retreat. She stood her ground and raised her palms high overhead. As the creature came down, now just feet away, she summoned all the power within her, every last ounce she had. An image of her mother flashed in her mind, an image of her power. She saw light surround her. Invincible, impregnable, light.

She knew that she was more than a normal woman. She was special. She carried a power inside her meant for a special destiny, a power that came once a generation. She hailed from Kings and Queens. And most of all, she was infused with the limitless power of God.

She could be stronger than this creature, she knew. She just had to allow her power—her full power—to summon forth.

As Alistair raised both arms, she felt an enormous heat flash from her and saw a yellow light shoot from her hands, a light brighter than any she had ever seen. The light impacted the beast's belly, right above her, and it stopped it in midair.

Alistair lifted her palms higher and higher, struggling with all her might, her arms and elbows shaking as she tried to hoist it.

Suddenly Alistair felt the power shoot through her, and she watched in awe as the creature went flying up with a screech, high up in the air, shooting up hundreds of feet, flailing, shrieking. She focused on pushing it up to the sky, and as she did, as it went flying farther and farther away, she felt dominion over the creature. She felt all-powerful.

Alistair directed her arms, and as she did, the beast went flying sideways. Alistair spotted the jagged rocks of the Dragon's Spine protruding straight up into the sky and she directed the creature until it was above them—then suddenly, she pulled back her arms with all her might.

The monster came plummeting straight down, arms and legs flailing, straight for the jagged points of the Spine. Alistair kept pulling it down, down, until finally it impacted with the sharp rocks, impaled from head to toe on the Dragon's Spine.

The monster lay there, grotesque, unmoving, rivers of blood dripping down from it into the sea.

Dead.

Alistair felt Erec and the others all turn and look at her in awe. She stood there, trembling, drained from the ordeal, and Erec came up beside her and draped an arm around her.

They were now near the end of the Dragon's Spine, the blue skies apparent just in front of them, and one more huge wave lifted up their ship and this time, instead of tossing it backwards, it propelled them forward, into a calm sea of sunny skies.

All was quiet as the wind stopped, the waves calmed, the ships righted themselves.

Alistair looked up in disbelief. They had made it.

CHAPTER TWENTY NINE

Luptius sat at the head of the Grand Council table, in the center of the Empire Capital's High Chambers, an immense, circular marble building built of shining, black granite, framed by a hundred columns, and he stared back at the Councilmen, all young, stupid men, with disgust. This was the not the Grand Council he once knew, the one that had consolidated the Empire to power and ruthlessness, the one that would never have allowed the conflicts that had erupted within the Empire these past moons. He was in a bitter mood, and ready to let it out on someone.

He sat in this building, meant to inspire fear, and looked around the table at the representatives from the Six Horns of the Empire, formidable men of nearly every Empire race. There were governors of regions, commanders of armies, all of them collectively representing the tens of millions of Empire citizens and countless provinces. Luptius studied the faces one at a time, pondering all their words and their opinions, which had gone on for hours in this endless meeting. They brought in reports from every corner of the Empire. The ripple effect from Andronicus's death, then Romulus's death, was still spreading to the provinces; power grabs and internal conflicts were never ending. This is what it meant to have an Empire, he knew, without a living supreme leader.

There came reports of Romulus's million men, still occupying the Ring, now leaderless, purposeless, causing havoc; there came reports of the assassination of Romulus at Volusia's hand; there came reports of Volusia's new army, of her attempted coup. It all fell into bickering, none of these men agreeing on a course of action, and all of them vying for power. All of them, Luptius knew, wanted to succeed Romulus. This meeting was as much an audition for power as a report of the state of the Empire.

Arguments continued over whether elections should be held, whether military commanders should rule, over which province should have greater power—even over whether the capital should be moved.

Luptius listened patiently to it all; there had been a much more democratic feeling in the air, and he had fostered it. After all, Andronicus and Romulus had been tyrants, and this Grand Council had had to bow to them and grant their every wish. Now, with them dead, Luptius relished the freedom, relished not having a single overbearing leader. It was more of a controlled chaos.

Yet they all at least looked Luptius to preside over them. As the oldest of the group, nearly eighty, with the fading yellow bald head indicative of his age, he aspired to be no commander. He preferred to pull the strings behind the scenes, as he had his entire life. There was an old Empire saying, which he lived by: Supreme Commanders come and go—but Council chairs rule forever.

Luptius waited for all the bickering to die down, letting these young stupid men argue until they were blue in the face, all of their arguing focusing on what to do about Volusia. He waited, until finally they all, with no resolution, turned to him.

When he was ready, he cleared his throat, and looked them all evenly in the eye. There was no aggression, he knew, like silence; his calm demeanor was more disconcerting to all of them than the commands of the fiercest general. When he finally spoke, it was with the voice of authority.

"This young girl who thinks she's a goddess," he said, "Volusia. Killing a few men does not make her a threat to the Empire. You forget we have millions of men at our disposal."

"And yet we have no one to lead them," answered one of the councilmen ominously. "More dangerous, I should think, to have thousands of men behind a strong leader than millions of men without one."

Luptius shook his head.

"The Empire soldiers will follow and execute the command of the Supreme Council as they always have," he said, shrugging it off.

"We shall meet her out in the field, stop her foolish advance before she gets any closer."

The men looked back at him, concern in their eyes.

"Do you think that wise?" a councilman asked. "Why not force her to march on the capital? Here we have the fortifications of the city, and a million men strong to guard it. Out there, we meet her on her own terms."

"That is precisely what we shall do, because that is what she shall not expect. Nor shall she expect our convoy's offer of peace."

The room fell silent as all the men looked to him in shock.

"*Peace!?*" one of them asked, outraged. "We offer her, a usurper, peace!?"

"You just said we had nothing to fear of her," another said. "Then why would we offer her peace?"

Luptius smiled, annoyed and impatient with the stupidity of all these men.

"I said we shall *offer* her peace," he explained. "I did not say we shall give it."

They all looked back at him, baffled. Luptius took a deep breath, annoyed. He was always one step ahead of this council—which was why none of them were fit to be Supreme Commander.

"We shall meet Volusia in the field and send a convoy to offer her a truce. I myself will lead it. When she arrives to talk terms, she will be surrounded and killed."

"And how will you manage that?" one of them asked.

"The commander of her army has been bought. He will betray her. I have paid him too well not to."

A thick silence fell over the room, and he could sense the others were impressed. They all looked to him now, hanging on his every word.

"Before tomorrow is through," Luptius concluded, smiling at the thought, "this young girl's head will be on a pike."

CHAPTER THIRTY

Godfrey reclined in a luxurious silk armchair, on a balcony made of gold, being fanned and fed grapes by a host of servants, and he marveled at how much his station had changed. But a few hours before he'd been locked in a stinking cell, on a floor of mud, surrounded by people who would all just as happily kill him as look at him. There had been no way out, no proposition before him but death and torture—death, if he was lucky, and torture if he was not. It seemed he would never rise again.

And yet now here he was, in a shining seaside villa made of marble and gold, on a luxurious balcony perched at the water's edge, overlooking one of the most spectacular vistas he'd ever seen. Before him lay a glistening harbor filled with shining ships, and at his feet, the ocean waves crashed beneath them. Godfrey was being fed one fine delicacy after the next, and he and Akorth, Fulton, Merek, and Ario were gorging themselves.

Godfrey sat back and belched as he finished his first sack of wine, washing down a meal of venison, caviar and exotic fruits. Beside him Akorth smeared yet another piece of bread with the softest butter Godfrey had ever tasted, and he wolfed down an entire loaf by himself. Godfrey had forgotten how hungry he was—he had not had a good meal in days. And this was the finest food he'd ever eaten.

Godfrey sat back in his silk chair, resting his arms on the golden, intricately carved arms, and he looked up at his captors, curious. Seated facing him, smiling, on the other side of the balcony, sat a half dozen Finians, seated in equally luxurious chairs, observing them. None of them ate or drank. None of them needed to: they had this bounty of food, Godfrey was certain, every day of their lives, and for them, this buffet of delicacies was routine. Instead, they sat back calmly, a smile on their faces, and studied Godfrey and his friends, seeming amused.

Godfrey wondered what they thought of them. They must've seemed a sorry sight, he realized. Godfrey was hardly the model of a shining warrior, and Akorth and Fulton were in far worse shape than he, both overweight, eating enough to satisfy a horse, and drinking twice as much. Merek, with his pockmarked face and darting eyes, clearly seemed a criminal, eyes always shifting, looking as if he would steal the silver out from underneath the table. And Ario looked like a boy who'd wandered off from his grandfather's house and got lost somewhere.

"I must say, you are the sorriest bunch of heroes I've ever met," said their leader, smiling. This man, who'd introduced himself as Fitus, sat in their center, and they all clearly deferred to him. Godfrey wondered what to make of these Finians; he had never encountered anyone quite like them. They sat there, perfectly at ease, with large, twinkling hazel eyes, bright red hair, too pale skin and pale freckles. Their hair was the most distracting of all. It was so bright, and sat so high on their heads, Godfrey found it hard to concentrate on anything else. They wore bright red robes and their long, skinny pale fingers stuck out at the end, as if the robes were too long for them, the fingertips barely touching.

Most of all, Godfrey could see in their faces that these men were rich. Pampered. He had never met anyone—not even kings—who came off as richer. There was something about their presence, an entitled feeling, that left him no doubt that these men were *spectacularly* rich. And, more ominously, that they always got what they wanted.

Somehow, facing off against these men was even scarier to him than facing off against knights or kings. Godfrey could detect a certain listlessness in their ways, a certain apathy, as if they would kill a man with a smile, and never break a sweat. Men like this spoke softly, he knew, and usually meant every word they said.

"And the hungriest," Akorth chimed in. "This meat is delicious. Have you any more?"

Their leader nodded, and a servant brought Akorth another platter.

"We are not heroes," Fulton said. "We are not even warriors."

"All just commoners," Akorth said. "Sorry to disappoint you."

"Except, of course, for Godfrey here," Fulton said. "He's royalty."

The Finian leader turned and examined Godfrey, eyes wide in surprise, and Godfrey felt himself redden; he hated being called that.

"Royalty, are you?" their leader asked.

Godfrey shrugged.

"In truth, my father would rather not have seen me that way, though I am indeed his son—even if the son with the least aspirations, the son never destined for the throne. I suppose none of that matters now, though. My kingdom is far away, across the sea, and it lies in ashes."

Fitus studied him and smiled wide.

"I like you, Godfrey, son of MacGil. You are an honest man. A self-effacing man. That is a rare thing in Volusia. You are also a daring and reckless man—and, I might add, a foolish man. Did you really think you would arrive in Volusia and achieve your goals? This seems almost naïve coming from a man of your position."

Godfrey shrugged.

"You'd be amazed at what desperation can do to a man's judgment," he replied. "Better to try than to face a certain death, wouldn't you say?"

Fitus slowly nodded back.

"It is admirable that you chose to fight for the slaves," he said, "to take up a cause not your own."

"I wish I could declare myself so selfless," he replied, "but truth be told my lord, it was a shared cause. We, too, wish to throw off the yoke of the Empire, and if they had slaughtered the slave village, we would have surely been next. I just chose to take preemptive action instead of waiting to fight in a battle I could not win."

"Not that he'd do much of the fighting," Akorth added, with a belch.

"Or that he'd win anyway," Fulton chimed in.

Fitus smiled, looking from them back to Godfrey.

"Nonetheless," Fitus said, "you were brave, and your cause was a noble one—however selfish it may have been and however clumsily you went about it. Did you really think buying off the right people would protect your people from doom?"

Godfrey shrugged.

"It has worked for me in the past. In my opinion, everyone can be bought."

Fitus smiled.

"You clearly have not met the Finians," he said. "We are the richest race in the Empire. Do you think a few sacks of gold would impress us? This balcony you are sitting on is worth a thousand times your sacks of gold."

Godfrey looked around, saw the solid gold everywhere, reflecting the light brilliantly, and realized that indeed it was. He had a point.

"I suppose I did not realize the extreme wealth of the Finians," Godfrey said.

"And yet the riches of the Finians are legendary," he said. "Your problem is that you attack a people, a region, of which you know nothing about. You know nothing of our people, our culture, our history. For example, you probably assumed that all free Volusians were of the Empire race and all other races were enslaved. Yet here we are, Finians, a race of humans, free, independent, and even more powerful than the Queen. You probably did not know that the leader of Volusia is herself human. We are a people of many paradoxes."

"No, I did not," Godfrey said, surprised.

"This is the problem that arises from ignorance. You must know your enemies well if you are to risk attacking them."

Fitus reached down and sipped tea from a dainty golden saucer as a servant handed it to him, and Godfrey studied the man, wondering. He was more intelligent than Godfrey had imagined.

"Well, I apologize for not reading up on my history before entering your city," Godfrey said. "I wasn't really in a scholarly mood—just in the mood to save my life. Perhaps even land a sack of wine, or a random woman."

The Finian leader smiled wide.

"You are an interesting man, Godfrey son of MacGil," he said slowly, summing him up. "You wish to appear to be humorous, brash, impetuous, even foolish. Yet I can see by observing you that you are anything but. You are a serious man beneath your façade—perhaps even as serious and studied as your father."

Godfrey looked at him in surprise, raising his eyebrows.

"And how would you know anything about my father?"

Fitus smiled and shook his head.

"King MacGil, the sixth of the MacGil kings. He began his reign twenty-three years ago, and named his second-eldest daughter Gwendolyn as heir, skipping over Luanda and Kendrick and Godfrey and Reece and yourself. A move that surprised them all."

Godfrey stared back, flabbergasted at this man's knowledge.

"How do you know so much about my family?"

Fitus smiled wide.

"Unlike yourself, I study my enemies well," he replied. "Not just locally, but abroad. I know everything about your family—probably more than you do. I know what happened four generations ago, when your great-great-grandfather abdicated the throne. But I won't bore you with the details. You see, we Finians are thorough. Knowledge is our trade. Knowledge is our weapon. How else do you think we could have survived here, in a hostile Empire, amidst a hostile race, for nine generations? Queens of Volusia have come and gone—yet we Finians have always been. And while we lurk in the shadows, we have always been more powerful than the Queens."

Godfrey studied them all with a new respect, seeing the wisdom in all of them, seeing how they were all survivors. Like he. They also had a certain cynicism, a certain ruthlessness that he could understand.

"So why bother with me?" Godfrey finally asked. "My gold can't buy you. And you already know more about me than I can tell. Why didn't you just leave us to the mercies of the Empire?"

Fitus laughed, a light, sharp, dangerous sound.

"As I have said, I like you, Godfrey son of MacGil. I like your cause. More importantly, I need your cause. We need your cause. And that is why you are here."

Godfrey stared back, puzzled.

"We have been watching you from the moment you entered our city," he said. "Of course, no one enters these gates without our knowing about it. We let you enter. I wanted to see where you would go, what you would do. We watched you place your gold. We didn't take it, because we wanted to see what you did with it. It was quite amusing, indeed, to watch you escape. When we had enough, we brought you here. We could not let you get killed because we need you—as much as you need us."

Godfrey stared back in surprise.

"How could you possibly need *us*?" he asked.

Fitus sighed, turned and looked at his people, and they nodded back silently.

"Let's just say we have a certain shared purpose," he continued. "You want the Empire overthrown. You want your slaves free. You want freedom for yourself. You probably even want to return to the Ring. We understand. We want the Empire race dead, too."

Godfrey gaped, his eyes opened wide, wondering if they were being serious.

"But you live peacefully with them," he said. "You have control, as you say. You have all the power."

Fitus sighed.

"Presently, we do. Yet things are changing. I don't like what I see for the future. The Empire is becoming ever-emboldened; their race is flourishing. There is a new generation of Empire, a generation that does not respect us the way their parents did; they feel more and more that the Finians are a relic of another time, are expendable. More and more their indignities against our people are being enacted. We do not wish to wake up five years from now and discover that our race has been outlawed, imprisoned by this bold new generation of Empire. We like our position of wealth and power very much, and we do not wish to see it disrupted."

"And what of Volusia?" Godfrey asked. "Will she not use her army to crush the uprising?"

Fitus sighed.

"Our spies tell us that Volusia, even now, leads her men to march on the Empire capital. She is leading them to slaughter. She has become delusional, like her mother, and cannot win. The Empire will crush her, and they will come here, seeking revenge. Which is another reason we want what you do, and we want it now: if the Empire army arrives to Volusia and finds a free and liberated city, with Volusia's forces all dead, then they will reconsider their vengeance. It is the only hope for survival of our people, of our great city."

Fitus smiled.

"You see, Godfrey son of MacGil," he concluded, "we are selfish preservationists, just like you. We are not heroes, just like you. The only thing that Finians are loyal to is survival itself."

Godfrey took it all in, wondering.

"So then what exactly do you ask of me?" Godfrey asked.

"I ask you to do exactly what you set out to do: to overthrow the Empire. To help your salves—and yourselves—be free. With the Empire dead, and the slaves in power, Volusia will be the first and only free city in the Empire. We Finians would rather share power with the slaves than the Empire. You will act as our intermediary, will tell the slaves the pivotal role we played in assuring their freedom, and assure we all live in peace and harmony, with the Finians, of course, assuming a primary position of power. You are a partner we can respect. A partner we can trust."

Godfrey welled with optimism at his words, feeling, for the first time since entering this city, that there might be hope for his people after all.

Fitus nodded, and one of his men handed him a quill and parchment.

"You will pen a letter to the slave leader, Darius," he added. "In your own hand, a hand, unlike ours, that his people can recognize and trust. You are going to tell him of our plan and ask him to follow your instructions. We will send this letter as soon as you are done on the next falcon. It will find him in his camp, in time for tonight."

"And what instructions are those?" Godfrey asked warily.

231

"Tonight, we will have all the Empire soldiers slaughtered at the rear gate of the city," he said. "On our signal, the gates to the city will be open for Darius to lead his men inside. You will tell him to be there, tonight, and to await our signal. The city will be his. And you, Godfrey son of MacGil, will be the hero that made it all happen."

Godfrey was elated at the thought, thinking of himself, for the first time, as a true hero.

Fitus stood, as did all of his men, smiled, and held out his hand.

Godfrey stood and shook it, and the Finian's pale fingers were icy cold to the touch, like shaking hands with a corpse.

"Congratulations to you, Godfrey son of MacGil," he said. "Tonight, the city shall be yours—and your people shall be free."

CHAPTER THIRTY ONE

Erec knelt beside Alistair at the side of the ship, holding her hand as she lay in a pile of furs, attended by several healers. He ran a hand softly along her face, damp with cool sweat, and brushed back her hair, flooded with concern. He squeezed her hand, overwhelmed with gratitude for her; once again, he owed her his life. He knew she was powerful—but he had no idea she had held powers like that. They had been facing a certain and cruel death at the hands of that monster, and it was only because of her they had survived.

She opened her eyes, smiling up at him weakly, her eyes filled with love and exhaustion.

"My love," he said. "Are you well?"

"I am fine," she replied, her voice weak.

"You don't look fine."

She shook her head gently.

"I am just spent from the use of my powers," she said. "My strength shall return to me. I just need time. Time and rest."

He nodded, relieved.

"Yours was the greatest display of power I have seen," he said. "All of us have our lives, thanks to you. You deserve to rest for a year."

Alistair smiled.

"I would do it again a thousand times over, my lord," she said.

"As I would walk through fire for you," he said. "This is getting to be a habit, your saving my life. Isn't it supposed to be the other way around? You will have to give me some opportunity, my lady. After all, a man needs to feel like he's a man."

She smiled wider.

"We have a long life together, if you choose," she said. "There shall be ample opportunity."

"If I choose?" he said. "I could make no other choice. It is not even a choice. You and I shall be together until the end of our days. Nothing will ever tear us apart—and that I vow."

Erec leaned over and kissed her, and she kissed him back, Alistair still looking so beautiful, even in her exhausted state.

"I will love you for the rest of my life," he said.

"As I will you, my lord," she said.

He could see her closing her eyes again, and he decided it best to let her rest.

"Sleep, my love," he said, kissing her one last time, then rising to his feet.

Erec stood and turned and as Strom came up beside him, he surveyed his men all about the boat with satisfaction. The sound of industry was in the air, hammers, anvils, men yelling instructions, creaking wood, hoisting sails. All of them were hard at work, repairing the mast, the oars, the rails, from all the damage sustained by the Dragon's Spine. The suns shone down, the waters could not be more calm, and Erec sailed, finally, with a great sense of peace. They had survived the worst of it: nothing in this ocean could hold worse fears.

Erec walked to the bow, Strom at this side, and looked out at the horizon, leaning his arms on the rail. He looked behind them and saw, on the horizon, fading away, the Dragon's Spine, looking so small, so harmless, from here. He spotted the remains of his ships crashed up against it, and of course, the remains of the monster's body, still impaled. He shook his head sadly as he thought of all the good men he'd lost.

Yet Erec also looked about at the remaining ships in his fleet, the remaining ships of Krov's fleet, Krov sailing right beside him, and he took heart in the fact that so many of his men had survived. The ships were all, of course, badly beaten, and yet, they had survived. Now there was nothing left in this stretch of sea between them and the Empire shores.

"Do you expect we shall have more encounters like that?" Strom asked.

Strom stood there, and Erec could see his younger brother had been shaken by it; his brother's unshakable confidence had met its first real challenge in life. Erec, a veteran of too many battles, understood the feeling.

"One never knows, my brother," he replied, after a measured silence. "Oftentimes, the greatest wars are fought *on the way* to war."

"*That* was a war," Strom said.

Erec nodded.

"Indeed it was."

Images still flashed in Erec's head of that awful creature bearing down on them, its teeth, its roar, its shriek. He tried to block from his mind the screams of his men, smashing against those rocks in the Dragon's Spine, the sight of the enormous waves, crashing down on them again and again.

He closed his eyes and shook them away. He had to move on. There was no choice in life but to move on, and he was determined to lead his men.

"I want to show you something," Strom said, and Erec snapped out of it and followed him across the deck.

Erec followed Strom across the boat, to the rear, all the men parting ways and nodding to him respectfully as he went. Strom stopped at the side rail and pointed out at the horizon.

"Those rocks," he said. "Why does our path take us so close to them?"

Erec looked out and saw, in the distance, a huge outcropping of rocks, rising up from the water, a good thirty feet high, and stretching for a mile in either direction.

"We won't be sailing into them, my brother," Erec said. "We will clear them by a good hundred yards."

"And yet," Strom replied, "this does not seem the most direct route to the Empire. We should be sailing more northeast than due east."

Erec turned and looked out at Krov's fleet, beside him and slightly ahead, leading.

"Krov knows these waters better than anyone," Erec said. "We follow his lead, as we have from the start."

"And yet our maps show otherwise, my lord," Strom said.

Erec furrowed his brow, wondering.

"He may be leading us around some shallow shoals," Erec said, "or some other unseen danger. He knows these waters. Father trusted him to guide him, and we must, too. Maps don't always tell the whole story."

Erec, though, was now intrigued, and he signaled for his watchmen to signal Krov's fleet.

Erec looked across the waters and saw Krov at the bow of his ship, leading his small fleet. He was perhaps fifty yards away, and as Erec's men signaled, he came close.

Erec leaned over the rail as they came within shouting distance.

"Your ship looks worse for wear," Erec called out with a smile.

Krov smiled back.

"That's what years of pirating will get you," he said. "They were weathered to begin with, and I didn't think they could look much worse. I should have known, following you for a day can do that to them."

"Do we sail in the right direction?" he yelled out.

Krov hesitated, surprised, as he looked back.

"Do you question this old sailor?" he yelled back, sounding offended. "Are you watching the maps? Don't mind them much. Shallow rocks up ahead. If we had followed them and sailed straight, your ships would likely be at the bottom of the ocean right now," he said with a roguish smile.

Erec, feeling reassured, turned back to Strom, who nodded, clearly reassured, too.

The two brothers turned and slowly made their way back toward the bow.

"It's a clear, calm day, my brother," Erec said, clasping his shoulder. "Try to relax. That was always your problem: you worried too much."

"When we reach the Empire," Strom said, studying the horizon, "I want to be first in battle. I'm going to kill the man that comes for you first. You can kill the man that comes for me—just the way they did in father's time. Or you can stand back and let me kill them both," he added with a smile.

Erec laughed, glad to see Strom back to his old confident self.

"Why don't I just let you fight the entire Empire by yourself?" Erec said.

Now Strom laughed.

"Now that would be a fine idea. How many Empire soldiers do you think I could take with this—"

Suddenly, they were interrupted by a shout cutting through the air.

"UP AHEAD!"

Erec turned, snapping out of it, and looked up at the mast; way up high, sitting perched at the top of the pole, was the lookout, pointing and shouting.

Erec, alarmed at the lookout's tone, turned and looked out at the horizon, puzzled, not seeing anything. Yet there was a mist on the horizon, and as Erec watched, it slowly began to rise.

Erec was shocked to see a hundred huge Empire ships, easily identifiable by the gleaming black and gold banners, emerging from behind the rocks. Thousands of Empire archers stood at the edge of the boat and had their arrows pointed down at their fleet, the tips flaming. Erec knew that with the slightest nod from their commander, his entire fleet would be destroyed.

They were too close to get away, and Erec suddenly realized, with dread, that they had been ambushed. There were no possible options—he could not run, and he could not fight without assuring a certain death for all of his men. The Empire had outsmarted them, and they were at their mercy, with no choice but to surrender.

Erec turned to Krov, immediately concerned for him, feeling guilty that he had led him, too, into an Empire trap.

Yet as Erec looked at Krov, he was confused: Krov did not look scared, or surprised, as Erec expected him to. Instead, Krov nodded to the Empire commander, who nodded back at him knowingly. Even more shocking was that none of Empire the arrows were aimed on Krov's boat; they were all aimed at Erec's.

That was when he realized: Krov had set all of this up, had led them here, to this vulnerable spot beside these rocks. He had betrayed them.

Krov's boat glided up along the Empire's, and Erec watched as one sack of gold after the next was thrown over the rail, landing on Krov's boat, and he flushed with indignation.

Erec could feel all of his men looking to him in the silence.

"Is this how you repay my trust?" Erec called out to Krov, his voice echoing over the silent waters.

Krov turned and faced Erec. He shook his head.

"It is your fault," he called back. "You never should have trusted me, Erec. Your father didn't. I've always told you I sell myself to the highest bidder—and your bid, my friend, was not the highest."

"Drop your swords!" shouted the Empire commander, a fierce soldier in gleaming armor, standing before all of his men.

Erec could feel the eyes of all of his men on him. Strom looked at him, too, and Erec turned and looked at Alistair, who lay there weakly, still spent. More than ever Erec wished for Alistair to be able to use her powers. But she lay there, so weak, and could barely lift her head. Without her help, he realized, there was no chance of victory.

"Don't," Strom urged. "Let us all die here, together."

Erec shook his head.

"That is a solution for a soldier," he said. "Not a leader."

Heart breaking inside, Erec slowly, gently, drew his sword and placed it on the deck. It hit the deck with a hollow thud, the sound piercing Erec's heart. It was the first time he'd ever laid down his sword before the enemy. But he knew he had no choice: it was that, or have all of his fine men, and Alistair, killed.

All around him, on all the ships of his fleet, his men followed his lead, and the air was soon filled with the sound of thousands of small swords placed on the decks, shattering the stillness around them.

"You have betrayed us, Krov!" Erec shouted. "You have given up your honor for a sack of gold."

Krov laughed.

"Honor?" he yelled. "Whoever said I had any to begin with?"

Krov laughed.

"You are Empire property now," he said. "And I am a very, very rich man."

CHAPTER THIRTY TWO

Loti walked with her mother, her brother Loc at her side, following her as they had been for hours, taken on a meandering trail, wondering how this all came about. She understood her mother needed her to help to help convince new villagers to join the cause, but she wanted to be back in the main camp, with Darius and the others, helping them fight.

Loc limped along beside them, sweating beneath the sun, and Loti wondered how much longer this would all go on.

"How much further?" Loti asked her mother, impatient.

Her mother, as she always did, ignored her, just hiking faster through the woods, pushing back branches that snapped in Loti's face.

It was impossible to get anything out of her. All Loti had been able to learn was that one of the neighboring villages, populated with the strongest slaves, was reluctant to join their cause and would only join if Loti urged them to. Her mother said they could bring a thousand slaves to the cause, nearly doubling the size of the army. She said they had great respect for Loti, that her fame had already spread, stories told and retold about what she had done to save her brother's life. Her legend was growing, as the one who had escaped from the Empire's clutches, the one who had managed to make it back to her village on her own. It was only she, her mother said, who could convince them.

As Loti thought about it, marching as they had been for hours, following her mother down the winding paths over the arid desert and in and out of forest trails, she felt a sense of optimism. While she was annoyed to be with her mother and not Darius, she was also thrilled to have a chance to do her part to help the cause. She felt a sense of purpose, a sense of being needed, and she felt honored that these villagers would even want to speak with her and her brother.

Finally, Loti was relieved to see the terrain open up, and they emerged from the forest and back out into the arid desert. Before them lay a small slave village, perched at the edge of the forest, and within it, hundreds of slaves milling about. She braced herself, ready to do whatever she could to convince them.

"Why do these people need an invitation?" Loc asked, beside her. "Shouldn't they be rushing to join our cause? Don't they realize that if they don't, they will be killed?"

Loti shrugged.

"Some are more proud than others, I guess," she replied.

They followed their mother and walked into the village, down its dusty path, and followed her as she weaved in and out of crowded streets.

Loti was a bit surprised. She had expected a welcoming committee, a group of villagers ready to greet her. And yet everyone here was bustling about, ignoring them, as if they did not even know they were coming.

"They want to speak with us," Loc said to his mother, "yet, there is no one to greet us. What is wrong? Have they changed their minds?"

"Shut your tongues and follow me!" their mother snapped, walking faster ahead of them, turning down side streets.

Loc came close to Loti.

"I don't like it," he said to her quietly, jostled by other passersby. "This whole thing stinks. Since when has Mother ever come around to our cause? Everything we've ever done she has resisted."

Loti began to wonder herself—she had to admit, it all did seem strange. But she didn't delve too deeply into it—all that she cared about was helping Darius, whatever the cost.

They turned a corner and their mother stopped before a large, black, horse-drawn carriage, with iron bars on its windows. Several large slaves stood before it, scowling down at them.

Loti stopped in her tracks, confused. None of this made any sense. The carriage before them was a slaver carriage—she had seen them a few times in her life. They traveled the country roads, going village to village, and used the carriages to trade slaves between villages. They were mercenary scum, the lowest of the low, those who captured their own kind, broke up families, chained them, and sold them to the highest bidder.

"That is a slaver's carriage," Loti said to her mother, annoyed. "What are they doing here? We shall not have slavers join our cause."

Loc turned to her, too. "Mother, I don't understand. Who are these people? Why have you led us here?"

As Loti stared at her mother, she watched her expression change; her stern face fell away, and instead was replaced with an expression of profound loss and sadness, even regret. She saw her mother's eyes well with tears, for the first time in her life.

"I'm sorry," her mother said. "There was no other way. You and your brother—you are too proud. You have always been too proud. You would have joined Darius's fight. And he, my children, is going to lose. They are *all* going to lose. The Empire always wins. *Always.*"

The slavers rushed forward, and before Loti knew what was happening, she felt her wrists being grabbed by big, strong calloused hands, felt her arms being wrenched behind her back, felt her wrists being shackled. She cried out and tried to resist, as did Loc, but it was too late for them both.

"Mother!" Loc shrieked. "How could you do this to us?!"

"I'm sorry, my children," their mother cried out, as they were dragged to the carriage. "We are all going to die in this war. But not you two. You two are too precious to me, you always have been. You always thought that I favored your brothers. But I favored you. And I will do whatever I have to, to protect you."

"Mother, don't do this!" Loti yelled, frantic, struggling desperately to get free, but to no avail.

Loti saw the rear door to the carriage open as she was dragged to it and as she was shoved from behind, she felt herself tumbling into it, Loc beside her.

She turned and tried to get out, but the iron door was immediately slammed and locked behind her. She kicked and shoved it, but it would not give.

Loti heard the crack of a whip, felt herself bounced roughly as the carriage began to move, and she scurried to her knees and grabbed the iron bars and looked out the window, watching the world go by.

The last thing she saw, before the village disappeared from sight, was her mother's face, standing there, weeping, watching them go.

"I'm sorry," her mother cried out after them. "Forgive me!"

CHAPTER THIRTY THREE

Darius stood in the captured fort of Volkara, surrounded by his huge camp of soldiers, Dray at his side, and examined the scroll in his hands. He read it again, then a third time, wondering if it could be true. Ever since the falcon had arrived with it, he had been able to think of little else.

Could it be true? he wondered. At first he was certain it had been some sort of trick, or perhaps that he had misread it. But as he read it again and again, he felt it was true: this was a genuine letter from Godfrey, the Queen's brother. Against all odds, somehow Godfrey, with his impossible mission, had succeeded. Darius could hardly believe that Godfrey, of all people, had come through. He had taken him for a drunk, perhaps even a fool—certainly not a competent warrior. It had taught Darius a great lesson—victory could come from the most unlikely of sources. Perhaps Godfrey had been right after all: there are many ways to win a war.

When the moon rises, approach the rear of the city. When you see a great torch lit atop the parapets, the gates shall be opened, and the great city of Volusia will be yours.

For the first time since this war had begun, Darius's heart welled with optimism. Darius looked everywhere for Loti, wanting to share this good news with her and Loc, to embrace her, to see how elated she would be. He was puzzled that he could not find her anywhere, and he resolved to find her later.

Darius passed the scroll around, to Raj, Desmond, Luzi, Kaz, Bokbu, all of his brothers, all of the elders. Each examined it and clapped their hands in joy, before passing it on to the other. One by one the joy spread, and a wave of optimism began to spread throughout the camp.

Before this arrived, the camp had been filled with anxiety, hundreds of former slaves milling about, wondering how they would hold this fort, how they would ever attack Volusia. Darius had met with all his men, with all the village leaders, the elders, all of them arguing over what to do next. Some argued over different ways to attack Volusia. They all knew its walls would be too high to scale, that thousands of soldiers would await them with fire, with boulders, with a myriad ways to stop a siege. They all knew that they, former slaves, were not professional soldiers with the professional equipment needed to siege a city like Volusia. Many of them had argued not to attack at all; some argued to hold this fort they had captured, and others argued to abandon it. Any way they looked at it, it seemed clear to all of them that they would lose a great deal of men no matter what they did.

And now this. This missive, this falcon. An open door into the city. That was what they needed. A sign. A sign to move forward, to attack. They could take this city—Darius felt certain of it.

"Brothers and sisters!" Darius suddenly yelled, jumping up onto a boulder in the center of the fort, ten feet above the crowd, demanding attention.

One by one, they all turned and quieted, as the organized chaos turned to rapt attention, all eyes on Darius.

"Tonight, we shall march on Volusia!" he called out. "Sharpen your swords, prepare yourselves: tonight is our night for victory, and no one, not any man, will take it away from us!"

The crowd cheered wildly as everyone raised their swords and banged them together, a clanking rising up and spreading all throughout the fort. Darius heard the first true wave of optimism he had heard since he began this war. He could see that all these people now looked to him with trust. With confidence. They could all taste freedom, as he could. After all these years, all these generations, it was so close.

Just one final battle away.

*

Darius led the charge through the night, Dray beside him, heart slamming in his ears as he led his men out of the safety of Volkara, opening its massive gates, and into the open desert. Hundreds of men, swords in hand, followed on his heels. They ran quickly, barefoot, as Darius had ordered, stealthily through the night, racing over the hardened desert ground towards Volusia, looming on the horizon. Beside him ran Raj, Desmond, Kaz and Luzi, along with dozens of his brothers, all of them running for their lives. This, Darius knew, could be their last attack before being completely free men. Darius imagined liberating all the slaves inside Volusia, and it urged him on to run even faster.

As they neared the city, Darius turned and led his men into the woods surrounding it, entering through the trails for cover, weaving in and out in the direction of Volusia. Darius was scratched by branches, but he didn't care; he took the trails, allowing them to lead him in a big circle around Volusia and toward its rear gate, as Godfrey had instructed.

Darius stopped and signaled for his men to stop behind him, at the periphery of the wood. He stood there, breathing hard, looking out at the city, tightening his grip on the hilt of his sword. He watched the black sky, waiting patiently for Godfrey's signal.

Behind him he could hear all his men, breathing hard in the night, could feel their anxiety, their excitement. Their desire for vengeance. For freedom. Their desire to end this war with one great battle. It was a desire that Darius shared.

Darius stood there, sweating, trying to stem his hard breathing as he looked into the night, proud of his people for being so silent, so patient, as they waited. They had much more will and discipline than he could have ever imagined. They had become a true army, one village blending with the next, all fighting seamlessly together, all united under one cause.

"Did he say a torch?" Raj asked, staring at the sky with all the others.

Darius watched, too, and it felt like forever.

Darius nodded, watching the starlit sky for any sign. A million doubts and worries passed through his mind as he did. What if the letter was wrong? A fake? What if the signal never came?

"What if it was all just bluster?" Desmond asked the question on all of their minds. "The ramblings of a drunken fool?"

Darius stared into the night, wondering.

"He may be a drunk," Darius said, "but he is the son of a King. Gwendolyn's brother. I see more in him. I see a King in him. A soldier's heart. He will come through."

"I hope you're right," Kaz said. "We risk the lives of all of our people to put our faith in him."

Darius stood there, watching the skies, his heart pounding in anticipation.

Godfrey, come on. Give me the sign.

Darius clenched and re-clenched the hilt on his word, his palms sweating, burning to use it.

Darius examined Volusia's stone walls, its rear gate, a massive gate, soaring fifty feet high, made of solid iron. Darius found it strange that the gate wasn't guarded. There should be dozens of guards both outside and inside it. He took hope in that. Perhaps Godfrey had paid off the right people in preparation.

Suddenly, Darius's heart soared as a great light filled the night sky: Darius looked up to see a single torch, burning, high atop the parapets of Volusia. He saw Godfrey standing there, beneath its light, holding it high overhead.

Godfrey threw the torch down, the flames cutting through the black night, until it hit the ground.

"NOW!" Darius yelled.

Darius and all his men burst forth, out of the woods, sprinting out for the city gate, perhaps a hundred yards ahead. They all ran silently, none of them cheering, as Darius had instructed. He could feel the anticipation in all of their hearts, could feel his own blood pumping in his ears.

Darius ran and ran for the huge gate, closing the gap, ever closer, hoping and willing that it would open, as Godfrey had promised, and not leave them all trapped out there, exposed. It was a run of faith.

They came ever closer, running over the small drawbridge, over the moat, all of it unguarded, running the final thirty yards, then twenty....

Come on, Darius thought. *Open the gate. Open it!*

Finally, the gate began to open, as planned, slowly, with a creak, higher and higher, and Darius felt a rush of relief as he and his men reached it, clearing it just in time, not having to slow as they all kept running and poured right into the streets of Volusia.

Darius raced forward, right into the streets of Volusia, amazed to actually be inside this legendary city, this place that had been so feared by his people for so long. He went charging into the streets, sword held high, as did the others, expecting to surprise Volusian soldiers. They ran and ran, deeper into the streets, and everywhere he went, he was perplexed.

There were no soldiers anywhere. The streets were deserted. There was not a sound to be heard.

Darius finally came to a stop, realizing something was wrong. He turned around and looked back over his shoulder and saw all of his men, who had followed him into the city, standing there, holding their swords, equally puzzled. They all eventually turned and looked to him for answers.

Darius looked behind them and saw in the distance, outside the open gate, Zirk. He stood outside the city walls, the other half of the slave army with him. For some reason, he was not following them all in.

Darius looked at him, confused, trying to understand what was happening.

Suddenly, the sound of a horn tore through the night, followed by a great outcry, sounding like the battle cry of a million men, echoing off the streets of Volusia.

Darius turned and he felt his stomach drop as he saw an endless stream of Empire soldiers charging them, pouring in behind them through the open city gates, swords held high, blocking their exit.

There came another cry, and Darius turned to see Empire soldiers pouring in for them from every direction, every street of Volusia. There must have been thousands of them. And they were all waiting. They had all been prepared.

They swarmed through the city, closing in on them like ants. Darius turned in every direction, with dread, to see that his men were completely surrounded.

In moments, great cries rose up, as the Empire began slaughtering, closing in on his men left and right. A great wave of blood and destruction was coming toward them. And there was absolutely nowhere left to turn.

Darius looked up high at the city wall, and the torch was now extinguished. All he could see was Godfrey's face, looking down, horrified, as if he, too, had been betrayed.

Darius could not believe it. He'd been led into a trap. He and everyone he knew and loved—all of them, all because of him. They'd all been betrayed. And now there remained nothing for any of them except cold, cruel death.

"So this is how it ends," Raj said beside him, drawing his other sword, facing the oncoming army fearlessly.

Darius, too, drew his second sword, and prepared to charge the Empire. Dray, at his side, loyal to the end, snarled at the enemy and awaited Darius' next move.

"We all knew we'd die someday," Darius said. "Let us at least go down with valor."

Darius and the others let out a cry, and he charged, Dray beside him, into the thick of soldiers, knowing death was but a moment away, and finally, after a lifetime of suffering, prepared to greet it.

*

Godfrey stood on the parapets of the rear gate of Volusia, Akorth, Fulton, Merek, and Ario on one side and Fitus on the other, joined by dozens of Finians—and he watched the scene below unfold in horror. His blood ran cold as he witnessed the slaughter below, not believing what he was seeing.

Godfrey was in shock; he had been so filled with optimism, so excited to see his men be free, their plan carried out perfectly. As he had stood there with the Finians and lit the torch and raised it high, he had been thrilled to watch it all unfold seamlessly. The back gate had opened, as the Finians had promised, and Darius's men had rushed in. Godfrey was certain it was all over, that the city was about to fall.

Then he had seen Zirk remain behind, with half the soldiers, not pass through the gate, and it was the first sign of something awry. He had watched, numb, as thousands of Empire soldiers, clearly alerted to some other plan, had flooded into the gate, behind Darius's men. They came pouring in with a great outcry, around the corners of the outside the castle, clearly having been lying in wait. It was all one huge ambush.

Godfrey had spun around, had watched in dismay as thousands more troops had flooded in from every corner of the city, completely surrounding Darius's men. He heard the cries ring out, saw the slaughter begin, and he had finally had to close his eyes and look away, feeling as if he were being stabbed himself. He could not bear to watch all of Darius's men, so close to freedom, all being murdered like animals—and all because of him.

Godfrey felt the torch being taken from his limp hand, too numb to react, and he looked over to see Fitus standing beside him; he took it and threw it down to the stone, and Godfrey watched the torch get extinguished beneath the starry night.

Godfrey, mouth open, stared back at Fitus, who stood there calmly, a slight smile on his face, staring back.

"Why?" Godfrey said, his voice too raspy, barely able to get out the words, realizing the Finians had betrayed him. "Why would you do this? I don't understand."

Fitus's smile widened as he stood there, silent, cryptic.

Godfrey couldn't believe how smug he was, couldn't understand why he would do such a thing.

"You said you wanted the Empire killed," Godfrey said. "You said you needed our men. I believed you."

Fitus sighed.

"There was some truth to all those things," Fitus finally replied. "I would have loved to see all the Empire killed. But it would never happen, not with your few hundred men. So I arranged the next best thing for our security: I used you as a pawn to lure Darius, then sold out your plot to the Empire, striking a new bargain with them. Now the Finians are assured security, and assured a place in this city's history. Now we are untouchable."

"And all my friends?" Godfrey asked, horrified.

He shrugged.

"Expendable," Fitus replied. "Pawns in a greater game. Everyone dies," he added. "Not everyone dies in the service of a game."

"This is no game," Godfrey insisted, red-faced, indignant, a great fury rising up within him, greater than he'd ever felt. "All those men down there are being slaughtered. Does that mean nothing to you?"

Fitus turned and looked down there, as if watching something of passing interest.

"Sacrifices are always made for the greater good. Your men, I'm sorry to say, are one of them."

"But how could you do that? Those were all good men. Innocent men. You've denied them their dreams. You've denied them their freedom."

Fitus smiled back at him.

"Oh, how foolish you are, Godfrey son of MacGil. Do you not know that freedom itself is a dream? None of us are truly free. Above all of us, there is some government, some ruler, some authority. Freedom does not exist. It is merely a commodity—to be bought and sold by the highest bidder."

Fitus reached out and placed a hand on Godfrey's shoulder.

"Look on the bright side," he added. "You're not down there with them. I like you, and I've decided not to have you slaughtered.

You will live in safety. You will, of course, have to rot away in our dungeons. But I might even visit you once in a while. We can discuss our family histories."

Fitus nodded, and Godfrey suddenly felt his arms grabbed roughly as soldiers descended on him from all sides, yanking his arms behind his back, shackling his wrists. Merek, Ario, Akorth, and Fulton, too, were pounced upon, all of them being dragged away with him.

For the first time in his life, Godfrey felt real grief, real shame; for the first time, he shook off his apathy and really *cared*. No longer was he the drunken and foolish tavern boy—now he was *responsible* for other people. All those men dying below, they were all his fault. They were all dying due to his stupidity. His naiveté. His trusting the wrong people. Godfrey realized what a fool he had been. He had been played

"NO!" Godfrey yelled as he was dragged away, his screams dwarfed by those below. "You will pay for this! By all the gods, I swear, you will pay for this!"

Fitus laughed, a menacing, hollow sound, fading as Godfrey was dragged further and further away.

"Somehow, I doubt that," Fitus said. "I doubt that very much."

CHAPTER THIRTY FOUR

Volusia stood at dawn in the Valley of Skulls, in the vast, open desert, her two hundred thousand men behind her, Soku, Aksan, Koolian and Vokin at her side, and stared out at the sight before her. In the distant horizon, illuminated by the first of the morning suns, were the gleaming, golden buildings of the Empire capital. But that was not what caught her eye. Instead, she focused on a sight perhaps a hundred yards before her, the spot where she had chosen to meet the delegation from the capital: a perfect circle carved out in the middle of an otherwise unextraordinary desert plane.

"The Circle of Skulls," said Soku. "A fitting place to meet, don't you think? A fitting place for you to ascend as Empress of the entire capital."

Volusia looked at it, studying it, thinking. She knew the history of this place, this magical circle carved on the desert floor, by whom or by what, no one knew, a place of true power, a place where so many kings of old had met to discuss terms of truce. Now it was her turn. She saw standing inside it, already waiting for her, Luptius, the acting ruler of the Empire Council, along with his dozen councilmen and a mere dozen soldiers. The Empire army was nowhere in sight.

"Exactly as agreed, Goddess," Soku said. "They bring but a dozen men. They are bringing you terms of truce. They are preparing to defer to you."

"It appears that they have not even brought an army," Aksan said.

Volusia scanned the horizon, thinking the same thing.

"Why do you hesitate, Goddess?" Soku pressed. "You stand with two hundred thousand men behind you. They stand there alone in the circle, with no one."

She turned her icy glare on Soku.

"I never hesitate," she replied. "I observe. When I feel ready, I will go."

Volusia stood there, staring, taking it all in, as her men grew silent around her. They were finally learning not to question her.

"Vokin," she said aloud.

Vokin, the Vok leader, turned and shuffled up beside her.

"You shall join me in the circle."

Soku stepped forward, looking concerned.

"Goddess, that is not a good idea," Soku said. "That is not what was agreed. A dozen men only. The Empire has outlawed the Voks. They will take it as a threat. Perhaps they shall withdraw the terms of peace."

"The Voks shall be treated will all honors in my Empire," Volusia replied harshly. "You had best treat them as such, if you wish to remain my commander."

Soku looked down to the floor, clearly not willing to argue with her.

Volusia took a deep breath, finally feeling ready.

"Let us go," she said.

Volusia mounted her horse, as did the others, and they all charged out, racing toward the lone circle in the middle of the desert, leaving behind her army, joined only by her dozen soldiers and Vokin.

Volusia reached the circle's edge and dismounted with the others. They walked toward the circle, towards the waiting contingent of Empire men, and as they reached the edge, Volusia nodded to her men stopped, and they all stopped at the edge and lined up at the periphery the circle, just as the Empire's men were. Except for Vokin, who remained by her side.

Volusia walked into the circle, just she and Vokin, facing off alone with Luptius, who stood there, smiling contentedly, hands folded before him, looking back at her. Now an elderly man with graying hair, he looked back at her with eyes that appeared to be kind. But she knew the legends about him too well to know he was anything but kind. He was a man who lurked in the shadows, who made Empire rulers—and broke them—at his whim. So many had come and gone. He had outlived them all.

"My Queen," he said. "Or shall I call you Goddess?"

"You may call me whatever you wish," she replied, her voice confident and firm. "It will not change the fact that I am a goddess."

He nodded.

"I welcome you to the capital, to our part of the Empire," he said.

"All parts of the Empire are mine," she said back, her voice cold.

His eyebrows raised just a bit.

"They are not, Empress."

"Goddess," she corrected. "I am Goddess Volusia."

He hesitated and she could see the anger building in his eyes. He looked shocked, but he quickly regained his composure, and put on a fake smile.

"Very well, then, Goddess."

He looked over her shoulder and he stopped, seeming disconcerted, at the sight of the Vok. But he held his tongue and quickly looked back at her.

"Do you know why we are meeting here today, Goddess?"

She nodded.

"To accept your truce," she said, "and your offer of the throne."

Luptius smirked.

"Not exactly," he replied. "We are here to broker a truce, that is correct. But it will be a one-way choose. Also known as a surrender. We are going to take your army; you will be stripped of power; this war will end; and you, I'm afraid, will not ascend to any throne. In fact, you are about to spend your final moments right here, in this circle, in this desert. But I do wish to congratulate you on what has been an extraordinary run. Just extraordinary. And to thank you for handing us your army."

Volusia stared back at him, amazed at his calm composure, at how expressionless he was, speaking in such a matter-of-fact way, as if he were reporting the weather. He merely nodded his head, and suddenly, she heard the sound of swords being drawn all around her, on all peripheries of the circle, and she felt two dozen blades pointed at her back.

Volusia glanced back, even though she did not need to, to know what happened. All of her men had betrayed her. Led by Soku, her trusted commanders had enacted a coup, teaming up with the Empire to kill her through treachery, through a false peace offering.

"There is a reason I did not bring an army, Goddess," Luptius continued, smiling. "Because I did not need to. Because I already have one here—yours. They've been bought, and I must say, their price was cheap. You've been brought to me like a lamb to slaughter. Indeed, I find it most fitting that we shall slaughter you here, in this circle, where so many rulers have died. You are a foolish girl to trust in the loyalty of your men. To believe in your own myth. And now you will pay the price."

He stared back at Volusia, clearly expecting her to be shocked or to lose her composure, or anything—and he seemed surprised when she stood there, equally calm, and merely smiled back.

"I find it amusing," she said, "that you think your soldiers' spears and swords can do me any harm, I, a goddess. I *am* a goddess. When I ascend to the throne, a statue shall be erected to me in every city in this realm. I am Volusia. I cannot be touched by any man, by any weapon—especially a lying, ineffectual old man like you. Tell me, Luptius: after I have killed you, will anyone remember your name?"

He looked at her, clearly shocked, and for the first time she saw him lose his composure; he gained it back quickly and smiled and shook his head.

"Just as they say about you," he said. "Delusional to the last. Just like your mother before you."

Luptius nodded, and suddenly all the men marched forward, closing in on her in the circle, preparing to murder her from all sides.

Volusia looked at Vokin, who looked back at her and nodded. He took out a small sack from his hand, reached over and turned it upside down in her palm. Red sand came pouring out, into her hands. She felt it trickle through her fingers and it felt nice and warm from the sun, as she closed her fist on it.

As she did, she closed her eyes and felt the power of this red sand.

The men closed in on her from all sides, now just feet away, and as they did, Volusia leaned back and suddenly threw the sand high up overhead, high into the air, a good ten feet. As she did, it morphed into smoke, a smoke that was blown by a breeze in all directions, covering the men on all sides of the circle.

Suddenly, the air was filled with the screams of men, as all around her men fell writhing on their backs, dropping their weapons. They cried out, their bodies convulsing, and Volusia slowly turned and looked at them all, shaking, convulsing, blood pouring from their ears and noses and mouths. Finally they stopped, eyes looking up at the sky, their faces frozen in a death agony.

Only Luptius still stood there, horrified, watching all of them die. Volusia bent over, grabbed a sword from a dying soldier, took two steps forward, and as the Empire leader looked back at her in shock, she plunged it through his heart.

He screamed out in agony, blood gushing from his mouth, and she smiled wide as she grabbed him with one hand on his chest and pulled him close, till their faces were almost touching. She held the sword deep in his heart as he gasped, not letting go.

"I almost wish it was harder to kill you," she said.

Finally, he slumped down, dead.

In the stillness that followed, Volusia looked at the dead bodies all around her, and she raised her arms to the skies and leaned back, triumphant.

She looked ahead to the horizon and she knew that now there lay nothing between her and the capital. Her destiny.

"VOLUSIA!" screamed the two hundred thousand men behind her. "VOLUSIA!"

CHAPTER THIRTY FIVE

Gwendolyn marched through the Great Waste, the beating sun shining down off the red desert, red dust swirling in the air, at her feet, and she felt as if she could not go on another step. It was hard to think clearly, with the sun beating down the way it was, sweat pouring down her cheeks, down the back of her neck, all of her possessions lost to her. She had dropped them long ago, as had all the others, she could not remember when, a long trail of objects left in the desert. It didn't matter. There was no food left now, no water left either. Every breath was an effort, her voice rasping, dried out days ago.

She was amazed they were still walking, all of them, like the walking dead, refusing to die. It had been days more of marching since the great revolt, since half her people had risen up against her. Gwen took some assurance in knowing those close to her were still marching with her.

Or were they? She was too tired to turn and look, and she couldn't remember the last time she did. And the red wind howled too loudly for her to hear anyone else—anyone but Krohn, who still walked by her feet, gasping, his fur on her ankles.

That was all that was left of the Ring, Gwen marveled. The once great and glorious country, with all its kings and queens and nobles and princes and Silver and Legion, with all of its ships and fleets and horses and armies—all reduced to this. Just this.

Gwen was amazed that any of them still followed her, that any of them still thought of her as Queen. She was a Queen without a kingdom, a queen without a people left to rule.

Krohn whined, and Gwen, out of reflex, reached down into the sack at her waist to give him of whatever food she had, as she had for days. And yet there was nothing left. It was empty.

I'm sorry, Krohn, she wanted to say. But she was too weak for the words to come out.

Krohn continued to walk alongside her, his fur brushing up against her leg, and she knew he would never leave her side—ever. She wished she had anything left to give him.

Gwen mustered all her remaining energy to glance up, at the horizon. She knew she shouldn't do it, knew she would find nothing but more of the monotony. More of the Great Waste.

She was right. She was crushed to see nothingness, spread out before her in all its cruelty.

They had been right all along: the Great Waste was a suicide mission. Godfrey might be dead in Volusia, and Darius might be dead on the battlefield. But at least they had died quick, merciful deaths. Gwen and the others would die long and torturous deaths, left as food for insects, as skeletons in the desert. Finally, she realized she had been foolish to attempt this, to overreach, to search for the Second Ring. Clearly, it had never existed.

Gwen heard a baby's weak cry, and she managed to turn and look over.

"Let me see my baby," Gwen somehow managed to say.

Illepra, shuffling alongside her, came over and laid the baby in Gwen's arms. The weight of her, as young as she was, was almost too much for Gwen to bear.

Gwen looked into the baby's beautiful blue eyes, dim from hunger.

No one deserves to die in this world without a name, Gwen thought.

Gwen closed her eyes and laid her palm on the child's forehead. Suddenly, it came to her. For some reason, she thought of her mother, how they had reconciled at the end, had even become close. And as she looked into this baby's eyes, the look in her eyes, somehow it reminded her of her.

"Krea," Gwen said, mustering the strength to speak one last word.

Illepra nodded back in satisfaction.

Gwen kept walking, clutching the baby, and as she looked out into the desert, she could have sworn she saw the face of her mother, beckoning her. The face of her father, waiting to greet her. She began to see the faces of everyone she had ever known and loved, most of them dead now.

Most of all, she saw the faces of Thorgrin, of Guwayne.

She closed her eyes as she marched now, her eyelids, caked down by the red dust, too heavy to keep open. As she marched she felt her thighs growing heavier, as if she were being dragged down to the center of the earth. She had nothing left now. All she had were these faces, these names, the names of all those who had loved her, and whom she had loved. And she realized that was worth more than any possession she'd ever had.

Gwen wanted to stop marching, to lie down a bit, just a bit. But she knew that the second she did, she would never rise again.

After how long she didn't know, Gwendolyn felt her knees buckling, felt her legs giving way beneath her. She stumbled, and then she could not stop the fall.

Gwen dropped down to the desert floor in a cloud of dust, turning her body to take the fall instead of the baby. She expected Illepra to cry out, to rush to grab her, or any of the others to.

But as she lay there and looked over, she was shocked to see that no one else was there. She was alone. They must have, she realized, collapsed somewhere else, long ago. She had been marching all alone for she did not know how long. Even Krohn was no longer there. Now, finally, it was just her. Gwendolyn, Queen of the Ring, clutching a baby and left alone to die in the midst of nothingness.

CHAPTER THIRTY SIX

Angel opened her eyes, shivering from the cold, to see the world rising up and down before her. She bobbed up and down slowly, gently rising and falling in the rolling waves of the ocean. She felt her body still immersed in the water, and she looked up to realize her head was just barely above water, and she was clinging to a piece of wood. Her entire body was freezing, immersed in the cold water, and as she looked up she saw the most beautiful sunrise she had ever seen, lighting up the ocean, spreading out over it like a blanket. She wondered how many days she had been floating here.

She rubbed the salty water from her eyes and tried to remember, and it all came rushing back to her in flashes: the ferocious storm, the tremendous waves, the sound of the wind and the crashing of the sea, the shouts of all the others in her ears. She remembered being thrown overboard, remembered the feeling of all that water crushing down on her, a feeling she would never forget. She felt as if her body were being split into a million pieces. She was sure she had died.

And then she remembered Thorgrin. She felt an icy cold grip around her waist, and she looked over and saw him, lying on the wood beside her, eyes closed, one arm draped over the piece of wood, the other still wrapped around her. He was unconscious, but still holding onto her, and she remembered his vow: that no matter what happened, he would never, ever let go of her.

Her heart rushed with gratitude now that she saw he had been good to his word. No one in her life had ever cared for her that much, had ever been good to their word. And yet there he lay, bobbing, unconscious, perhaps dead, she could not tell, and yet his hand was still clasped around her waist, helping to keep her afloat, making sure they never got separated.

"Thorgrin," she said.

She reached over and shook him, and he did not respond.

Her heart sank. She looked closely and saw his chest was indeed rising and falling. She was relieved: that meant he was breathing. His face was out of the water, even if the rest of his body was in it, so he had not drowned. Had he slipped into a coma?

Angel looked all around, hoping to see signs of the others, of the wreckage—anything. She expected to see Reece and Selese, Elden and Indra, Matus and O'Connor, all floating nearby, all clutching to their own pieces of wood.

But as she looked around, her heart sank as she saw no sign of them. To her dismay, there was nothing but a vast and open sea, no debris, no sign of anyone or anything. That could only mean one thing: they had all died in the storm. She and Thorgrin were the only survivors.

"Look what the tide dragged in," suddenly came a voice from somewhere behind her.

Angel's heart lifted, relieved to hear another human voice, someone else alive in these rough seas. But then as she turned all the way around, she saw the source of the voice, and her heart fell: before her was a huge, black ship, gleaming in the sun, the most powerful ship she'd ever seen, flying the red and black banner of cutthroats. A sinister breed, making even pirates seem friendly. She saw their ugly faces, grinning down as if looking at prey, and her stomach fell. She remembered the stories the other lepers had told her, that her parents had been killed by cutthroats—and she'd always wanted vengeance. She wished the tides would take them away, anywhere but here.

Angel reached up and began splashing at the water, trying to swim, to pull them away from the boat.

The men laughed behind her, clearly amused by her efforts.

Suddenly a heavy rope-net came flying down through the air, landing on her and Thor so heavily it hurt; she tried to shake it off, but it was useless: she felt her and Thor hopelessly entangled in the net, and soon hoisted up out of the water and into the air.

She wriggled and screamed, trying to break free as she was lifted ever higher, her arms sticking out of the large holes in the net.

"Thorgrin!" she yelled shoving him. "Wake up! Please!"

But he did not respond.

As they neared the deck, Angel spun in the net and saw dozens of pirates standing close to the edge, looking down at her. A particularly fierce-looking one, unshaven, with rotting teeth, stringy hair, and a necklace of real shrunken heads, stared down her, smiling, licking his lips.

"Bring her up," he said. "I'm going to have some fun with this one."

She was lifted higher and higher, like some fish caught for the day, and the laughter of the cutthroats filled the air as she was raised to eye level, dripping wet, over the deck.

"Let me go!" she yelled, kicking and writhing.

"And why would you want that, little sister?" one of them asked in his raspy voice. "Would you rather be at the mercy of the sharks? Or wouldn't you rather be up here and alive here with us?"

She spat, right through the net, onto their face:

"I would rather be dead a thousand times than be with you on your ship. At least the sharks I can trust."

The other cutthroats mocked the leader as he wiped the spit off his face, hooting and hollering at him.

"Looks like it took a little girl to put you in your place."

The leader's laughter quickly turned to rage.

"Don't worry," he snarled at her, "when we're done with you, maybe I'll throw you to the fish after all. At least what's left of you."

She sneered back at him, deciding to bluff.

"My friends will find me," she snapped. "I have very powerful friends on my ship. They are all alive, and coming for me right now."

The cutthroats laughed uproariously.

"Are they?" they asked. "Then we shall be quivering in our boots."

"Thorgrin!" she yelled again, elbowing him in the ribs again and again. "Wake up! I beg you! Wherever you are, wake up!"

She elbowed Thor again and again, but he just hung there, limp-necked, not responding. Maybe he really was dead, she thought.

"Looks like your friend is dead," the captain said, as he pulled them in close, pulling her right at eye level, and reached out and grabbed her though the net, yanking her close. He stared at her through the net, but a few inches away, his awful breath in her face.

"Don't worry," he said. "We've got a cure for dead meat."

Angel looked down and watched him draw a dagger from his waist, the longest dagger she had ever seen, and watched him reach up and aim for her. She screamed and braced herself, assuming he was going to stab her.

Instead, though, she heard the sound of cutting rope and she realized what they were doing: they were cutting away the portion of the net that held Thorgrin.

Angel reacted. She wrapped her legs around Thor quick and squeezed as tight as she could, using all of her strength to hang onto the net and keep him from plunging. She strained and struggled, holding on for dear life, as Thor swung beneath her, unconscious, dangling over the ocean, held only by her legs. She knew that if he fell, in his state, he would surely drown.

"Let him go!" the cutthroat yelled. "If you don't, you'll go right down to the sea with him—then you'll both be dead!"

"Never!" she yelled defiantly.

Angel hung on for dear life, while the cutthroats poked and prodded her with sticks, trying to make her let go. Still she hung on, every muscle in her body shaking, determined to never let Thorgrin go.

"Thorgrin!" she yelled. "Please! I beg you. Wake up! I need you!"

Suddenly, another cutthroat stepped forward, took a long club, wound back, swung it wide, and cracked her on the legs.

Angel cried out, the pain feeling as if it would smash her in half. Involuntarily, she loosened her grip and let go of Thor.

Angel's heart broke as she watched him plummet down through the air, into the ocean. There he went, the only person who had ever cared for her in her life, who had risked his life for her, who had been good to his word and had held onto her no matter what. And she had let him go. She hadn't reciprocated his loyalty—and loyalty mattered more to her than her life.

Angel made a sudden decision. She could not let Thor go. No matter what.

As the cutthroats began to pull the net over the deck, Angel suddenly let go and leapt away from the ship.

She dove down, headfirst, aiming right for the icy waters below, aiming for Thor's body, which she could already see sinking beneath the waves.

From up here, she was able to look out and see the entire ocean, and she glanced out and looked for any sign of the others, Thor's brothers, floating somewhere out there, maybe clinging to debris.

But there was none. They were all dead. All of Thor's legion brothers. All dead.

Now, it was only she and Thor.

As she dove down for the frigid waters, she knew the ocean would kill them both. But that meant nothing to her.

Having a chance to save Thorgrin's life was all that mattered. And she would take it—no matter what the cost.

COMING SOON!

BOOK #15 IN THE SORCERER'S RING

Books by Morgan Rice

THE SORCERER'S RING
A QUEST OF HEROES
A MARCH OF KINGS
A FATE OF DRAGONS
A CRY OF HONOR
A VOW OF GLORY
A CHARGE OF VALOR
A RITE OF SWORDS
A GRANT OF ARMS
A SKY OF SPELLS
A SEA OF SHIELDS
A REIGN OF STEEL
A LAND OF FIRE
A RULE OF QUEENS
AN OATH OF BROTHERS

THE SURVIVAL TRILOGY
ARENA ONE (Book #1)
ARENA TWO (Book #2)

the Vampire Journals
turned (book #1)
loved (book #2)
betrayed (book #3)
destined (book #4)
desired (book #5)
betrothed (book #6)
vowed (book #7)
found (book #8)
resurrected (book #9)
craved (book #10)
fated (book #11)

About Morgan Rice

Morgan Rice is the #1 bestselling author of THE VAMPIRE JOURNALS, a young adult series comprising eleven books (and counting); the #1 bestselling series THE SURVIVAL TRILOGY, a post-apocalyptic thriller comprising two books (and counting); and the #1 bestselling epic fantasy series THE SORCERER'S RING, comprising thirteen books (and counting).

Morgan's books are available in audio and print editions, and translations of the books are available in German, French, Italian, Spanish, Portugese, Japanese, Chinese, Swedish, Dutch, Turkish, Hungarian, Czech and Slovak (with more languages forthcoming).

Morgan loves to hear from you, so please feel free to visit www.morganricebooks.com to join the email list, receive a free book, receive free giveaways, download the free app, get the latest exclusive news, connect on Facebook and Twitter, and stay in touch!

CPSIA information can be obtained at www.ICGtesting.com
Printed in the USA
BVOW08s2032280815

415127BV00001B/8/P

9 781632 910622